Miss Arnott's Marriage

Richard Marsh

CHAPTER I
ROBERT CHAMPION'S WIFE

"Robert Champion, you are sentenced to twelve months' hard labour."

As the chairman of the Sessions Court pronounced the words, the prisoner turned right round in the dock, and glanced towards where he knew his wife was standing. He caught her eye, and smiled. What meaning, if any, the smile conveyed, he perhaps knew. She could only guess. It was possibly intended to be a more careless, a more light-hearted smile than it in reality appeared. Robert Champion had probably not such complete control over his facial muscles as he would have desired. There was a hunted, anxious look about the eyes, a suggestion of uncomfortable pallor about the whole countenance which rather detracted from the impression which she had no doubt that he had intended to make. She knew the man well enough to be aware that nothing would please him better than that she should suppose that he regarded the whole proceedings with gay bravado, with complete indifference, both for the powers that were and for the punishment which they had meted out to him. But even if the expression on his face had not shown that the cur in the man had, for the moment, the upper hand, the unceremonious fashion in which the warders bundled him down the staircase, and out of sight, would have been sufficient to prevent any impression being left behind that he had departed from the scene in a halo of dignity.

As regards his wife, the effect made upon her by the whole proceedings was an overwhelming consciousness of unbearable shame. When the man with the cheap good looks was hustled away, as if he were some inferior thing, the realisation that this was indeed her husband, was more than she could endure. She reached out with her hand, as if in search of some support, and, finding none, sank to the floor of the court in a swoon.

"Poor dear!" said a woman, standing near. "I expect she's something to do with that scamp of a fellow--maybe she's his wife."

"This sort of thing often is hardest on those who are left behind," chimed in a man. "Sometimes it isn't those who are in prison who suffer most; it's those who are outside."

When, having regained some of her senses, Violet Champion found herself in the street, she was inclined to call herself hard names for having gone near the court at all. She had only gone because she feared that if she stayed away she might not have learned how the thing had ended. This crime of which Robert Champion had been guilty was such a petty, such a paltry thing, that, so far as she knew, the earlier stages of the case had not been reported at all. One or other of the few score journals which London issues might have noticed it at some time, somewhere. If so, it had escaped her observation. Her knowledge of London papers was limited. They contained little which was likely to be of interest to her. She hardly knew where to look for such comments. The idea was not to be borne that she should be left in ignorance as to how the case had gone, as to what had become of Robert Champion. Anything rather than that. Her want of knowledge would have been to her as a perpetual nightmare. She would have scarcely dared to show herself in the streets for fear of encountering him.

Yet, now that it was all over, and she knew the worst-- or best-- her disposition was to blame herself for having strayed within the tainted purlieus of that crime-haunted court. She felt as if the atmosphere of the place had infected her with some loathsome bacillus. She also thought it possible that he might have misconstrued the meaning of her presence. He was in error if he had supposed that it was intended as a mark of sympathy. In her complete ignorance of such matters she had no notion as to the nature of the punishment to which he had rendered himself liable. If he were sentenced to a long term of penal servitude she simply wished to know it, that was all. In such a situation any sort of certainty was better than none. But sympathy! If he had been sentenced to be hung, her dominant sensation would have been one of relief. The gallows would have been a way of escape.

No one seeing the tall, handsome girl strolling listlessly along the street would have connected her with such a sordid tragedy. But it seemed to her that the stigma of Robert Champion's shame was branded large all over her, that passers-by had only to glance at her to perceive at once the depths into which she had fallen.

And they were depths. Only just turned twenty-one; still a girl, and already a wife who was no wife. For what sort of wife can she be called who is mated to a convicted felon? And Robert Champion was one of nature's felons; a rogue who preferred to be a rogue, who loved crooked ways because of their crookedness, who would not run straight though the chance were offered him. He was a man who, to the end of his life, though he might manage to keep his carcase out of the actual hands of the law, would render himself continually liable to its penalties. Twelve months ago he was still a stranger. The next twelve months he was to spend in gaol. When his term of imprisonment was completed would their acquaintance be recommenced?

At the thought of such a prospect the dizziness which had prostrated her in court returned. At present she dared not dwell on it.

She came at last to the house in Percy Street in which she had hired a lodging. A single room, at the top of the house, the rent of which, little though it was, was already proving a severe drain on her limited resources. From the moment in which, at an early hour in the morning, her husband had been dragged out of bed by policemen, she had relinquished his name. There was nothing else of his she could relinquish. The rent for the rooms they occupied was in arrears; debts were due on every side. Broadly speaking, they owed for everything-- always had done since the day they were married. There were a few articles of dress, and of personal adornment, which she felt that she was reasonably justified in considering her own. Most of these she had turned into cash, and had been living--or starving--on the proceeds ever since. The occupant of the "top floor back" was known as Miss Arnott. She had returned to her maiden name. She paid six shillings a week for the accommodation she received, which consisted of the bare lodging, and what--ironically-- was called "attendance." Her rent had been settled up to yesterday, and she was still in possession of twenty-seven shillings.

When she reached her room she became conscious that she was hungry--which was not strange, since she had eaten nothing since breakfast, which had consisted of a cup of tea and some bread and butter. But of late she had been nearly always hungry. Exhausted, mentally and bodily, she sank on to the side of the bed, which made a more comfortable seat than the only chair which the room contained; and thought and thought and thought. If only certain puzzles could be solved by dint of sheer hard thinking! But her brain was in such a state of chaos that she could only think confusedly, in a vicious circle, from which her mind was incapable of escaping. To only one conclusion could she arrive--that it would be a very good thing if she might be permitted to lie down on the bed, just as she was, and stay there till she was dead. For her life was at an end already at twenty-one. She had put a period to it when she had suffered herself to become that man's wife.

She was still vaguely wondering if it might not be possible for her to take advantage of some such means of escape when she was startled by a sudden knocking at the door. Taken unawares, she sprang up from the bed, and, without pausing to consider who might be there, she cried,--

"Come in!"

Her invitation was accepted just as she was beginning to realise that it had been precipitately made. The door was opened; a voice--a masculine voice--inquired,--

"May I see Miss Arnott?"

The speaker remained on the other side of the open door, in such a position that, from where she was, he was still invisible.

"What do you want? Who are you?" she demanded.

"My name is Gardner--Edward Gardner. I occupy the dining-room. If you will allow me to come in I will explain the reason of my intrusion. I think you will find my explanation a sufficient one."

She hesitated. The fact that the speaker was a man made her at once distrustful. Since her marriage day she had been developing a continually increasing distaste for everything masculine--seeing in every male creature a possible replica of her husband. The moment, too, was unpropitious. Yet, since the stranger was already partly in the room, she saw no alternative to letting him come a little farther.

"Come in," she repeated.

There entered an undersized, sparely-built man, probably between forty and fifty years of age. He was clean-shaven, nearly bald--what little hair he had was iron grey--and was plainly but neatly dressed in black. He spoke with an air of nervous deprecation, as if conscious that he was taking what might be regarded as a liberty, and was anxious to show cause why it should not be resented.

"As I said just now, I occupy the dining-rooms and my name is Gardner. I am a solicitor's clerk. My employers are Messrs Stacey, Morris & Binns, of Bedford Row. Perhaps you are acquainted with the firm?"

He paused as if for a reply. She was still wondering more and more what the man could possibly be wanting; oppressed by the foreboding, as he mentioned that he was a solicitor's clerk, that he was a harbinger of further trouble. With her law and trouble were synonyms. He went on, his nervousness visibly increasing. He was rendered uneasy by the statuesque immobility of her attitude, by the strange fashion in which she kept her eyes fixed on his face. It was also almost with a sense of shock that he perceived how young she was, and how beautiful.

"It is only within the last few minutes that I learned, from the landlady, that your name was Arnott. It is a somewhat unusual name; and, as my employers have been for some time searching for a person bearing it, I beg that you will allow me to ask you one or two questions. Of course, I understand that my errand will quite probably prove to be a futile one; but, at the same time, let me assure you that any information you may give will only be used for your advantage; and should you, by a strange coincidence, turn out to be a member of the family for whom search has been made, you will benefit by the discovery of the fact. May I ask if, to your knowledge, you ever had a relation named Septimus Arnott?"

"He was my uncle. My father's name was Sextus Arnott. My grandfather had seven sons and no daughters. He was an eccentric man, I believe--I never saw him; and he called them all by Latin numerals. My father was the sixth son, Sextus; the brother to whom you refer, the seventh and youngest, Septimus."

"Dear, dear! how extraordinary! almost wonderful!"

"I don't know why you should call it wonderful. It was perhaps curious; but, in this world, people do curious things."

"Quite so!--exactly!--not a doubt of it! It was the coincidence which I was speaking of as almost wonderful, not your grandfather's method of naming his sons; I should not presume so far. And where, may I further be allowed to ask, is your father now, and his brothers?"

"They are all dead."

"All dead! Dear! dear!"

"My father's brothers all died when they were young men. My father himself died three years ago--at Scarsdale, in Cumberland. My mother died twelve months afterwards. I am their only child."

"Their only child! You must suffer me to say, Miss Arnott, that it almost seems as if the hand of God had brought you to this house and moved me to intrude myself upon you. I take it that you can furnish proofs of the correctness of what you say?"

"Of course I can prove who I am, and who my father was, and his father."

"Just so; that is precisely what I mean--exactly. Miss Arnott, Mr Stacey, the senior partner in our firm, resides in Pembridge Gardens,

Bayswater. I have reason to believe that, if I go at once, I shall find him at home. When I tell him what I have learnt I am sure that he will come to you at once. May I ask you to await his arrival? I think I can assure you that you shall not be kept waiting more than an hour."

"What can the person of whom you speak have to say to me?"

"As I have told you, I am only a servant. It is not for me to betray my employer's confidence; but so much I may tell you--if you are the niece of the Septimus Arnott for whom we are acting you are a very fortunate young lady. And, in any case, I do assure you that you will not regret affording Mr Stacey an opportunity of an immediate interview."

Mr Gardner went; the girl consented to await his return. Almost as soon as he was gone the landlady--Mrs Sayers--paid her a visit. It soon appeared that she had been prompted by the solicitor's clerk.

"I understand, Miss Arnott, from Mr Gardner, who has had my dining-room now going on for five years, that his chief governor, Mr Stacey, is coming to call on you, as it were, at any moment. If you'd like to receive him in my sitting-room, I'm sure you're very welcome; and you shall be as private as you please."

The girl eyed the speaker. Hitherto civility had not been her strongest point. Her sudden friendly impulse could only have been induced by some very sufficient reason of her own. The girl declined her offer. Mrs Sayers became effusive, almost insistent.

"I am sure, my dear, that you will see for yourself that it's not quite the thing for a young lady to receive a gentleman, and maybe two, in a room like this, which she uses for sleeping. You're perfectly welcome to my little sitting-room for half an hour, or even more, where you'll be most snug and comfortable; and as for making you a charge, or anything of that sort, I shouldn't think of it, so don't let yourself be influenced by any fears of that kind."

But the girl would have nothing to do with Mrs Sayers' sitting-room. This woman had regarded her askance ever since she had entered the house, had treated her with something worse than incivility. Miss Arnott was not disposed, even in so trifling a matter, to place herself under an obligation to her now. Mrs Sayers was difficult to convince; but the girl was rid of her at last, and was alone to ask herself what this new turn of fortune's wheel might portend. On this already sufficiently eventful day, of what new experiment was she to be made the subject? What was this stranger coming to tell her about Septimus Arnott--the uncle from whom her father had differed, as he himself was wont to phrase it, on eleven points out of ten? She was, it appeared, to be asked certain questions. Good; she would be prepared to answer them, up to a certain point. But where, exactly, was that point? And what would happen after it was reached?

She was ready and willing to give a full and detailed account of all that had ever happened to her--up to the time of her coming to London. And how much afterwards? She did not, at present, know how it could be done; but if, by any means whatever, the thing were possible, she meant to conceal--from the whole world!--the shameful fact that she was Robert Champion's wife. Nothing, save the direst unescapable pressure, should ever induce her to even admit that she had known the man. That entire episode should be erased from her life, as if it had never been, if it were feasible. And she would make it feasible.

The matter she had at present to consider was, how much--or how little--she should tell her coming visitors.

CHAPTER II
THE WOMAN ON THE PAVEMENT

Mr Stacey was a tall, portly gentleman, quite an accepted type of family lawyer. He was white-headed and inclined to be red-faced. He carried a pair of nose glasses, which were as often between his fingers as on his nose. His manner was urbane, with a tendency towards pomposity; and when he smiled, which was often, he showed a set of teeth which were as white and regular as the dentist could make them. He was followed into the room by Mr Gardner; and when the apartment contained three persons it was filled to overflowing.

"Miss Arnott, my excellent friend, Mr Gardner here, has brought me most important news--most important. He actually tells me that you are--eh--the Miss Arnott for whom we have been so long in search."

"I am Miss Arnott. I am not aware, however, that anyone has searched for me. I don't know why they should."

Mr Gardner, who had been showing a vivid consciousness of scanty space, proffered a suggestion.

"If I might make so bold, sir, as to ask Miss Arnott to honour me by stepping down to my poor parlour, we should, at least, have a little more room to move."

"Mrs Sayers has already made me a similar proposal. I declined it, as I decline yours. What you wish to say to me you will be so good as to say to me here. This room, such as it is, is at anyrate my own--for the present."

"For the present; quite so!--quite so! A fine spirit of independence--a fine spirit. I think, Miss Arnott, that before long you will have other rooms of your own, where you will be able to be independent in another sense. I understand that you claim to be the only surviving relative of Septimus Arnott, of Exham Park, Hampshire."

"You understand quite wrongly; I claim nothing. I merely say that I am the only child of Sextus Arnott, and that I had an uncle whose name was Septimus. When they were young men my father and his brother were both artists. But, after a time, Uncle Septimus came to the conclusion that there was not much money to be made out of painting. He wanted my father to give it up. My father, who loved painting better than anything else in the world"--the words were uttered with more than a shade of bitterness--"wouldn't. They quarrelled and parted. My father never saw his brother again, and I have never seen him at all."

"You don't know, then, that he is dead?"

"I know nothing except what my father has told me. He remained what he called 'true to his art' to the end of his life, and never forgave his brother for turning his back on it."

"Pardon my putting to you a somewhat delicate question. Did your father make much money by his painting?"

"Much money!" The girl's lip curled. "When he died there was just enough left to keep my mother till she died."

"And then?"

"I came to London in search of fortune."

"And found it?"

"Do I look as if I had--in this attic, which contains all that I have in the world? No; fortune does not come to such as I am. I should be tolerably content if I were sure of daily bread. But why do you ask such questions? Why do you pry into my private affairs? I am not conscious of a desire to thrust them on your notice--or on anyone's."

"Miss Arnott, I beg that you will not suppose that I am actuated by common curiosity. Let me explain the situation in half-a-dozen words. Your Uncle Septimus, after he left your father, went to South

America. There, after divers adventures, he went in for cattle breeding. In that pursuit he amassed one of those large fortunes which are characteristic of modern times. Eventually he came to England, bought a property, settled himself on it, and there died. We acted as his legal advisers. He left his whole property to his brother Sextus; or, in the event of his brother predeceasing him, to his brother's children. You must understand that he himself lived and died a bachelor. His own death occurred three years ago."

"My father also died three years ago--on the 18th of March."

"This is very remarkable, Miss Arnott; they must have died on the same day!"

"My father died at five minutes to six in the evening. His last words were, 'Well, Septimus.' My mother and I, who were at his bedside, wondered why he had said it-- which he did so plainly that we both turned round to see if anyone had come into the room. Until then he had not mentioned his brother's name for a long time."

"Miss Arnott, this is more and more remarkable; quite apart from any legal proof there can be no sort of doubt that you are the person we are seeking. It happened that I was present at your uncle's deathbed--partly as a friend and partly as his professional adviser. For I should tell you that he was a very lonely man. He seemed to have no friends, and was chary of making acquaintances; in that great house he lived the life of a lonely recluse. He died just as the clock was striking six; and just before he died he sat up in bed, held out his hand, and exclaimed in quite his old, hearty voice, 'Hullo, Sextus.' No one there knew to what the reference was made; but from what you say it would almost appear as if their spirits were already meeting." Mr Stacey blew his nose as if all at once conscious that they were touching a subject which was not strictly professional. "Before entering further into matters, I presume that--merely for form's sake--you are in a position to prove, Miss Arnott, that you are you."

"Certainly, I can do that, to some extent, at once." She took an envelope from a shabby old handbag; from the envelope some papers. "This is my mother's marriage certificate; this is the certificate of my own birth; this--" the paper of which she had taken hold chanced to be a copy of the document which certified that a marriage had taken place between Robert Champion, bachelor, and Violet Arnott, spinster. For the moment she had forgotten its existence. When she recognised what it was her heart seemed to sink in her bosom; her voice trembled; it was only with an effort that she was able to keep herself from handing it to the man of law in front of her. "No," she stammered, "that's the wrong paper." Just in time she drew it back. If he had only had one glance at it the whole course of her life would have been different. She went on, with as complete a show of calmness as she was capable of, "This is the paper I meant to give you--it is a copy of the certificate of my father's death; and this is a copy of my mother's. They are both buried in the same grave in the cemetery at Scarsdale."

He took the papers she passed to him, seemingly unconscious that there was anything curious in her manner. That other paper, crumpling it up, she slipped between the buttons of her bodice. He looked through the documents she had given him.

"They appear to be perfectly in order--perfectly in order, and I have no doubt that on investigation they will be ascertained to be. By the way, Miss Arnott, I notice that you were born just one-and-twenty years ago."

"Yes; my twenty-first birthday was on the 9th of last month--five weeks ago."

She did not think it necessary to mention that the memory of it would be with her for ever, since it had been celebrated by the arrest of her husband.

"Five weeks ago? A pity that it couldn't have been next month instead of last; then the date of your coming of age might have been made a great occasion. However, it shall still be to you a memorable year. You will, of course, understand that there are certain forms which must be gone through; but I don't think I am premature in expressing to you my personal conviction that you are the person who is intended to benefit under the will of the late Mr Septimus Arnott. Your uncle was one of our multi-millionaires. I cannot, at this moment, state the exact value of his estate; but this I can inform you--that your income will be considerably over one hundred thousand pounds a year."

"One hundred thousand pounds a year!" She gripped, with her right hand, the back of the room's one chair. "Do you mean it?"

"Beyond the shadow of a doubt. I am free to admit that I am fond of a jest; but a fortune of that magnitude is not a fit subject for a joke. Believe me, you will find it a serious matter when you come to be directly responsible for its administration."

"It seems a large sum of money."

He observed her a little curiously; she showed so few signs of emotion, none of elation. In her position, at her age, on receipt of such news, one would have looked for her cheeks to flush, for her lips to be parted by a smile, for a new brightness to come into her eyes--for these things at least. So far as he was able to perceive, not the slightest change took place in her bearing, her manner, her appearance; except that perhaps she became a little paler. The communication he had just made might have been of interest to a third party, but of none to her, so striking was the suggestion of indifference which her demeanour conveyed.

He decided that the explanation was that as yet she was incapable of realising her own good fortune.

"Seems a large sum? It is a large sum! How large I lack words to enable you to clearly comprehend. When we talk of millions we speak of figures anything like the full meaning of which the ordinary imagination is altogether incapable to grasp. I think, Miss Arnott, that some time will probably elapse vast is the responsibility which is about to be placed upon you. In the meantime I would make two remarks--first, that until matters are placed in regular order I shall be happy to place at your disposition any amount of ready cash you may require; and second, that until everything is arranged, Mrs Stacey and myself will be only too glad to extend to you our hospitality at Pembridge Gardens."

"I think, if you don't mind, I should like to remain here at anyrate to-night. I shall have a great many things to consider; I should prefer to do so alone. If you wish it I will call on you in the morning at your offices, and then we will go into everything more fully."

"Very good. As you choose, Miss Arnott. It is for you to command, for me to obey. You are your own mistress in a sense, and to a degree which I fancy you don't at present understand. I took the precaution to provide myself, before leaving home, with a certain amount of ready money. Permit me to place at your service this hundred pounds; you will find that there are twenty five-pound notes. I need scarcely add that the money is your own property. Now as to to-morrow. We have had so much difficulty in finding you, and it is by such a seeming miracle that we have lighted on you at last, that I am reluctant to lose sight of you even for a single night--until, that is, everything is in due order, and you have happily released us from the great weight of responsibility which has lain so long upon us. May I take it that we shall certainly see you to-morrow at our offices at noon?"

"Yes; I will be with you to-morrow at noon." It was on that understanding they parted. Before he left the house Mr Stacey said to his clerk,--

"Gardner, that's a singular young woman. So young, so beautiful, and yet so cold, so frigid, so--stolid. She didn't even thank me for bringing her the good news, neither by a word nor look did she so much as hint that the news had gratified her; indeed, I am not at all sure that she thinks it is good news. In one so young, so charming--because, so far as looks are concerned, she is charming, and she will be particularly so when she is well dressed--it isn't natural, Gardner, it isn't natural."

In the top floor back the girl was contemplating the twenty five-pound notes. She had never before been the owner of so much money, or anything like so much. Had she been the possessor of such a fortune when she came to town she might never have become a "model" in the costume department of the world-famed Messrs Glover & Silk, she might never have made the acquaintance of Robert Champion, she would certainly never have become his wife. The glamour which had seemed to surround him had been the result of the circumstances in which she had first encountered him. Had her own position not been such a pitiable one she would never have been duped by him, by his impudent assurance, his brazen lies, his reckless promises. She had seen that clearly, long ago.

A hundred pounds! Why, the fraud for which, at that moment, he was in gaol had had for its objective a sum of less than twenty pounds. She writhed as she thought of it. Was he already in prisoner's clothes, marked with the broad arrow? Was he thinking of her in his felon's cell? She tried to put the vision from her, as one too horrible for contemplation. Would it persistently recur to her, in season and out, her whole life long? God forbid! Rather than that, better death, despite her uncle's fortune.

In any case she could at least afford to treat herself to a sufficient meal. She went to a quiet restaurant in Oxford Street, and there fared sumptuously--that is, sumptuously in comparison to the fashion in which she had fared this many and many a day. Afterwards, she strolled along the now lamp-lit street. As she went she met a girl of about her own age who was decked out in tawdry splendours. They had nearly passed before they knew each other. Then recognition came. The other girl stopped and turned.

"Why, Vi!" she exclaimed. "Who'd have dreamt of seeing you?"

The girl addressed did not attempt to return the greeting. She did not even acknowledge it. Instead she rushed off the pavement into a "crawling" hansom, saying to the driver as she entered his vehicle,--

"Drive me to the city--anywhere; only be quick and get away from here!"

When she concluded that she was well out of that other girl's sight she instructed the man to drive her to Percy Street. At the corner of the street she alighted. Once more in her attic she did as she had done on her previous return to it--she sank down on to the side of the bed, trembling from head to foot.

The woman who had spoken to her in Oxford Street was Sarah Stevens, who had been a fellow employee at Messrs Glover & Silk's. It was she who had introduced her to Robert Champion. It was largely owing to the tales she had told of him, and to her eager advocacy of his suit, that she had been jockeyed into becoming his wife. It was only afterwards, when it was too late, that she had learnt that the girl was as bad as--if not worse than--the man to whom she had betrayed her. From the beginning the pair had been co-conspirators; Violet Arnott had been their victim.

Was she to be haunted always by the fear of such encounters? Rather than run that risk she would never again set foot in London. Certainly, the sooner she was out of it the better.

CHAPTER III
HE HEIRESS ENTERS INTO HER OWN

During the days and weeks which followed it was as though she were the chief personage in a strange, continuous dream. Always she expected an awakening--of a kind of which she did not dare to think. But the dream continued. All at once her path was strewn with roses; up to then she had seemed to have to pick her way, barefooted, amid stones and thistles. No obstacle of any kind arose. Everything was smooth and easy. Her claim to be her uncle's niece was admitted as soon as it was made. Under her uncle's will Mr Stacey was the sole trustee. To all intents and purposes his trusteeship was at an end when she was found. She was of age; the property was hers to do with exactly as she would. By no conditions was she bound. She was her own mistress; in sole control of that great fortune. It was a singular position for a young girl to find herself suddenly occupying.

She was glad enough to leave her affairs in the hands of Messrs Stacey, Morris & Binns. In those early days the mere attempt to understand them was beyond her power. They were anxious enough to place before her an exact statement of the position she had now to occupy. To some extent she grasped its meaning. But the details she insisted on being allowed to assimilate by degrees.

"If I know pretty well what I have and what I haven't, what I can do and what I can't, and what my duties and responsibilities are, say, in three, or even six months' time, I'll be content. In the meanwhile you must continue to do precisely what you have been doing during the time in which I was still not found. I understand sufficiently to know that you have managed all things better than I am ever likely to."

She provided herself with what she deemed an ample, and, indeed, extravagant supply of clothing at Mrs Stacey's urgent request. That lady's ideas, however, were much more gorgeous than her own. The solicitor's wife insisted that it was only right and proper that she should have a wardrobe which, as she put it, "was suitable to her position." That meant, apparently, that, in the way of wearing apparel, she should supply herself with the contents of a good-sized London shop. To that Miss Arnott objected.

"What do you suppose I shall do with all those things?" she demanded. "I am going into the country to stay there. I am going to live all alone, as my uncle did. I sha'n't see a creature from week's end to week's end--a heap of new dresses won't be wanted for that. They'll all be out of fashion long before I have a chance of wearing them."

Mrs Stacey smiled; she was a lady of ample proportions, who had herself a taste for sumptuous raiment.

"I fancy, dear Miss Arnott, that even now you don't realise your own situation. Do you really suppose that--as you suggest--you will be allowed to live all alone at Exham Park, without seeing a creature from week's end to week's end?"

"Who is going to prevent me?"

"Dear Miss Arnott, you are positively amusing. Before you have been there a fortnight the whole county, at least, will have been inside your doors."

"I hope not."

The look of distress on the young lady's countenance was almost comical.

"You speak, I think, without reflection. I, personally, should be both grieved and disappointed if anything else were to happen."

"You would be grieved and disappointed? Good gracious! Mrs Stacey, why?"

"It is only in accordance with the requirements of common decency that a person in your position should receive adequate recognition. If everyone did not call on you you would be subjected to an injurious slight."

"Certainly that point of view did not occur to me. Up to now no one worth speaking of has recognised my existence in the slightest degree. The idea, therefore, that it has suddenly become everyone's duty to do so is, to say the least, a novel one.

"So I imagined. It is, however, as I say; you see, circumstances are altered. Quite apart from the period when you will possess a town residence--"

"That period will be never."

"Never is a long while--a very long while. I say, quite apart from that period, what I cannot but call your unique position will certainly entitle you to act as one of the leaders of county society."

"How dreadful! I'm beginning to wish my position wasn't so unique."

"You speak, if you will forgive my saying so, as a child. Providence has seen fit to place you in a position in which you will be an object of universal admiration. With your youth, your appearance, your fortune, not only all Hampshire, but all England, will be at your feet.

"All England! Mrs Stacey, isn't that just a little exaggerated?"

"Not in the least. On the contrary, my language, if anything, errs on the side of being too guarded. A beautiful young girl of twenty-one, all alone in the world, with more than a hundred thousand pounds a year entirely under her own control--princes from all parts of the world will tumble over each other in their desire to find favour in your eyes."

"Then princes must be much more foolish persons than I supposed."

"My dear, of that we will say nothing. Don't let us speak evil of dignitaries. I was always brought up to think of them with respect. To return to the subject of your wardrobe. I have merely made these few remarks in order to point out to you how essential it is that you should be furnished, at the outset, with a wardrobe likely to prove equal to all the demands which are certain to be made on one in your position."

"All the same, I won't have five hundred dresses. Position or no position, I know I shall be much happier with five."

It is an undoubted fact that the young lady's equipment of costumes extended to more than five, though it stopped far short of the number which her feminine mentor considered adequate. Indeed, Mrs Stacey made no secret of her opinion that, from the social point of view, her arrangements were scarcely decent.

"At the very first serious call which is made upon your resources, you will find yourself absolutely without a thing to wear. Then you'll have to rush up to town and have clothes made for you in red-hot haste, than which nothing can be more unsatisfactory."

"I shall have to chance that. I hate shops and I hate shopping."

"My dear!"

"I do. I don't care how it is with other girls, it's like that with me. I've already had more than enough of dressmakers; for ever so long I promise you that I won't go near one for another single thing. I'm going to the country, and I'm going to live a country life; and for the kind of country life I mean to live you don't want frocks."

Mrs Stacey lifted up her hands and sighed. To her such sentiments seemed almost improper. It was obvious that Miss Arnott meant to be her own mistress in something more than name. On one question, however, she was over-ruled. That was on the question of a companion.

It was perfectly clear, both to her legal advisers and to the senior partner's wife, that it was altogether impossible for her to live at Exham Park entirely companionless.

"What harm will there be?" she demanded. "I shall be quite alone."

"My dear," returned Mrs Stacey, "you won't understand. It is precisely that which is impossible--you must not be quite alone; a young girl, a mere child like you. People will not only think things, they will say them-- and they will be right in doing so. The idea is monstrous, not to be entertained for a moment. You must have some sort of a companion."

Miss Arnott emitted a sound which might have been meant for a groan.

"Very well then, if I must I must--but she shall be younger than I am; or, at anyrate, not much older."

Mrs Stacey looked as if the suggestion had rendered her temporarily speechless.

"My dear," she finally gasped, "that would be worse than ever.

Two young girls alone together in such a house--what a scandal there would be!"

"Why should there be any scandal?"

Miss Arnott's manner was a little defiant.

"If you cannot see for yourself I would rather you did not force me to explain. I can only assure you that if you are not extremely careful your innocence of evil will lead you into very great difficulties. What you want is a woman of mature age, of wide knowledge of the world; above all, of impregnable respectability. One who will, in a sense, fill the place of a mother, officiate--nominally--as the head of your household, who will help you in entertaining visitors--"

"There will be no visitors to entertain."

The elder lady indulged in what she intended for an enigmatic smile.

"When you have been at Exham Park for six months you will blush at the recollection of your own simplicity. At present I can only ask you to take my word for it that there will be shoals of visitors."

"Then that companion of mine will have to entertain them, that's all. One thing I stipulate: you will have to discover her, I sha'n't."

To this Mrs Stacey willingly acceded. The companion was discovered. She was a Mrs Plummer; of whom her discoverer spoke in tones of chastened solemnity.

"Mrs Plummer is a distant connection of Mr Stacey. As such, he has known her all his life; and can therefore vouch for her in every respect. She has known trouble; and, as trouble always does, it has left its impress upon her. But she is a true woman, with a great heart and a beautiful nature. She is devoted to young people. You will find in her a firm friend, one who will make your interests her own, and who will be able and willing to give you sound advice on all occasions in which you find yourself in difficulty. I am convinced that you will become greatly attached to her; you will find her such a very present help in all times of trouble."

When, a few days before they went down together to Exham Park, Miss Arnott was introduced to Mrs Plummer in Mrs Stacey's drawing-room, in some way, which the young lady would have found it hard to define, she did not accord with her patroness's description. As her custom sometimes was, Miss Arnott plunged headforemost into the midst of things.

"I am told that you are to be my companion. I am very sorry for you, because I am not at all a companionable sort of creature."

"You need not be sorry. I think you will find that I understand the situation. Convention declines to allow a young woman to live alone in her own house; I shall be the necessary figurehead which the proprieties require. I shall never intrude myself. I shall be always in the background--except on occasions when I perceive that you would sooner occupy that place yourself. I shall be quick to see when those occasions arise; and, believe me, they will be more frequent than you may at this moment suspect. As for freedom--you will have more freedom under the ægis of my wing, which will be purely an affair of the imagination, than without it; since, under its imaginary shelter, you will be able to do all manner of things which, otherwise, you would hardly be able to do unchallenged. In fact, with me as cover, you will be able to do exactly as you please; and still remain in the inner sanctuary of Mrs Grundy."

Mrs Plummer spoke with a degree of frankness for which Miss Arnott was unprepared. She looked at her more closely, to find that she was a little woman, apparently younger than she had expected. Her dark brown hair was just beginning to turn grey. She was by no means ugly; the prominent characteristic of her face being the smallness of the features. She had a small mouth, thinly lipped, which, when it was closed, was tightly closed. She had a small, slenderly-fashioned aquiline nose, the nostrils of which were very fine and delicate. Her eyes were small and somewhat prominent, of a curious shade in blue, having about them a quality which suggested that, while they saw everything which was taking place around her, they served as masks which prevented you seeing anything which was transpiring at the back of them. She was dressed like a lady; she spoke like a lady; she looked a lady. Miss Arnott had not been long in her society before she perceived, though perhaps a little dimly, what Mrs Stacey had meant by saying that trouble had left its impress on her. There was in her voice, her face, her bearing, her manner, a something which spoke of habitual self-repression, which was quite possibly the outcome of some season of disaster which, for her, had changed the whole aspect of the world.

The day arrived, at last, when the heiress made her first appearance at Exham Park. The house had been shut up, and practically dismantled, for so long, that the task of putting it in order, collecting an adequate staff of servants, and getting it generally ready for its new mistress, occupied some time. Miss Arnott journeyed with Mrs Plummer; it was the first occasion on which they had been companions. The young lady's sensations, as the train bore her through the sunlit country, were of a very singular nature; the little woman in the opposite corner of the compartment had not the faintest notion how singular.

Mr Stacey met the travellers at the station, ushering them into a landau, the door of which was held open by a gigantic footman in powdered hair and silk stockings. Soon after they had started, Miss Arnott asked a question,--

"Is this my carriage?"

The gentleman replied, with some show of pomposity,--

"It is one of them, Miss Arnott, one of them. You will find, in your coach-houses, a variety of vehicles; but, of course, I do not for a moment pretend that you will find there every kind of conveyance you require. Indeed, the idea has rather been that you should fill the inevitable vacancies in accordance with the dictates of your own taste."

"Whose idea is the flour and the silk stockings?"

She was looking up at the coachman and footman on the box.

"The--eh?--oh, I perceive; you allude to the men's liveries. The liveries, Miss Arnott, were chosen by your late uncle; I think you will admit that they are very handsome ones. It has been felt that, in deference to him, they should be continued, until you thought proper to rule otherwise."

"Then I'm afraid that they won't be continued much longer. In such matters my uncle's tastes were--I hope it isn't treason to say so--perhaps a trifle florid. Mine are all the other way. I don't like floured heads, silk stockings, or crimson velvet breeches; I like everything about me to be plain to the verge of severity. My father's ideal millionaire was mine; shall I tell you what that was?"

"If you will be so good."

"He held that a man with five thousand a year, if he were really a gentleman, would do his best not to allow it to be obvious to the man who only had five hundred that he had more than he had."

"There is something to be said for that point of view; on the other hand, there is a great deal to be said for the other side."

"No doubt. There is always a great deal to be said for the other side. I am only hinting at the one towards which I personally incline." Presently they were passing along an avenue of trees. "Where are we now?"

"We are on your property--this is the drive to the house."

"There seems to be a good deal of it."

"It is rather more than three miles long; there are lodge gates at either end; the house stands almost in the centre."

"It seems rather pretty."

"Pretty! Exham Park is one of the finest seats in the country. That is why your uncle purchased it."

After a while they came in sight of the house.

"Is that the house? It looks more like a palace. Fancy my living all alone in a place like that! Now I understand why a companion was an absolute necessity. It strikes me, Mrs Plummer, that you will want a companion as much as I shall. What shall we two lone, lorn women do in that magnificent abode?"

As they stepped in front of the splendid portico there came down the steps a man who held his hat in his hand, with whom Mr Stacey at once went through the ceremony of introduction.

"Miss Arnott, this is Mr Arthur Cavanagh, your steward."

She found herself confronted by a person who was apparently not much more than thirty years of age; erect, well-built, with short, curly hair, inclined to be ruddy, a huge moustache, and a pair of the merriest blue eyes she had ever seen. When they were in the house, and Mr Stacey was again alone with the two ladies, he observed, with something which approximated to an air of mystery,--

"You must understand, Miss Arnott, that, as regards Mr Cavanagh, we--my partners and myself--have been in a delicate position. He was your uncle's particular protégé. I have reason to know that he came to England at his express request. We have hardly seen our way--acting merely on our own initiative--to displace him."

"Displace him? Why should he be displaced? Isn't he a good steward?"

"As regards that, good stewards are not difficult to find. Under the circumstances, the drawbacks in his case are, I may almost say, notorious. He is young, even absurdly young; he is not ill-looking, and he is unmarried."

Miss Arnott smiled, as if Mr Stacey had been guilty of perpetrating a joke.

"It's not his fault that he is young; it's not my fault that I am young. It's nice not to be ill-looking, and-- I rather fancy--it's nice to be unmarried." She said to Mrs Plummer as, a little later, they were going upstairs together, side by side, "What odd things Mr Stacey does say. Fancy regarding them as drawbacks being young, good-looking and unmarried. What can he be thinking of?"

"I must refer you to him. It is one of the many questions to which I am unable to supply an answer of my own."

When she was in her own room, two faces persisted in getting in front of Miss Arnott's eyes. One was the face of Mr Arthur Cavanagh, the other was that of the man who was serving a term of twelve months' hard labour, and which was always getting, as it were, between her and the daylight.

CHAPTER IV
THE EARL OF PECKHAM'S PROPOSAL

Miss Arnott soon realised what Mrs Stacey had meant by insisting on the impossibility of her living a solitary life. So soon as she arrived upon the scene, visitors began to appear at Exham Park in a constant stream. The day after she came calls were made by two detachments of the clergy, and by the representatives of three medical men. But, as Mrs Plummer somewhat unkindly put it, these might be regarded as professional calls; or, in other words, requests for custom.

"Since you are the patron of these livings, their present holders were bound to haste and make obeisance--though it would seem that, in that respect, one of them is still a defaulter. The way in which those two doctors and their wives, who happened to come together, glowered at each other was beautiful. One quite expected to see them lapse into mutual charges of unprofessional conduct. Which of the three do you propose to favour?"

"Mr Cavanagh says that uncle used to patronise all three. He had one for the servants on the estate one for the indoor servants, and one for himself."

"And which of the three was it who killed him?"

"There came a time when all three were called together to consult upon his case. That finished uncle at once. He died within four-and-twenty hours. So Mr Cavanagh says."

"I suppose Mr Cavanagh is able to supply you with little interesting details on all sorts of recondite subjects?"

"Oh yes; he is like a walking encyclopedia of information on all matters connected with the estate. Whenever I want to know anything I simply go to him; he always knows. It is most convenient."

"And I presume that he is always willing to tell you what you want to know."

"Most willing. I never met a more obliging person. And so good-humoured. Have you noticed his smile?"

"I can't say that I have paid particular attention to his smile."

"It's wonderful; it lights up all his face and makes him positively handsome. I think he's a most delightful person, and so clever. I'm sure he's immensely popular with everyone; not at all like the hard-as-nails stewards one reads about. I can't imagine what Mr Stacey meant by almost expressing a regret that he had not displaced him, can you?"

"Some people sometimes say such extraordinary things that it's no use trying to imagine what they mean."

The answer was a trifle vague; but it seemed to satisfy Miss Arnott. Neither of the ladies looked to see if the other was smiling.

Mrs Stacey's sibylline utterance was prophetic; in a fortnight the whole county had called--that is, so much of it as was within anything like calling distance, and in the country in these days "calling distance" is a term which covers a considerable expanse of ground. Practically the only abstentions were caused by people's absence from home. It was said that some came purposely from London, and even farther, so that they might not lose an opportunity of making Miss Arnott's acquaintance.

For instance, there was the case of the Dowager Countess of Peckham. It happened that the old lady's dower house was at Stevening, some fourteen or fifteen miles from Exham Park. Since she had never occupied it since the time it came into her possession, having always preferred to let it furnished to whoever might come along, one would scarcely have supposed that she would have called herself Miss Arnott's neighbour. When, however, a little bird whispered in her ear what a very charming millionairess was in practically solitary occupation of Exham Park, it chanced that, for the moment, her own house was untenanted, and, within four-and-twenty hours of the receipt of that whispered communication, for the first time in her life she was under its roof. On the following day she covered the fourteen miles which lay between her and Exham Park in a hired fly, was so fortunate as to find Miss Arnott at home, and was so agreeably impressed by the lady herself, by her surroundings, and by all that she heard of her, that she stopped at the village post office on her homeward journey to send a peremptory telegram to her son to come at once. The Earl of Peckham came. He had nothing particular to do just then; or, at least, nothing which he could not easily shirk. He might as well run down to his mother. So he ran down on his automobile. Immediately on his arrival she favoured him with a few home truths; as she had done on many previous occasions, and peremptorily bundled him over to Exham Park.

"Mind! you now have a chance such as you never had before; and such as you certainly will never have again. The girl has untold wealth absolutely at her own command; she hasn't a relation in the world; she is alone with a woman who is perfectly ready to be hoodwinked; she knows nobody worth speaking of. You will have her all to yourself, it will be your own fault if she's not engaged to you in a fortnight, and your wife within six weeks. Think of it, a quarter of a million a year, not as representing her capital, you understand, but a year! and absolutely no relations. None of that crowd of miserable hangers-on which so often represents the mushroom millionaire's family connections. If you don't take advantage of this heaven-sent opportunity, Peckham, you are past praying for--that's all I can say."

Peckham sighed. According to her that always was all she could say, and she had said it so many times. He motored over to Exham Park in a frame of mind which was not in keeping with the character of a light-hearted wooer. He had wanted his mother to accompany him. But she had a conservative objection to motor cars, nothing would induce her to trust herself on one. So, reluctantly enough, he went alone.

"You ask Miss Arnott to lunch to-morrow; you can go over yourself and bring her on your car, it will be an excellent opening. And when she is here I will do the honours. But I have no intention of risking my own life on one of those horrible machines."

As he reached the bottom of a rather steep slope, his lordship met a lady and a gentleman, who were strolling side by side. Stopping, he addressed the gentleman,--

"I beg your pardon, but can you tell me if I am going right for Exham Park? There were crossroads some way back, at the top of the hill, but I was going so fast that I couldn't see what was on the direction posts. I mean Miss Arnott's."

"You will find the lodge gate on your right, about half a mile further on." The speaker hesitated, then added, "This is Miss Arnott."

Off came his lordship's hat again.

"I am very fortunate. I am Peckham--I mean the Earl of Peckham. My mother has sent me with a message."

The lady was regarding the car with interested eyes.

"I never have been on a motor car, but if you could find room for me on yours, you might take me up to the house, and--give me the message."

In a trice the mechanician was in the tonneau, and the lady by his lordship's side. As Mr Cavanagh, left alone, gazed after the retreating car, it was not the good-humoured expression of his countenance which would have struck Miss Arnott most.

The young lady's tastes were plainly altogether different from the old one's--at anyrate, so far as motor cars were concerned. Obviously she did not consider them to be horrible machines. She showed the liveliest interest in this, the first one of which she had had any actual experience. They went for quite a lengthy drive together, three times up and down the drive, which meant nearly nine miles. Once, at the lady's request, the driver showed what his car could do. As it was a machine of the highest grade, and of twenty-four horse power, it could do a good deal. Miss Arnott expressed her approbation of the performance.

"How splendid! I could go on like that for ever; it blows one about a bit, but if one were sensibly dressed that wouldn't matter. How fast were we going?"

"Oh, somewhere about fifty miles an hour. It's all right in a place like this; but, the worst of it is, there are such a lot of beastly policemen about. It's no fun having always to pay fines for excessive speed, and damages for running over people, and that kind of thing."

"I should think not, indeed. Have you ever run over anyone?"

"Well, not exactly; only, accidents will happen, you know."

As she observed that young man's face, a suspicion dawned upon her mind, that--when he was driving--they occasionally would.

Ere she descended she received some elementary lessons in the art of controlling a motor car. And, altogether, by the time they reached the house, and the message was delivered, they were on terms of considerable intimacy.

The acquaintance, thus auspiciously begun, rapidly ripened. The Earl did not find the business on which he was engaged anything like such a nuisance as he had feared; on the contrary, he found it an agreeable occupation. He was of opinion that the girl was not half a bad sort; that, in fact, she was a very good sort indeed. He actually decided that she would have been eligible for a place in the portrait gallery of the Countesses of Peckham even if she had not been set in such a desirable frame. That motor car was a great aid to intimacy. He drove her; and he taught her to drive him. Sometimes, the chauffeur being left behind, they had the car to themselves. It was on such an occasion, when their acquaintance hardly extended beyond his mother's suggested fortnight, that he made her an offer of his hand and heart. She was driving at the time, and going at a pretty good pace, which was possibly on the wrong side of the legal limit; but when she began to have an inkling of what he was talking about, she instantly put on the brakes, and pulled up dead. She was so taken by surprise, and her own hideous position was so continually present to her mind's eye, that it was some seconds before she perceived that the young man at her side must, of necessity, be completely unconscious of the monstrous nature of his proposal. She was silent for several moments, then she answered, while the car was still at a standstill in the middle of the road,--

"Thank you. No doubt your offer is not meant unkindly; but acceptance on my part is altogether out of the question."

"Why?"

"Why? Because it is. I am sorry you should have spoken like this, because I was beginning to like you."

"Isn't that a reason why I should speak? If you are beginning to like me, by degrees you may get to like me more and more."

"I think not. Because this little contretemps will necessarily put a period to our acquaintance."

"Oh, rats! that isn't fair! If I'd thought it would worry you I wouldn't have said a word. Only--I should like to ask if there is anybody else."

"Do you mean, is there anyone else to whom I am engaged to be married? There is not--and there never will be."

"I say, Miss Arnott! Every man in England--who can get within reach of you--will have tried his luck before the end of the season. You will have to take one of them, to save yourself from being bothered."

"Shall I? You think so? You are wrong. If you don't mind, I will turn the car round, and take it to the lodge gate; then I will get out, and walk home. Only there must be no more conversation of this sort on the way, or I shall get out at once."

"You need not fear that I shall offend again; put her round."

She "put her round." They gained the lodge gate. The lady descended.

"Good-bye, Lord Peckham. I have to thank you for some very pleasant rides, and for much valuable instruction. I'm sorry I couldn't do what you wanted, but--it's impossible."

"I sha'n't forget the jolly time I've had with you, and shall hope to meet you again when you come to town. You are inclined to treat me with severity, but I assure you that if you intend to treat every man severely, merely because he proposes, you have set yourself a task which would have been too much for the strength of Hercules."

His lordship returned then and there to London. On the road he sent a telegram to his mother which contained these two words only: "Been refused."

On her part, Miss Arnott did not at once return to the house. She chose instead a winding path which led to a certain woodland glade which she had already learned to love. There, amidst the trees, the bushes, the gorse, the wild flowers, the tall grasses and the bracken, she could enjoy solitary communion with her own thoughts. Just then she had plenty to think about. There was not only Lord Peckham's strange conduct, there was also his parting words.

Her knowledge of the world was very scanty, especially of that sort of world in which she so suddenly found herself. But she was a girl of quick intuitions; and already she had noticed a something in the demeanour of some of the masculine acquaintances she had made which she had not altogether relished. Could what Lord Peckham had said be true? Would every man who came within reach of her try his luck--in a certain sense? If so, a most unpleasant prospect was in store for her. There was one way out of the difficulty. She had only to announce that she was a married woman and that sort of persecution would cease at once. She doubted, however, if the remedy would not be worse than the disease. She had grown to regard her matrimonial fetters with such loathing, that, rather than acknowledge, voluntarily, that she was bound about by them, and admit that her husband was an unspeakable creature in a felon's cell, she believed that she was ready to endure anything. Certainly she would sooner reject a dozen men a day.

She came to the woodland glade she sought. It so chanced that the particular nook which she had learned, from experience, was the best to recline in was just on the other side of a rough fence. She crossed the fence, reclined at her ease on the mossy bank; and thought, and thought, and thought. On a sudden she was roused from her deepest day-dream by a voice which addressed to her an inquiry from above,--

"Are you trespassing--or am I?"

CHAPTER V
TRESPASSING

She looked up with a start--to find that a man was observing her who seemed to be unusually tall. She lay in a hollow, he stood on the top of the bank; so that perhaps their relative positions tended to exaggerate his apparent inches. But that he was tall was beyond a doubt. He was also broad. Her first feeling was, that she had never seen a man who was at once so tall and so broad across the shoulders. He was rather untidily dressed--in a grey tweed knickerbocker suit, with a Norfolk jacket, and a huge cap which was crammed right down on his head. He wore a flannel shirt, and a dark blue knitted tie, which was tied in a scrambling sailor's knot. Both hands were in the pockets of his jacket, which was wide open; and, altogether, the impression was conveyed to her, as she lay so far beneath him, that he was of a monstrous size.

It struck her that his being where he was was an impertinence, which was rendered much greater by his venturing to address her; especially with such an inquiry. Merely raising herself on her elbow, she favoured him with a glance which was intended to crush him.

"There can be no doubt as to who is trespassing as you must be perfectly well aware--you are."

"I quite agree with you in thinking that there can be no doubt as to who is trespassing; but there, unfortunately, our agreement ends, because, as it happens, you are."

"Do you suppose that I don't know which is my own property? I am Miss Arnott, of Exham Park--this is part of my ground."

"I fancy, with all possible deference, that I know which is my property better than you appear to know which is yours. I am Hugh Morice, of Oak Dene, and, beyond the slightest shadow of a doubt, the ground on which we both are is mine."

She rose to her feet a little hurriedly.

"What authority have you for what you say? Are you trying to amuse yourself at my expense?"

"Allow me to explain. You see that fence, which is in rather a doddering condition--it forms the boundary line between Exham Park and Oak Dene, a fact which I have a particular reason to remember.

Once, before this was my ground, I was shooting in these woods. My bird-- it was only a pigeon--dropped on the other side of that fence. I was no better acquainted with the landmarks then than you appear to be now. Not aware that there was any difference between this side and that, I was scrambling over the fence to retrieve my pigeon when I was pulled up short by some very plain words, pronounced in a very plain tone of voice. I won't tell you what the words were, because you might like them even less than I did. I looked up; and there was an old gentleman, who was flanked by two persons who were evidently keepers. He was one of the most eloquent old gentlemen I had ever met. He commenced by wanting to know what I meant by being about to defile his ground by the intrusion of my person. I replied that I wasn't aware that it was his ground, and that I wanted my pigeon. He asked me who I was. When I told him he informed me that he was Septimus Arnott, and desired me to inform all persons bearing my name what he thought of them. He thought a good deal--in a sense. He wound up by remarking that he would instruct his keepers, if ever they caught me on the wrong side of that fence, to put a charge of lead into me at sight. Towards the end of the interview I was as genially disposed as he was; so I retorted by assuring him that if ever I caught anyone from Exham Park on this side, I'd do the honours with a charge of lead. This is the exact spot on which that interview took place--he was there and I here. But the circumstances have changed--it is Exham Park who is now the trespasser. Shall I put a charge of lead into you?"

"By all means--if you wish to."

"I am not quite sure that I do wish to."

"If you have the slightest inclination in that direction, pray don't hesitate."

"You mightn't like it."

"Don't consider my feelings, I beg. In such a matter surely you wouldn't allow my feelings to count."

"No? You think not? I don't know. Perhaps you're right; but, you see, I haven't a gun. I can't put charges of lead into anything, or anyone, without one.

"Pray don't let any trifling obstacle of that kind stand in your way. Permit me to send for one."

"Would you? You're very good. Who would you send?"

"Of course I would myself fetch you the indispensable weapon."

"And how long would you be, do you imagine? Should I have

time to smoke a pipe while you were going there and back?"

Suddenly the lady drew herself up with a gesture which was possibly meant to be expressive of a judicious mingling of scorn with hauteur.

"It is possible, if you prefer it. I will admit that it is probable that my uncle was rude to you. Do you intend to continue the tradition, and be rude to me?"

"I was simply telling you a little anecdote, Miss Arnott."

"I am obliged to you for taking so much trouble. Now, with your permission, I will return to what you state to be my side of the fence."

"I state? Don't you state that that side of the fence is yours?"

"My impression was that both sides were mine. I will have the matter carefully inquired into. If your statement proves to be correct I will see that a communication is sent to you, conveying my apologies for having been an unwitting trespasser on your estate."

"Thank you. Can I lift you over?"

"Lift me over!"

The air of red-hot indignation with which his proposition was declined ought to have scorched him. It seemed, however, to have no effect on him of any sort. He continued to regard her from the top of the bank, with an air of indolent nonchalance, which was rapidly driving her to the conclusion that he was the most insolent person she had ever encountered. With a view, possibly, of showing the full absurdity of his offer of assistance, she placed both hands on the top of the fence, with the intention of vaulting over it. The intention was only partially fulfilled. During her wanderings with her father among their Cumberland hills she had become skilled in all manner of athletic exercises. Ordinarily she would have thought nothing of vaulting--or, for the matter of that, jumping--an insignificant fence. Perhaps her nervous system was more disorganised than she imagined. She caught her knee against the bar, and, instead of alighting gracefully on her feet, she rolled ignominiously over. She was up almost as soon as she was down, but not before he had cleared the fence at a bound, and was standing at her side. She exhibited no sign of gratitude for the rapidity with which he had come to her assistance. She merely put to him an icy question,--

"Was it necessary that you should trespass also?"

"Are you sure that you are not hurt? ankle not twisted, or anything of that kind?"

"Quite sure. Be so good as to return to your own side."

As he seemed to hesitate, a voice exclaimed, in husky tones,--

"By----, I've a mind to shoot you now."

He turned to see a man, between forty and fifty years of age, in the unmistakable habiliments of a gamekeeper, standing some twenty feet off, holding a gun in a fashion which suggested that it would need very little to induce him to put it to his shoulder and pull the trigger. Hugh Morice greeted him as if he were an old acquaintance.

"Hullo, Jim Baker! So you're still in the land of the living?"

Mr Baker displayed something more than surliness in his reply.

"So are you, worse luck! What are you doing here? Didn't Mr Arnott tell me if I saw you on our land to let fly, and pepper you?"

"I was just telling Miss Arnott the story. Odd that you should come upon the scene as corroborating evidence."

"For two pins I'd let fly!"

"Now, Baker, don't be an idiot. Take care how you handle that gun, or there'll be trouble; your hands don't seem too steady. You don't want me to give you another thrashing, do you? Have you forgotten the last one I gave you?"

"Have I forgotten?" The man cursed his questioner with a vigour which was startling. "I'll never forget--trust me. I'll be even with you yet, trust me. By ---- if you say another word about it I'll let fly at you now!"

Up went the stock of the gun to the speaker's shoulder, the muzzle pointing direct at Mr Morice. That gentleman neither moved nor spoke; Miss Arnott did both.

"Baker, are you mad? Put down that gun. How dare you so misbehave yourself?"

The gun was lowered with evident reluctance.

"Mr Arnott, he told me to shoot him if ever I see him this side the fence."

"I am mistress here now. You may think yourself fortunate if you're not presently introduced to a policeman."

"I was only obeying orders, that's all I was doing."

"Orders! How long ago is it since the orders to which you refer were given you?"

Mr Morice interposed an answer,--

"It's more than four years since I was near the place."

The keeper turned towards him with a vindictive snarl.

"Four years! what's four years? An order's an order if it's four years or forty. How was I to know that things are different, and that now you're to come poaching and trespassing whenever you please?"

Miss Arnott was very stern.

"Baker, take yourself away from here at once. You will hear of this again. Do you hear me? Go! without a word!"

Mr Baker went, but as he went he delivered himself of several words. They were uttered to himself rather than to the general public, but they were pretty audible all the same. When he was out of sight and sound, the lady put a question to the gentleman,--

"Do you think it possible that he could have been in earnest, and that he would have shot you?"

"I daresay. I suspect that few things would have pleased him better. Why not? He would only have been carrying out instructions received."

"But--Mr Morice, I wish you would not jest on such a subject! Has he a personal grudge against you?"

"It depends upon what you call a grudge; you heard what he said. He used to live in that cottage near the gravel pits; and may do so still for all I know. Once, when I was passing, I heard a terrible hullabaloo. I invited myself inside to find that Mr Baker was correcting Mrs Baker with what seemed to me such unnecessary vigour that--I corrected him. The incident seems to linger in his memory, in spite of the passage of the years; and I shouldn't be at all surprised if, in his turn, he is still quite willing to correct me, with the aid of a few pellets of lead."

"But he must be a dangerous character."

"He's a character, at anyrate. I've always felt he was a little mad; when he's drunk he's stark mad. He's perhaps been having half a gallon now. Let me hasten to assure you that, I fancy, Baker's qualities were regarded by Mr Septimus Arnott, in the main, as virtues. Mr Arnott was himself a character; if I may be excused for saying so."

"I never saw my uncle in his life, and knew absolutely nothing about him, except what my father used to tell me of the days when they were boys together."

"If, in those days, he was anything like what he was afterwards, he must have been a curiosity. To make the whole position clear to you I should mention that my uncle was also a character. I am not sure that, taking him altogether, he was not the more remarkable character of the two. The Morices, of course, have been here since the flood. But when your uncle came my uncle detected in him a kindred spirit. They became intimates; inseparable chums, and a pair of curios I promise you they were, until they quarrelled--over a game of chess."

"Of chess?"

"Of chess. They used to play together three or four times a week--tremendous games. Until one evening my uncle insisted that your uncle had taken his hand off a piece, and wouldn't allow him to withdraw his move. Then the fur flew. Each called the other everything he could think of, and both had an extensive répertoire. The war which followed raged unceasingly; it's a mystery to me how they both managed to die in their beds."

"And all because of a dispute over a game of chess?"

"My uncle could quarrel about a less serious matter than a game of chess; he was a master of the art. He quarrelled with me--but that's another story; since when I've been in the out-of-the-way-corners of the world. I was in Northern Rhodesia when I heard that he was dead, and had left me Oak Dene. I don't know why-- except that there has always been a Morice at Oak Dene, and that I am the only remaining specimen of the breed."

"How strange. It is only recently that I learned--to my complete surprise--that Exham Park was mine."

"It seems that we are both of us indebted to our uncles, dead; though apparently we neither of us owed much to them while they still were living. Well, are the orders to be perpetuated that I'm to be shot when seen on this side of the fence?"

"I do not myself practise such methods."

"They are drastic; though there are occasions on which drastic methods are the kindest. Since I only arrived yesterday I take it that I am the latest comer. It is your duty, therefore, to call on me. Do you propose to do your duty?"

"I certainly do not propose to call on you, if that's what you mean."

"Good. Then I'll call on you. I shall have the pleasure, Miss Arnott, of waiting on you, on this side of the fence, at a very early date. Do you keep a shot gun in the hall?"

"Do you consider it good taste to persist in harping on a subject which you must perceive is distasteful?"

"My taste was always bad."

"That I can easily imagine."

"There is something which I also can easily imagine."

"Indeed?"

"I can imagine that your uncle left you something besides Exham

Park."

"What is that?"

"A little of his temper."

"Mr Morice! I have no wish to exchange retorts with you, but, from what you say, it is quite obvious that your uncle left you all his manners."

"Thank you. Anything else?"

"Yes, Mr Morice, there is something else. It is not my fault that we are neighbours."

"Don't say that it's my misfortune."

"And since you must have left many inconsolable friends behind you in Rhodesia there is no reason why we should continue to be neighbours."

"Quite so."

"Of course, whether you return to Rhodesia or remain here is a matter of complete indifference to me."

"Precisely."

"But, should you elect to stay, you will be so good as to understand that, if you do call at Exham Park, you will be told that I am not at home. Good afternoon, Mr Morice, and good-bye."

"Good-bye, Miss Arnott. I had a sort of premonition that those orders would be re-issued, and that I should be shot if I was seen this side."

She had already gone some distance; but, on hearing this, stopping, she turned towards him again.

"Possibly if we raise the fence to a sufficient height, that will keep you out."

"Oh, I can scale any fence. No fence was ever constructed that I couldn't negotiate. You'll have to shoot."

"Shall we? We shall see."

"We shall--Miss Arnott?"

She stopped again.

"What is it you wish to say to me?"

"Merely that I have in my mind some half-formed intention to call on you to-morrow."

"You dare!"

"You have no notion what I do dare."

This time she was not tempted to a further rejoinder. He watched her as, straight as a dart, her head in the air, striding along the winding path, she vanished among the trees. He ruminated after she had gone,--

"She's splendid! she magnificent! How she holds herself, and how she looks at you, and what eyes they are with which to look. I never saw anything like her, and I hope, for her own sake, she never saw anything like me. What a brute she must think me, and what a brute I am. I don't care; there's something about her which sets all my blood on fire, which rouses in me the instinct of the hunter. I wish old Baker would come along just now; gun or no gun, we'd have a pretty little argument. It might do me good. There's no doubt that what I said was true--the girl has her uncle's temper, if I've my uncle's manners; as I'm a sinful man I've as good as half a mind to marry her."

The lady was unconscious of the compliments which, mentally, the gentleman was paying her. When, returning home, she entered the apartment where Mrs Plummer, apparently just roused from a peaceful doze, was waiting for her tea, she was in a flame of passion.

"I have just left the most unendurable person I ever yet encountered, the most ill-mannered, the most clumsy, the most cowardly, the most stupid, the most absurd, the most unspeakable!"

"My dear! who is this very superlative individual? what is his delightful name?"

"His name!" For some occult reason Mrs Plummer's, under the circumstances, mild request, seemed to cause her passion to flame up higher. "What do I care what his name is? So far as I am concerned such a creature has no name!"

CHAPTER VI
AN AUTHORITY ON THE LAW OF MARRIAGE

The next day Mr Hugh Morice fulfilled his threat--he paid his ceremonial call at Exham Park. The word "ceremonial" is used advisedly, since nothing could have been more formal and decorous than his demeanour throughout.

Miss Arnott and Mrs Plummer happened to be entertaining four or five people that afternoon, among them a Mr Pyecroft, a curate attached to one of Miss Arnott's three livings. He was favouring that lady with a graphic account of the difficulties encountered in endeavouring, in a country place, to arouse interest on any subject whatever, and was illustrating the position by describing the disappointments he had met with in the course of an attempt he had made to organise a series of local entertainments in aid of a new church organ, when his listener suddenly became conscious that a person had just entered the room, who, if she could believe her eyes, was none other than the unspeakable individual of the previous day. Not only was it unmistakably he, but he was actually--with an air of complete self-possession--marching straight across the room towards her. When he stood in front of her, he bowed and said,--

"Permit me, Miss Arnott, to introduce myself to you. I am Hugh Morice, of Oak Dene, which, as you are probably aware, adjoins Exham Park. I only arrived two days ago, and, so soon as I learned that I was honoured by having you as a neighbour, I ventured to lose no time in--with your permission--making myself known to you."

Miss Arnott looked at him with an expression on her countenance which was hardly encouraging. His own assurance was so perfect that it deprived her, for the moment, of her presence of mind. He wore a suit of dark blue serge, which made him seem huger even than he had done the day before. In the presence of Mr Pyecroft, and of the other people, she could scarcely assail this smiling giant, and remind him, pointedly, that she had forbidden him to call. Some sort of explanation would have to be forthcoming, and it was exactly an explanation which she desired to avoid. Observing that she seemed tongue-tied, the visitor continued,--

"I have been so long a wanderer among savages that I have almost forgotten the teachings of my guide to good manners. I am quite unaware, for example, what, as regards calling, is the correct etiquette on an occasion when an unmarried man finds himself the next-door neighbour to an unmarried lady. As I could hardly expect you to call upon me I dared to take the initiative. What I feared most was that I might not find you in."

The invitation was so obvious that the lady at once accepted it.

"It is only by the merest accident that you have done so."

Mr Morice was equal to the occasion. "I fancy, Miss Arnott, that for some of the happiest hours of our lives we are indebted to accidents. Ah, Pyecroft, so you have not deserted us."

Mr Morice shook hands with Mr Pyecroft--Miss Arnott thought they looked a most incongruous couple--with an air of old comradeship, and presently was exchanging greetings with others of those present with a degree of heartiness which, to his hostess, made it seem impossible that she should have him shown the door. When all the other visitors had gone--including the unspeakable man--she found, to her amazement, that he had made a most favourable impression on Mrs Plummer. That lady began almost as soon as his back was turned.

"What a delightful person Mr Morice is." Miss Arnott was so taken by surprise that she could do nothing but stare. Mrs Plummer went placidly on, "It is nice to be able just to look at him, the mere sight of him's a satisfaction. To a little woman the idea of a man of his size is such a comfort."

The young lady's manner was not effusive.

"We're not all of us fond of monstrosities."

"Monstrosities! my dear! He's not a monstrosity, he's a perfect figure of a man, magnificently proportioned. You must admit that."

"I don't."

"And then his manners are so charming."

"They never struck me like that."

"No? I suppose one judges people as one finds them. I know he was particularly nice to me. By the way, that dreadful person you spoke of yesterday, you might tell me what his name is, so that I might be on my guard against him, should our paths happen to cross."

"I repeat what I have already told you that, so far as I am concerned, he has no name; and anyhow, you wouldn't recognise him from my description if you did meet."

It was odd, considering how much Miss Arnott disliked Mr Morice, how frequently he was destined to come, at anyrate, within her line of vision. And yet, perhaps, it was natural--because, although their houses were a couple of miles apart, their estates joined--they were neighbours. And then Miss Arnott was inclined to suspect that the gentleman went out of his way to bring about a meeting. Situated as they were, it was not a difficult thing to do.

To a certain extent, the lady had accepted the position. That is, she had allowed the acquaintance to continue; being, indeed, more than half disposed to fear that she might not find it easy to refuse to know him altogether. But she had been careful to avoid any reference to that curious first encounter. He, on his part, had shown no disposition to allude to it. So there grew up between them a sort of casual intimacy. They saw each other often. When he spoke to her she spoke to him, though never at any greater length than, as it seemed to her, she could help.

With the lessons she had received from the Earl of Peckham still fresh in her mind she bought herself a motor car; almost simultaneously with its appearance on the scene her relations with Hugh Morice began to be on a friendlier footing. She was sitting in it one day, talking to the lodge-keeper, when Mr Morice came striding by. At sight of it he at once approached.

"That's a strange beast."

She had become somewhat accustomed to his odd tricks of speech, and merely smiled a wintry smile.

"You think so?"

"It's not only a strange, it's a wonderful beast, since it holds in its hands no small portion of the future history of the world."

"Are you referring to this particular machine?"

"I am referring to all the machines of which that one's a type. They're going to repeat the performance of Puffing' Billy--produce a revolution. I wish you'd give me a ride."

"I was just thinking of going in."

"Put off going in for a few minutes--take me for a run."

She looked at the chauffeur, who was quick to take the hint. Presently they were bowling along between the hedgerows, she conscious that his eyes were paying more attention to her than she quite relished. A fact of which his words immediately gave evidence.

"You like it. This feeling of flight through the air, which you can command by touching a handle, supplies you with an evanescent interest in life which, in ordinary, everyday existence you find lacking."

"What do you mean?"

"Is it necessary that I should tell you? Do you wish me to?"

"Do you mean that, as a general rule, I don't take an interest in things?"

"Do you? At your age, in your position, you ought to take an interest in everything. But the impression you convey to my mind is that you don't, that you take an interest in nothing. You try to, sometimes, pretty hard. But you never quite succeed. I don't know why. You remind me, in some odd way, of the impersonal attitude of a spectator who looks on at something with which he never expects to have any personal concern."

"I don't know what you're talking about, I don't believe you do either. You say the strangest things."

"You don't find them strange, you understand them better than I do. I am many years older than you--ye Goths, how many! I am tolerably blasé, as befits my age. But you, you are tired--mortally tired-

-of everything already. I've not yet reached that stage. You don't know what keenness means; thank goodness there are still a good many things which I am keen about. Just as something turns up for which you're on the point of really caring, a shadow steps from the back of your mind to the front, and stops you. I don't know what it is, but I know it's there."

"I'm going back."

As this man spoke something tugged at her heartstrings which filled her with a sort of terror. If he was beginning to regard her attitude towards life--of which she herself was only too hideously conscious--as a problem, the solution of which he had set himself to find out, what might the consequences not be? Then she could not stop to think. She swung the car round towards home. As if in obedience to her unspoken hint he changed the subject, speaking with that calm assumption of authority which galled her the more because she found herself so frequently compelled to submission.

"You must teach me to drive this machine of yours."

"My mechanician will be able to do that better than I can, I am myself only a tyro."

"Thank you, I prefer that you should teach me. Which handle do you move to stop?" She showed him. "And which to start?" She showed him again.

Before they parted, she had put him, however unwillingly, through quite a small course of elementary instruction. In consequence of which she had a bad quarter of an hour, when, later, she was in her own sitting-room, alone.

"He frightens me! He makes me do things I don't want to do; and then--he seems to know me better than I know myself. Is it so obvious that I find it difficult to take a real interest in things? or has he a preternaturally keen sense of perception? Either way it isn't nice for me. It's true enough; nothing does interest me. How should it? What does money, and all that matter; when there's that--shadow--in the prison, coming closer to me, day by day? I believe that being where I am--Miss Arnott of Exham Park--makes it worse, because if it weren't for the shadow, it would be so different--so different!"

That night she dreamed of Hugh Morice. She and he were on the motor car together, flying through the sunshine, on and on and on, happy as the day was bright, and the road was fair. Suddenly the sun became obscured, all the world was dark; they were approaching a chasm. Although it was so dark she knew that it was there. In a wild frenzy of fear she tried to stop the car, to find, all at once, that it had no brake. She made to leap out on to the road, but Mr Morice seized her round the waist and held her. In another moment they were dashing over the edge of an abyss, into the nameless horrors which lay below.

It was not a pleasant dream, it did not leave an agreeable impression on her mind after she was awake. But dreams are only dreams. Sensible people pay no heed to them. Miss Arnott proved herself to be sensible at least in that respect. She did not, ever afterwards, refuse him a seat in her car, because she had once, in a nightmare, come to grief in his society. On the contrary, she not only took him for other drives, but-- imitating her own experience with the Earl of Peckham, when, after a while--it was a very little while--he had attained to a certain degree of proficiency, she suffered him to drive her. And, as she had done, he liked driving so much that, before long, he also had an automobile of his own.

Then a new phase of the affair commenced. It was, of course, necessary that--with a view of extending her experience, and increasing her knowledge of motor cars--she should try her hand at driving his. She tried her hand, a first and a second time, perhaps a third. She admitted that his car was not a bad one. It had its points--but slight vibration, little noise, scarcely any smell. It ran sweetly, was a good climber, easy to steer. Certainly a capital car. So much she was ready to allow. But, at the same time, she could not but express her opinion that, on the whole, hers was a better one. There they joined issue. At first, Mr Morice was disposed to doubt, he was inclined to think that perhaps, for certain reasons, the lady's car might be a shade the superior. But, by degrees, as he became more accustomed to his new possession, he changed his mind. He was moved to state his conviction that, as a matter of fact, the superiority lay with his own car.

Whereupon both parties proceeded to demonstrate with which of the pair the palm of merit really lay. They ran all sorts of trials together--trials which sometimes resulted in extremely warm arguments; and by which, somehow, very little was proved. At anyrate, each party was always ready to discount the value of the conclusion at which the other had arrived.

One fact was noticeable--as evidence of the keen spirit of emulation. Wherever one car was the other was nearly sure to be somewhere near at hand.

Mrs Plummer, who had a gift of silence, said little. But one remark she made did strike Miss Arnott as peculiar.

"Mr Morice doesn't seem to have so many friends, or even acquaintances, as I should have expected in a man in his position."

"How do you know he hasn't?"

"I say he doesn't seem to have. He never has anyone at his own house, and he never goes to anyone else's. He always seems to be alone."

Miss Arnott was still. Mrs Plummer had not accentuated it in the slightest degree; yet the young lady wondered in what sense--in that construction--she had used the word "alone."

One day, when she was in town, Miss Arnott did a singular thing. Having deposited Mrs Plummer in a large drapery establishment, with peremptory instructions to make certain considerable purchases, she went off in a hansom by herself to an address in the Temple. Having arrived, she perceived in the hall of the house she had entered a board, on which were painted a number of names. Her glance rested on one--First floor, Mr Whitcomb. Without hesitation she ascended to the first floor, until she found herself confronted by a door on which that name appeared in black letters. She knocked; the door was opened by a very young gentleman.

"Can I see Mr Whitcomb?" she inquired.

"What name? Have you an appointment?"

"I have not an appointment, and my name is of no consequence. I wish to see Mr Whitcomb on very particular business."

The young gentleman looked at her askance, as if he was of opinion--which he emphatically was--that she was not at all the sort of person he was accustomed to see outside that door.

"Mr Whitcomb doesn't generally see people without an appointment, especially if he doesn't know their names; but if you'll step inside, I'll see if he's engaged."

She stepped inside to find herself in an apartment in which there were several other young gentlemen, of somewhat riper years; one and all of whom, she immediately became conscious, began to take the liveliest interest in her. Soon there appeared a grey-haired man, who held a pair of spectacles between the fingers of his right hand.

"May I ask what your name is? and what is the nature of the business on which you wish to see Mr Whitcomb?"

"I have already explained that my name doesn't matter. And I can only state my business to Mr Whitcomb himself." Then she added, as if struck by the look of doubt in the grey-haired man's face, "Pray don't imagine that I am here to beg for subscriptions to a charity or any nonsense of that kind. I wish to see Mr Whitcomb about something very important."

The grey-headed man smiled faintly, apparently amused by something in the caller's manner, or appearance. Departing whence he came he almost immediately reappeared, and beckoned to her with his hand.

"Mr Whitcomb is very much engaged, but he will manage to spare you five minutes."

"I daresay I sha'n't want to keep him longer."

She found herself in a spacious room, which was principally furnished, as it seemed to her, with books. At a table, which was almost entirely covered with books, both open and shut, stood a tall man, with snow-white hair, who bowed to her as she entered.

"You wish to see me?"

"You are Mr Whitcomb?"

"That is my name. How can I serve you?"

She seated herself on the chair towards which he pointed. Each looked at the other for some seconds, in silence. Then she spoke.

"I want you to tell me on what grounds a wife can obtain a divorce from her husband."

Mr Whitcomb raised his eyebrows and smiled.

"I think, madam, that it may have been a solicitor you wanted. I, unfortunately, am only a barrister. I fear you have made a mistake."

"I have not made a mistake; how have I made a mistake? I saw in a paper the other day that you were the greatest living authority on the law of marriage."

"It was very good of the paper to say so. Since I am indebted for your presence here to so handsome a compliment, I will waive the point of etiquette and inform you--of what you, surely, must be already aware--that the grounds on which a divorce may be obtained are various."

"I know that; that isn't what I mean. What I specially want to know is this--can a woman get a divorce from her husband because he gets sent to prison?"

"Because he gets sent to prison? For doing what?"

"For--for swindling; because he's a scoundrel."

Mr Whitcomb's eyebrows went up again.

"The idea that a marriage may be dissolved because one of the parties is guilty of felony, and is consequently sentenced to a term of imprisonment, is a novel one to me."

"Not if a girl finds out that the man who has married her is a villain and a thief? A thief, mind."

He shook his head.

"I find that that would be no ground for dissolution."

"Are you sure?"

"My dear young lady, you were good enough to say that some paper or other credited me with a knowledge of the laws dealing with the subject of marriage. I can assure you that on that point there is no doubt whatever."

"Is that so?" The girl's lips were tightly compressed, her brows knit. "Then there are no means whatever by which a wife can be rid of a husband whom she discovers to be a rogue and a rascal?"

"Not merely because he is a rogue and a rascal; except by the act of God."

"What do you mean by the act of God?"

"If, for example, he should die."

"If he should die? I see! There is no way by which she can be released from him except by--death. Thank you, that is all I wanted to know."

She laid on his table what, to his surprise, he perceived to be a twenty-pound note.

"My dear young lady, what is this?"

"That is your fee. I don't want to occupy your time or obtain information from you for nothing."

"But you have done neither. Permit me to return you this. That is not the way in which I do business; in this instance, the honour of having been consulted by you is a sufficient payment. Before you go, however, let me give a piece of really valuable advice. If you have a friend who is in any matrimonial trouble, persuade her to see a respectable solicitor at once, and to place the whole facts before him unreservedly. He may be able to show her a way out of her difficulty which would never have occurred to her."

He commented--inwardly--on his visitor, after her departure.

"That's either a very simple-minded young woman or a most unusual character. Fancy her coming to me with such an inquiry! She has got herself into some matrimonial mess, most probably, without the cognisance of her friends. Unless I am mistaken she is the kind of young woman who, if she has made up her mind to get out of it, will get out of it; if not by fair means, then-- though I hope not!--by foul."

CHAPTER VII
MR MORICE PRESUMES

One day a desire seized Miss Arnott to revisit the place where she had first met Mr Morice. She had not been there since. That memorable encounter had spoilt it for her. It had been her custom to wander there nearly every fine day. But, since it had been defiled by such a memory, for her, its charm had fled.

Still, as the weeks went by, it dawned upon her by degrees, that, after all, there was no substantial reason why she should turn her back on it for ever. It was a delightful spot; so secluded, so suited to solitary meditation.

"I certainly do not intend," she told herself, "to allow that man"--with an accent on the "that"--"to prevent my occasionally visiting one of the prettiest parts of my own property. It would be mere affectation on my part to pretend that the place will ever be to me the same again; but that is no reason why I should never take a walk in that direction."

It was pleasant weather, sunny, not too warm and little wind. Just the weather for a woodland stroll, and, also, just the weather for a motor ride. That latter fact was particularly present to her mind, because she happened to be undergoing one of those little experiences which temper an automobilist's joys. The machine was in hospital. She had intended to go for a long run to-day, but yesterday something had all at once gone wrong with the differential, the clutch, the bevel gear or something or other. She herself did not quite know what, or, apparently, anyone else either. As a result, the car, instead of flying with her over the sun-lit roads, was being overhauled by the nearest local experts.

That was bad enough. But what almost made it worse was the additional fact that Hugh Morice's car was flying over the aforesaid country roads with him. That her car should have broken down, though ever so slightly, and his should not--that altogether inferior article, of which he was continually boasting in the most absurd manner--was gall and wormwood.

The accident, which had rendered her own car for the moment unavailable, had something to do with her stroll; the consciousness that "that man" was miles away on his had more.

"At anyrate I sha'n't run the risk of any more impertinent interferences with my privacy. Fortunately, so far as I know, there is no one else in the neighbourhood who behaves quite as he does. So, as he is risking his life on that noisy machine of his, I am safe. I only hope he won't break his neck on it; there never was such a reckless driver."

This pious wish of hers was destined to receive an instant answer. Hardly had the words been uttered, than, emerging from the narrow path, winding among the trees and bushes, along which she had been wandering, she received ample proof that Mr Morice's neck still remained unbroken. The gentleman himself was standing not fifty paces from where she was. So disagreeably was she taken by surprise that she would have immediately withdrawn, and returned at the top of her speed by the way she had come, had it not been for two things. One was that he saw her as soon as she saw him; and the other that she also saw something else, the sight of which filled her with amazement.

The first reason would not have been sufficient to detain her; although, so soon as he caught sight of her, he hailed her in his usual hearty tones. The terms of courtesy--or rather of discourtesy--on which these two stood towards each other were of such a nature that she held herself at liberty wholly to ignore him whenever she felt inclined. More than once when they had parted they had been on something less than speaking terms. For days together she had done her very best to cut him dead. Then, when at last, owing to his calm persistency, the acquaintance was renewed, he evinced not the slightest consciousness of its having ever been interrupted. Therefore she would not have hesitated to have turned on her heels, and walked away without a word--in spite of his salutation, had it not been for the something which amazed her.

The fence had been moved!

At first she thought that her eyes, or her senses, were playing her a trick. But a moment's inspection showed her that the thing was so. The old wooden, lichen-covered rails had been taken away for a space of sixty or seventy feet; and, instead, a little distance farther back, on the Oak Dene land, a solid, brand-new fence had been erected; standing in a position which conveyed the impression that the sheltered nook to which--in her ignorance of boundaries--Miss Arnott had been so attached, and in which Mr Morice first discovered her, was part and parcel of Exham Park instead of Oak Dene.

It was some seconds before the lady realised exactly what had happened. When she did, she burst out on Mr Morice with a question.

"Who has done this?"

The gentleman, who stood with his back against a huge beech tree, took his pipe from between his lips, and smiled.

"The fairies."

"Then the fairies will soon be introduced to a policeman. You did it."

"Not with my own hands, I assure you. At my time of life I am beyond that sort of thing."

"How dare you cause my fence to be removed?"

"Your fence? I was not aware it was your fence."

"You said it was my fence."

"Pardon me--never. I could not be guilty of such a perversion of the truth."

"Then whose fence was it?"

"It was mine. That is, it was my uncle's, and so, in the natural course of things, it became mine. It was like this. At one time, hereabouts, there was no visible boundary line between the two properties. I fancy it was a question of who should be at the expense of erecting one. Finally, my uncle loosed his purse-strings. He built this fence, with the wood out of his own plantations--even your friend Mr Baker will be able to tell you so much--the object being to keep out trespassers from Exham Park."

"Then, as you have removed your fence, I shall have to put up one of my own. I have no intention of allowing innocent persons, connected with Exham Park, to trespass--unconsciously--on land belonging to Oak Dene."

"Miss Arnott, permit your servant to present a humble petition."

He held his cap in his hands, suggesting deference; but in the eyes was that continual suspicion of laughter which made it difficult to tell when he was serious. It annoyed Miss Arnott to find that whenever she encountered that glimmer of merriment she found it so difficult to preserve the rigidity of decorum which she so ardently desired. Now, although she meant to be angry, and was angry, when she encountered that peculiar quality in his glance, it was really hard to be as angry as she wished.

"What objectionable remark have you to make now?"

"This--your servant desires to be forgiven."

"If the fence was yours, you were at liberty to do what you liked with it. You don't want to be forgiven for doing what you choose with your own. You can pull down all the fence for all I care."

"Exactly; that is very good of you. It is not precisely for that I craved forgiveness. Your servant has ventured to do a bold thing."

"Please don't call yourself my servant. If there is a ridiculous thing which you can say it seems as if you were bound to say it. Nothing you can do would surprise me. Pray, what particular thing have you been doing now? I thought you were going to Southampton on your car?"

"The car's in trouble."

"What's the matter with it?"

"One man says one thing; another says another. I say-- since this is the second time it's been in trouble this week--the thing's only fit for a rummage sale."

"I have never concealed my opinion from you."

"You haven't. Your opinion, being unbiassed by facts, is always the same; mine--depends. What, by the way, is just now your opinion of your own one? Lately it never seems to be in going order."

"That's preposterous nonsense, as you are perfectly well aware. But I don't mean to be drawn into a senseless wrangle. I came here hoping to escape that sort of thing."

"And you found me, which is tragic. However, we are wandering from the subject on to breezy heights. As I previously remarked, I have ventured to do a bold thing."

"And I have already inquired, what unusually bold thing is it you have done?"

"This."

They were at some little distance from each other; he on one side of the newly-made fence, she, where freshly-turned sods showed that the old fence used to be. He took a paper from his pocket, and, going close up to his side of the fence, held it out to her in his outstretched hand. She, afar off, observed both it and him distrustfully.

"What is it?"

"This? It's a paper with something written on it. We'll call it a document. Come and look at it. It's harmless. It's not a pistol--or a gun."

"I doubt if it contains anything which is likely to be of the slightest interest to me. Read what is on it."

"I would rather you read it yourself. Come and take it, if you please."

He spoke in that tone of calm assurance which was wont to affect her in a fashion which she herself was at a loss to understand. She resented bitterly its suggestion of authority; yet, before she was able to give adequate expression to her resentment, she was apt to find herself yielding entire obedience, as on the present occasion. In her indignation at the thought that he should issue his orders to her, as if she were his servant, she was more than half disposed to pick up a clod of earth, or a stone, and, like some street boy, hurl it at him and run away. She refrained from doing this, being aware that such a proceeding would not increase her dignity; and, also, because she did what he told her. She marched up to the fence and took the paper from his hand.

"I don't want it; you needn't suppose so. I've not the faintest desire to know what's on it." He simply looked at her with a glint of laughter in his big grey eyes. "I've half a mind to tear it in half and return it to you."

"You won't do that."

"Then I'll take it with me and look at it when I get home, if I look at it at all."

"Read it now."

She opened and read it; or tried to. "I don't understand what it's about; it seems to be so much gibberish. What is the thing?"

"It's a conveyance."

"A conveyance? What do you mean?"

"Being interpreted, it's a legal instrument which conveys to you and to your heirs for ever the fee-simple of--that."

"That?"

"That." He was pointing to the piece of land which lay within the confines of the newly-made fence. "That nook--that dell--that haven in which I saw you first, because you were under the impression it was yours. I was idiot enough to disabuse your mind, not being conscious, then, of what a fool I was. My idiocy has rankled ever since. However, it may have been of aforetime your lying there, cradled on that turf, has made of it consecrated ground. I guessed it then; I know it now. Then you fancied it was your own; now it assuredly is, you hold the conveyance in your hand."

"Mr Morice, what are you talking about? I don't in the least understand.'

"I was only endeavouring to explain what is the nature of the document you hold. Henceforward that rood of land--or thereabouts-- is yours. If I set foot on it, you will be entitled to put into me a charge of lead."

49

"Do you mean to say that you have given it me? Do you expect me to accept a gift--"

"Miss Arnott, the time for saying things is past. The transaction is concluded--past redemption. That land is yours as certainly as you are now standing on it; nothing you can say or do can alter that well-established fact by so much as one jot or tittle. The matter is signed, sealed and settled; entered in the archives of the law. Protest from you will be a mere waste of time."

"I don't believe it."

"As you please. Take that document to your lawyer; lay it before him; he will soon tell you whether or not I speak the truth. By the way, I will take advantage of this opportunity to make a few remarks to you upon another subject. Miss Arnott, I object to you for one reason."

"For one reason only? That is very good of you. I thought you objected to me for a thousand reasons."

"Your irony is justified. Then we will put it that I object to you for one reason chiefly."

"Mr Morice, do you imagine that I care why you object to me? Aren't you aware that you are paying me the highest compliment within your power by letting me know that you do object to me? Do you suppose that, in any case, I will stand here and listen to your impertinent attempts at personal criticism?"

"You will stand there, and you will listen; but I don't propose to criticise you, either impertinently or otherwise, but you will stand and listen to what I have to say." Such a sudden flame came into Mr Hugh Morice's eyes that the girl, half frightened, half she knew not what, remained speechless there in front of him. He seemed all at once to have grown taller, and to be towering above her like some giant against whose irresistible force it was vain to try and struggle. "The chief reason why I object to you, Miss Arnott, is because you are so rich."

"Mr Morice!"

"In my small way, I'm well to do. I can afford to buy myself a motor. I can even afford to pay for its repairs; and, in the case of a car like mine, that means something."

"I can believe that, easily."

"Of course you can. But, relatively, compared to you, I'm a pauper, and I don't like it."

"And yet you think that I'll accept gifts from you-- valuable gifts?"

50

"What I would like is, that a flaw should be found in your uncle's will; or the rightful heir turn up; or something happen which would entail your losing every penny you have in the world."

"What delightful things you say."

"Then, if you were actually and literally a pauper I might feel that you were more on an equality with me.

"Why should you wish to be on an equality with me?"

"Why? Don't you know?" On a sudden she began to tremble so that she could scarcely stand. "I see that you do know. I see it by the way the blood comes and goes in your cheeks; by the light which shines out of your eyes; by the fashion in which, as you see what is in mine, you stand shivering there. You know that I would like to be on an equality with you because I love you; and because it isn't flattering to my pride to know that, in every respect, you are so transcendently above me, and that, compared to you, I am altogether such a thing of clay. I don't want to receive everything and to give nothing. I am one of those sordid animals who like to think that their wives-who-are-to-be will be indebted to them for something besides their bare affection."

"How dare you talk to me like this?"

She felt as if she would have given anything to have been able to turn and flee, instead of seeming to stultify herself by so halting a rejoinder; but her feet were as if they were rooted to the ground.

"Do you mean, how dare I tell you that I love you? Why, I'd dare to tell you if you were a queen upon your throne and I your most insignificant subject. I'd dare to tell you if I knew that the telling would bring the heavens down. I'd dare to tell you if all the gamekeepers on your estate were behind you there, pointing their guns at me, and I was assured they'd pull their triggers the instant I had told. Why should I not dare to tell you that I love you? I'm a man; and, after all, you're but a woman, though so rare an one. I dare to tell you more. I dare to tell you that the first time I saw you lying there, on that grassy cushion, I began to love you then. And it has grown since, until now, it consumes me as with fire. It has grown to be so great, that, mysterious and strange--and indeed, incredible though it seems--I've a sort of inkling somewhere in my bosom, that one day yet I'll win you for my wife. What do you say to that?"

"I say that you don't know what you're talking about. That you're insane."

"If that be so, I've a fancy that it's a sort of insanity which, in howsoever so slight a degree, is shared by you. Come closer."

He leaned over the fence. Almost before she knew it, he had his arms about her; had drawn her close to him, and had kissed her on the mouth. She struck at him with her clenched fists; and, fighting like some wild thing, tearing herself loose, rushed headlong down the woodland path, as if Satan were at her heels.

CHAPTER VIII
THE LADY WANDERS

That was the beginning of a very bad time for Mrs Plummer.

She was sitting peacefully reading--she was not one of those ladies who indulge in "fancy work," and was always ready to confess that never, under any circumstances, if she could help it, would she have a needle in her hand--when Miss Arnott came rushing into the room in a condition which would have been mildly described as dishevelled. She was a young lady who was a little given to vigorous entrances and exits, and was not generally, as regards her appearance, a disciple of what has been spoken of as "the bandbox brigade." But on that occasion she moved Mrs Plummer, who was not easily moved in that direction, to an exhibition of surprise.

"My dear child! what have you been doing to yourself, and where have you been?"

"I've been to the woods. Mrs Plummer, I've come to tell you that we're going abroad."

"Going abroad? Isn't that rather a sudden resolution? I thought you had arranged--"

"Never mind what I've arranged. We're going abroad to-morrow, if we can't get away to-night."

"To-morrow? To-night? My child, are you in earnest?"

"Very much so. That is, I don't wish to put any constraint on you. You, of course, are at liberty to go or stay, exactly as you please. I merely wish to say that I am going abroad, whether you come with me or whether you don't; and that I intend to start either to-night or to-morrow morning."

They left the next morning. The packing was done that night. At an early hour they went up to town; at eleven o'clock they started for the Continent. That evening they dined in Paris. Mrs Plummer would have liked to remonstrate--and did remonstrate so far as she dared; but it needed less sagacity than she possessed to enable her to see that, in Miss Arnott's present mood, the limits of daring might easily be passed. When she ventured to suggest that before their departure Mr Stacey should be consulted, the young lady favoured her with a little plain speaking.

"Why should I consult Mr Stacey? He is only my servant."

"Your servant? My dear!"

"He renders me certain services, for which I pay him. Doesn't that mean that, in a certain sense, he's my servant? I have authority over him, but he has none over me--not one iota. He was my trustee; but, as I understand it, his trusteeship ceased when I entered into actual possession of my uncle's property. He does as I tell him, that's all. I shouldn't dream of consulting him as to my personal movements-- nor anyone. As, in the future, my movements may appear to you to be erratic, please, Mrs Plummer, let us understand each other now. You are my companion--good! I have no objection. When we first met, you told me that my liberty would be more complete with you than without you. I assure you, on my part, that I do not intend to allow you to interfere with my perfect freedom of action in the least degree. I mean to go where I please, when I please, how I please, and I want no criticism. You can do exactly as you choose; I shall do as I choose. I don't intend to allow you, in any way whatever, to be a clog upon my movements. The sooner we understand each other perfectly on that point the better it will be for both sides. Don't you think so?"

Mrs Plummer had to think so.

"I'm sure that if you told me you meant to start in ten minutes for the North Pole, you'd find me willing; that is, if you'd be willing to take me with you."

"Oh, I'd be willing to take you, so long as you don't even hint at a disinclination to be taken."

They stayed in Paris for two days. Then they wandered hither and thither in Switzerland. Everywhere, it seemed, there were too many people.

"I want to be alone," declared Miss Arnott. "Where there isn't a soul to speak to except you and Evans,"-- Evans was her maid--"you two don't count. But I can't get away from the crowds; they're even on the tops of the mountains. I hate them."

Mrs Plummer sighed; being careful, however, to conceal the sigh from Miss Arnott. It seemed to her that the young lady had an incomprehensible objection to everything that appealed to anyone else.

She avoided hotels where the cooking was decent, because other people patronised them. She eschewed places where there was something to be obtained in the way of amusement, because other reasonable creatures showed a desire to be amused. She shunned beauty spots, merely because she was not the only person in the world who liked to look upon the beauties of nature. Having hit upon an apparently inaccessible retreat, from the ordinary tourist point of view, in the upper Engadine, where, according to Mrs Plummer, the hotel was horrible, and there was nothing to do, and nowhere to go, there not being a level hundred yards within miles, the roads being mere tracks on the mountain sides, she did show some disposition to rest awhile. Indeed, she showed an inclination to stay much longer than either Mrs Plummer or Evans desired. Those two were far from happy.

"What a young lady in her position can see in a place like this beats me altogether. The food isn't fit for a Christian, and look at the room we have to eat it in; it isn't even decently furnished. There's not a soul to speak to, and nothing to do except climb up and down the side of a wall. She'll be brought in one day--if they ever find her--nothing but a bag of bones; you see if she isn't!"

In that strain Evans frequently eased her mind, or tried to.

To this remote hamlet, however, in course of time, other people began to come. They not only filled the hotel, which was easy, since Miss Arnott already had most of it, and would have had all, if the landlord, who was a character, had not insisted on keeping certain rooms for other guests; but they also overflowed into the neighbouring houses. These newcomers filled Miss Arnott with dark suspicions. When indulging in her solitary expeditions one young man in particular, named Blenkinsop, developed an extraordinary knack of turning up when she least expected him.

"I believe I'm indebted to you for these people coming here."

This charge she levelled at Mrs Plummer, who was amazed.

"To me! Why, they're all complete strangers to me; I never saw one of them before, and haven't the faintest notion where they come from or who they are."

"All the same, I believe I am; to you or to Evans; probably to both."

"My dear, what do you mean? The things you say!"

"It's the things you say, that's what I mean. You and Evans have been talking to the people here; you have been telling them who I am, and a great many things you have no right to tell them. They've been telling people down in the valley, and the thing has spread; how the rich Arnott girl, who has so much money she herself doesn't know how much, is stopping up here all alone. I know. These creatures have come up in consequence. That man Blenkinsop as good as told me this afternoon that he only came because he heard that I was here."

"My dear, what can you expect? You can't hide your light under a bushel. You would have much more real solitude in a crowd than in a place like this."

"Should I? We shall see. If this sort of thing occurs again I shall send you and Evans home. I shall drop my own name, and take a pseudonym; and I shall go into lodgings, and live on fifty francs a week--then we'll see if I sha'n't be left alone."

When Mrs Plummer retailed these remarks to Evans, the lady's maid--who had already been the recipient of a few observations on her own account--expressed herself with considerable frankness on the subject of her mistress.

"I believe she's mad--I do really. I don't mean that she's bad enough for a lunatic asylum or anything like that; but that she has a screw loose, and that there's something wrong with her, I'm pretty nearly sure. Look at the fits of depression she has--with her quite young and everything to make her all the other way. Look how she broods. She might be like the party in the play who'd murdered sleep, the way she keeps awake of nights. I know she reads till goodness knows what time; and often and often I don't believe she has a wink of sleep all night It isn't natural--I know I shouldn't like it if it was me. She might have done some dreadful crime, and be haunted by it, the way that she goes on-- she might really."

It was, perhaps, owing to the fact that the unfortunate lady practically had no human society except the lady's maid's that Mrs Plummer did not rebuke her more sharply for indulging in such free and easy comments on the lady to whom they were both indebted. She did observe that Evans ought not to say such things; but, judging from certain passages in a letter which, later on, she sent to Mrs Stacey, it is possible that the woman's words had made a greater impression than she had cared to admit.

They passed from the Engadine to Salmezzo, a little village which nestles among the hills which overlook Lake Como. It was from there that the letter in question was written. After a page or two about nothing in particular it went on like this:--

"I don't want to make mountains out of molehills, and I don't wish you to misunderstand me; but I am beginning to wonder if there is not something abnormal about the young lady whom I am supposed to chaperon. In so rich, so young, and so beautiful a girl--and I think she grows more beautiful daily--this horror of one's fellow-creatures--carried to the extent she carries it--is in itself abnormal. But, lately, there has been something more. She is physically, or mentally, unwell; which of the two I can't decide. I am not in the least bit morbid; but, really, if you had been watching her--and, circumstanced as I am, you can't help watching her--you would begin to think she must be haunted. It's getting on my nerves. Usually, I should describe her as one of the most self-possessed persons I had ever met; but, during the last week or two, she has taken to starting--literally--at shadows.

"The other day, at the end of the little avenue of trees which runs in front of my bedroom, right before my eyes, she stopped and leaned against one of the trees, as if for support. I wondered what she meant by it--the attitude was such an odd one. Presently a man came along the road, and strode past the gate. The nearer he came the more she slunk behind the tree. When he had passed she crouched down behind the tree, and began to cry. How she did cry! While I was hesitating whether I ought to go to her or not, apparently becoming conscious that she might be overlooked, she suddenly got up and--still crying--rushed off among the trees.

"Now who did she think that man was she heard coming along the road? Why did she cry like that when she found it wasn't he? Were they tears of relief or disappointment? It seemed very odd.

"Again, one afternoon she went for a drive with me; it is not often that she will go anywhere with me, especially for a drive, but that afternoon the suggestion actually came from her. After we had gone some distance we alighted from the vehicle to walk to a point from which a famous view can be obtained. All at once, stopping, she caught me by the arm.

"'Who's that speaking?' she asked. Up to then I had not been conscious that anyone was speaking. But, as we stood listening, I gradually became conscious, in the intense silence, of a distant murmur of voices which was just, and only just, audible. Her hearing must be very acute. 'It is an English voice which is speaking,' she said. She dragged me off the path among the shadow of the trees. She really did drag; but I was so taken aback by the extraordinary look which came upon her face, and by the strangeness of her tone, that I was incapable of offering the least resistance. On a sudden she had become an altogether different person; a dreadful one, it seemed to me. Although I was conscious of the absurdity of our crouching there among the trees, I could not say so--simply because I was afraid of her. At last she said, as if to herself, 'It's not his voice.' Then she gave a gasp, or a groan, or sigh-- I don't know what it was. I could feel her shuddering; it affected me most unpleasantly. Presently two perfectly inoffensive young Englishmen, who were staying at our hotel, came strolling by. Fortunately they did not look round. If they had seen us hiding there among the trees I don't know what they would have thought.

"I have only given you two instances. But recently, she is always doing ridiculous things like that, which, although they are ridiculous, are disconcerting. She certainly is unwell mentally, or physically, or both; but not only so. I seriously do believe she's haunted. Not by anything supernatural, but by something, perhaps, quite ordinary. There may be some episode in her life which we know nothing of, and which it might be much better for her if we did, and that haunts her. I should not like to venture to hint at what may be its exact nature; because I have no idea; but I would not mind hazarding a guess that it has something to do with a man."

Mrs Plummer's sagacity was not at fault; it had something to do with a man--her husband. She had hoped that constant wandering might help her to banish him from her mind--him and another man. The contrary proved to be the case. The farther she went the more present he seemed to be--they both seemed to be.

And, lately, the thing had become worse. She had begun to count the hours which still remained before the prison gates should be reopened. So swiftly the time grew shorter. When they were reopened, what would happen then? Now she was haunted; what Mrs Plummer had written was true. Day and night she feared to see his face; she trembled lest every unknown footstep might be his. A strange voice made her heart stand still.

The absurdity of the thing did not occur to her? she was so wholly obsessed by its horror. Again Mrs Plummer was right, she was unwell both mentally and physically. The burden which was weighing on her, body and soul, was rapidly becoming heavier than she could bear. She magnified it till it filled her whole horizon. Look where she would it was there, the monster who--it seemed to her, at any moment--might spring out at her from behind the prison gates. The clearness of her mental vision was becoming obscured, the things she saw were distorted out of their true proportions.

As a matter of fact, the hour of Robert Champion's release was drawing near. The twelve months were coming to an end. The probability was that they had seemed much longer to him than to her. To her it seemed that the hour of his release would sound the knell of the end of all things. She awaited it as a condemned wretch might await the summons to the gallows. As, with the approaching hour, the tension grew tighter, the balance of her mind became disturbed. Temporarily, she was certainly not quite sane.

One afternoon she crowned her display of eccentricity by rushing off home almost at a moment's notice. On the previous day--a Tuesday--she had arranged with the landlord to continue in his hotel for a further indefinite period. On the Wednesday, after lunch, she came to Mrs Plummer and announced that they were going home at once. Although Mrs Plummer was taken wholly by surprise, the suggestion being a complete reversal of all the plans they had made, Miss Arnott's manner was so singular, and the proposition was in itself so welcome, that the elder lady fell in with the notion there and then, without even a show of remonstrance. The truth is that she had something more than a suspicion that Miss Arnott would be only too glad to avail herself of any excuse which might offer, and return to England alone, leaving her--Mrs Plummer-- alone with Evans. Why the young lady should wish to do such a thing she had no idea, but that she did wish to do it she felt uncomfortably convinced. The companion managing to impress the lady's maid with her aspect of the position, the trunks were packed in less than no time, so that the entire cortège was driven over to catch the afternoon train, leaving the smiling landlord with a thumping cheque, to compensate him for the rapidity with which the eccentric young Englishwoman thought proper to break the engagements into which she had solemnly entered.

That was on the Wednesday. On the Saturday--by dint of losing no time upon the way--they arrived at Exham Park. On the Sunday Robert Champion's term of imprisonment was to come to an end; on that day he would have been twelve months in jail. What a rigid account she had kept of it all, like the schoolboy who keeps count of the days which bar him from his holidays. But with what a different feeling in her heart! She had seen that Sunday coming at her from afar off--nearer and nearer. What would happen when it came, and he was free to get at her again, she did not know. What she did know was that she meant to have an hour or two at Exham Park before the Sunday dawned, and the monster was set free again. She had come at headlong speed from the Lake of Como to have it.

CHAPTER IX
THE BEECH TREE

When the travellers returned it was after nine o'clock. So soon as they set foot indoors they were informed that dinner was ready to be served; an announcement which, as they had been travelling all day, and had only had a scanty lunch on the train, Mrs Plummer was inclined to hail with rapture. Miss Arnott, however--as she was only too frequently wont to be--was of a different mind.

"I don't want any dinner," she announced.

"Not want any dinner!" Mrs Plummer stared. The limits of human forbearance must be reached some time, and the idea that that erratic young woman could not want dinner was beyond nature. "But you must want dinner--you're starving; I'm sure you are."

"Indeed? I don't see how you can be sure. I assure you, on my part, that I am not even hungry. However, as you probably mean that yours is a case of starvation, far be it from me to stand in the way of your being properly fed. Come! let us go in to dinner at once."

The imperious young woman marched her unresisting companion straight off into the dining-room, without even affording her an opportunity to remove the stains of travel. Not that Mrs Plummer was unwilling to be led, having arrived at that stage in which the satisfaction of the appetite was the primary consideration.

Miss Arnott herself made but an unsubstantial meal; watching the conscientious manner in which the elder lady did justice to the excellent fare with ill-concealed and growing impatience. At last--when they had only reached the entrées--her feeling found vent.

"Really, Mrs Plummer, you must excuse me. I'm not in the least bit hungry, and am in that state of mind in which even the sight of food upsets me--I must have some fresh air."

"Fresh air! But, my dear child, surely you must recently have had enough fresh air."

"Not of the kind I want. You stay there and continue to recruit exhausted nature; don't let my vagaries make any difference to you.

I'm going out--to breathe."

"After travelling for three whole days where can you be going to at this time of night? It's ten o'clock."

"I'm going--" From the way in which she looked at her Mrs Plummer deemed it quite possible that her charge was going to request her to mind her own business. But, suddenly, Miss Arnott stopped; seemed to change her mind, and said with a smile wrinkling her lips, "Oh, I'm going out into the woods."

Before the other could speak again she was gone.

Left alone, Mrs Plummer put down her knife and fork, and stared at the door through which the lady had vanished. Had there been someone to say it to she might have said something to the point. The only persons present were the butler and his attendant minions. To them she could hardly address herself on such a subject. It was not even desirable that any action of hers should acquaint them with the fact that there was something which she was burning to say. She controlled her feelings, composed her countenance, took up her knife and fork and resumed her meal.

And Miss Arnott went out into the woods.

She was in a curious mood, or she would never have gone out on such a frolic. Directly she found herself out in the cool night air, stretching out her arms and opening her chest, she drank in great draughts of it; not one or two, but half a dozen. When she reached the shadow of the trees she paused. So far the sky had been obscured by clouds. The woods stretched out in front of her in seemingly impenetrable darkness. It was impossible to pick out a footpath in that blackness. But all at once the clouds passed from before the moon. Shafts of light began to penetrate the forest fastness, and to illuminate its mysteries. The footpath was revealed, not over clearly, yet with sufficient distinctness to make its existence obvious. Unhesitatingly she began to follow it. It was not easy walking. The moon kept coming and going. When it was at its brightest its rays were not sufficiently vivid to make perfectly plain the intricacies of the path. When it vanished she found herself in a darkness which might almost have been felt. Progression was practically impossible. In spite of her putting out her hands to feel the way she was continually coming into contact with trees, and shrubs, and all sorts of unseen obstacles. Not only so, there was the risk of her losing the path--all sense of direction being nonexistent.

"If I don't take care I shall be lost utterly, and shall have to spend the night, alone with the birds and beasts, in this sweet wilderness. Sensible people would take advantage of the first chance which offers to turn back. But I sha'n't; I shall go on and on."

Presently the opportunity to do so came again. The moon returned; this time to stay. It seemed brighter now. As her eyes became accustomed to its peculiar glamour she moved more surely towards the goal she had in view. The light, the scene, the hour, were all three fitted to her mood; which certainly would have defied her own analysis. It seemed to her, by degrees, that she was bewitched--under the influence of some strange spell. This was a fairy forest through which she was passing, at the witching hour. Invisible shapes walked by her. Immaterial forms peopled the air. It was as though she was one of a great company; moving with an aerial bodyguard through a forest of faerie.

What it all meant she did not know; or why she was there; or whither, exactly, she was going. Until, on a sudden, the knowledge came.

Unexpectedly, before she supposed she had gone so far, she came to the end of the path. There, right ahead, was the mossy glade, the fee-simple of which had been presented to her in such queer fashion the last time she came that way. Coming from the shadow of the forest path it stood out in the full radiance of the moon; every object showing out as clearly as at high noon. The new-made fence, with its novelty already fading; the turf on which she loved to lie; the unevenness on the slope which had seemed to have been made for the express purpose of providing cushions for her head and back. These things she saw, as distinctly as if the sun were high in the heavens; and something else she saw as well, which made her heart stand still.

Under the giant beech, whose spreading branches cast such grateful shade, when the sun was hot, over the nook which she had chosen as a couch, stood a man--who was himself by way of being a giant. Never before had his height so struck her. Whether it was the clothes he wore, the position in which he stood, or a trick of the moonlight, she could not tell. She only knew that, as he appeared so instantly before her, he was like some creature out of Brobdingnag, seeming to fill all space with his presence.

The man was Hugh Morice.

He was so absorbed in what he was doing, and she was still some little distance from him, and had come so quietly; that she saw him while he still remained unconscious of her neighbourhood. She had ample time to withdraw. She had only to take a few steps back, and he would never know she had been near him. So the incident would be closed. Her instinct told her that in that way she would be safest. And for a moment or two she all but turned to go.

Her retreat, however, was delayed by one or two considerations. One was that the sight of him affected her so strangely that, for some seconds, she was genuinely incapable of going either backward or forward. Her feet seemed shod with lead, her knees seemed to be giving way beneath her, she was trembling from head to foot. Then she was divided between conflicting desires, the one saying go, the other stay; and while her instinct warned her to do the one, her inclination pointed to the other. In the third place there was her woman's curiosity. While she hesitated this began to gain the upper hand. She wondered what it was he was doing which absorbed him so completely that he never ceased from doing it to look about him.

He was in a dinner suit, and was apparently hatless. He had something in his hand, with which he was doing something to the tree in front of which he stood. What was he doing? She had no right to ask; she had no right to be there at all; still--she wondered. She moved a little farther out into the open space, to enable her to see. As she did so it seemed that he finished what he was doing. Standing up straight he drew back from the tree the better to enable him to examine his handiwork; and--then he turned and saw her.

There was silence. Neither moved. Each continued to look at the other, as if at some strange, mysterious being. Then he spoke.

"Are you a ghost?--I think not. I fancy you're material. But I haunt this place so constantly myself-- defying Jim Baker's charge of lead--that I should not be one whit surprised if your spirit actually did appear to keep me company. Do you believe in telepathy?"

"I don't know what it is."

"Do you believe that A, by dint of taking thought, can induce B to think of him? or--more--can draw, B to his side? I'm not sure that I believe; but it certainly is queer that I should have been thinking of you so strenuously just then, longing for you, and should turn and find you here. I thought you were over the hills and far away, haunting the shores of the Italian lakes."

"On Wednesday we came away from Como."

"On Wednesday? That's still stranger. It was on Wednesday my fever came to a head. I rushed down here, bent, if I could not be with you, on being where you had been. Since my arrival I've longed--with how great a longing--to use all sorts of conjurations which should bring you back to Exham; and, it seems, I conjured wiser than I knew."

"I left Como because I could no longer stay."

"From Exham? or from me? Speak sweetly; see how great my longing is."

"I had to return to say good-bye."

"To both of us? That's good; since our goodbyes will take so long in saying. Come and see what I have done." She went to the tree. There, newly cut in the bark, plain in the moonlight, were letters and figures. "Your initials and mine, joined by the date on which we met--beneath this tree. I brought my hunting knife out with me to do it--you see how sharp a point and edge it has." She saw that he held a great knife in his hand. "As I cut the letters you can believe I thought--I so thought of you with my whole heart and soul that you've come back to me from Como."

"Did I not say I've returned to say good-bye?"

"What sort of good-bye do you imagine I will let you say, now that you've returned? That tree shall be to us a family chronicle. The first important date's inscribed on it; the others shall follow; they'll be so many. But the trunk's of a generous size. We'll find room on it for all. That's the date on which I first loved you. What's the date on which you first loved me?"

"I have not said I ever loved you."

"No; but you do."

"Yes; I do. Now I know that I do. No, you must not touch me."

"No need to draw yourself away; I do not mean to, yet. Some happinesses are all the sweeter for being a little postponed. And when did the knowledge first come to you? We must have the date upon the tree."

"That you never shall. Such tales are not for trees to tell, even if I knew, which I don't. I'm afraid to think; it's all so horrible."

"Love is horrible? I think not."

"But I know. You don't understand--I do."

"My dear, I think it is you who do not understand."

"Nor must you call me your dear; for that I shall never be."

"Not even when you're my wife?"

"I shall never be your wife!"

"Lady, these are strange things of which you speak. I would rather that, just now, you did not talk only in riddles."

"It is the plain truth--I shall never be your wife."

"How's that? Since my love has brought you back from Como, to tell me that you also love? Though, mind you, I do not stand in positive need of being told. Because, now that I see you face to face, and feel you there so close to me, your heart speaks to mine--I can hear it speaking; I can hear, sweetheart, what it says. So that I know you love me, without depending for the knowledge on the utterance of your lips."

"Still, I shall never be your wife."

"But why, sweetheart, but why?"

"Because--I am a wife already."

CHAPTER X
THE TALE WHICH WAS TOLD

They were silent. To her it seemed that the silence shrieked aloud. He looked at her with an expression on his face which she was destined never to forget--as if he were hard of hearing, or fancied that his senses played him a trick, or that she had indulged in some ill-timed jest.

"What did you say?"

"I said that I am a wife already."

His look had become one of inquiry; as if desirous of learning if she were really in earnest. She felt her heart beating against her ribs, or seeming to--a habit of which it had been too fond of late. When it behaved like that it was only with an uncomfortable effort that she could keep a hold upon her consciousness; being fearful that it might slip away from her, in spite of all that she might be able to do. When he spoke again his tone had changed; as if he were puzzled. She had a sudden feeling that he was speaking to her as he might have spoken to a child.

"Do you know what you are saying? and do you mean what you say?"

"Of course I do."

"But--pardon me--I don't see the of course at all. Do you--seriously--wish me to understand that you're--a married woman?"

"Whether you understand it or not, I am."

"But you are scarcely more than a child. How old are you?"

"I am twenty-two."

"And how long do you wish me to understand that you've been married?"

"Two years."

"Two years? Then--you were married before you came here?"

"Of course."

"Of course? But everyone here has always spoken to me of you as Miss Arnott."

"That is because no one who knows me here knows that I am married."

He put his arms down to his sides, and drew himself up still straighter, so that she had to look right up at him, and knit his brows, as if he found himself confronted by a problem which was incapable of solution.

"I believe that I am the least curious of men, I say it seriously; but it appears to me that this is a situation in which curiosity is justified. You made yourself known to me as Miss Arnott; as Miss Arnott there have previously been certain passages between us; as Miss Arnott you have permitted me to tell you that I love you; you have even admitted that you love me. It is only when I take it for granted--as I am entitled to do--that the mutual confession involves your becoming my wife, that you inform me--that you are already a married woman. Under the circumstances I think I have a right to ask for information at least on certain points; as, for instance, so that I may know how to address you--what is your husband's name?"

"Robert Champion."

"Robert Champion? Then--you are Mrs Champion?"

"I am."

"Am I to take it that Mr Champion is alive?"

"So far as I know."

"So far as you know? That does not suggest very intimate--or very recent knowledge. When did you hear from him last?"

"I saw him twelve months ago."

"You saw him twelve months ago? That was not long before you came here. Why did he not accompany you when you came?"

"He couldn't."

"He couldn't? Why?"

"He was in prison."

"In--" He stopped, looked at her with, in his eyes, an altogether different expression; then, throwing his head back, seemed to be staring straight at the moon, as if he were endeavouring to read something which was written on her surface. Presently he spoke in an entirely altered tone of voice. "Now I understand, or, rather, now I begin to understand. It dawns on me that here is a position which will want some understanding." As if seized with sudden restlessness he began to pace to and fro, keeping to the same piece of ground, of which he seemed to be making mental measurements; she meanwhile, watching him, silent, motionless, as if she were waiting for him to pronounce judgment. After a while he broke into speech, while he still continued pacing to and fro. "Now I begin to see daylight everywhere; the meaning of the things which puzzled me. Why you seemed to take no interest in anything; why you were so fond of solitude; why, in the middle of a conversation, one found that your thoughts had strayed. The life you were living in public was not the one you were living to yourself. It's not nice to be like that. Poor child! And I have laughed at you, because I thought you were a character, and--you were. How many fools escape being kicked just at those moments when a kicking would do them good. It occurs to me, Mrs Champion--"

"Don't call me that!"

"But--if it's your name?"

"It's not my name to you; I wish you always to think of me as Miss Arnott."

"Then--" He paused; ceased to walk; looked at her, and went and stood with his back against the tree. "I fancy that what you stand most in need of is a friend. I can be that to you, if I can be nothing else. Come, tell me all about it--it will ease your mind."

"I've wanted to tell someone all the time; but I've told no one. I couldn't."

"I know what you mean; and I think I know what it feels like. Tell me--you'll find me an excellent father confessor."

"I shall have to begin at the beginning."

"Do. If I am to be of any assistance, and it's possible I may be, I shall have to understand it all quite clearly."

"My father died first, and then my mother, and when she died I was left with only quite a little money."

"And no relations?"

"No--no relations."

"And no friends?"

"No--no friends."

"Poor child!"

"You mustn't talk like that, or I sha'n't be able to go on, and I want to go straight on. I wasn't yet eighteen. There wasn't anything to be done in the country--we had lived quite out of the world--so I went to London. I was strange to London; but I thought I should have more chance there than in Scarsdale, so I went. But, when I got there, I soon found that I wasn't much better off than before, I'm not sure I wasn't worse. It was so lonely and so--so strange. My money went so fast, I began to be afraid, there seemed to be no means of earning more--I didn't know what to do. Then I saw an advertisement in a paper, of a shop where they wanted models in the costume department; they had to be tall and of good appearance. I didn't know what the advertisement meant; but I thought I was that, so I went, and they engaged me. I was to have board and lodging, and a few shillings a week. It was horrible. I had to keep putting on new dresses, and walk up and down in them in front of strange women, and sometimes men, and show them off. I had always been used to the open air, and to solitude; sometimes I thought I was going mad. Then the food was bad--at least, I thought it was bad--and, there were all sorts of things. But I had come so close to my last few shillings--and been so afraid--that I didn't dare to leave. There was one girl, who was also a model, whom I almost trusted; now that I look back I know that I never did quite. I used to walk about with her in the streets; I couldn't walk about alone, and there was nowhere else to walk, and I had to have some fresh air. She introduced me to a friend of hers--a man. She said he was a gentleman, but I knew better than that. She made out that he was very rich, and everything he ought to be. Directly he was introduced he began to make love. I so hated being a model; and I saw no prospect of doing anything else, and--besides, I wasn't well--I wasn't myself the whole of the time. She laughed when I said I didn't like him, and, therefore, couldn't be his wife. She declared that I was throwing away the best chance a girl in my position ever had; and said he would make the most perfect husband I could possibly want. He promised all sorts of things; he said we should live in the country, he even took me to see a house which he said he had taken. I grew to hate being a model more and more; I was miserable and ill, and they all made fun of me. At last, after he had asked me I don't know how many times, I said yes. We were married. We went to Margate for our honeymoon. Within four-and-twenty hours I knew what kind of a man he was."

    She stopped; putting her hands up before her face. He could see her trembling in the moonlight, and could only stand and watch. He dared not trust himself to speak.

Presently she went on.

"I lived with him twelve months."

"Twelve months!"

"When I think of it now I wonder why I didn't kill him. I had chances, but I daren't even run away. All the life had gone out of me, and all the spirit too. I didn't even try to defend myself when he struck me."

"Struck you?"

"Oh, he often did that. But I was a weak and helpless creature. I seemed to myself to be half-witted. He used to say that he believed I had a tile loose. I had, then. Then they locked him up."

"What for?"

"He put an advertisement in the paper for a person to fill a position of trust. When someone applied he got them to make what he termed a 'deposit' of a few pounds. Then he stole it. Of course there was no position of trust to fill. That was how he made his living. I always wondered where he got his money from. After he was arrested I understood."

"And he was sentenced?"

"To twelve months' hard labour."

"Only twelve months' hard labour? Then his term of imprisonment will soon be drawing to a close."

"To-morrow."

"To-morrow! You poor child!"

"Now you perceive why I hurried back from Lake Como to say good-bye."

"I hope I need not tell you, in words, how intensely I sympathise with you."

"Thank you, I would rather you didn't; I know."

"We will speak of such matters later. In the meantime, obviously, what you want is a friend; as I guessed. As a friend, let me assure you that your position is not by any means so hopeless as you appear to imagine."

"Not with my husband coming out of prison to-morrow? You don't know him."

"If you can do nothing else, you can keep him at arm's length."

"How do you mean?"

"You have money, he hasn't. You can at least place yourself in a position in which he can't get at you."

"Can't he compel me to give him money?"

"Emphatically, no. He has no claim to a penny of yours, not to a farthing. The marriage laws are still quite capable of being improved, but one crying injustice they have abolished. What a woman has is her own, and hers only, be she married or single. If Mr Champion wants money he will have to earn it. He has not a scintilla of right to any of yours, or anything that is yours. So, at anyrate, you should have no difficulty in placing yourself beyond his reach. But there is something more. You should experience no trouble in freeing yourself from him altogether. There is such a place as the divorce court. Plainly, it would be easy to show cruelty, and probably something else as well."

"I don't know. I knew nothing of what he did, and cared nothing, so long as he left me alone."

"Quite so. This is a matter which will be better managed by other hands than yours. Only--there are abundant ways and means of dealing with a person of his kind. What I want you to do now is not to worry. One moment! it's not a counsel of perfection! I see clearly what this means to you, what it has meant, but--forgive me for saying so--the burden has been made much heavier by your insisting on bearing it alone."

"I couldn't blurt out my shame to everyone--to anyone!"

"Well, you have told me now, thank goodness! And you may rely on this, that man sha'n't be allowed to come near you; if necessary, I will make it my business to prevent him. I will think things over to-night; be sure that I shall find a way out. To-morrow I will come and tell you what I've thought about, when the conditions are more normal."

"Rather than that he should again be able to claim me for his wife, even for an hour, I would kill him."

"Certainly; I will kill him for you if it comes to that. I have lived in countries where they make nothing of killing vermin of his particular type. But there'll be no necessity for such a drastic remedy. Now, I want you to go home and promise not to worry, because your case is now in hands which are well qualified to relieve you of all cause for apprehension of any sort or kind. I beg you will believe it. Good-night."

She hesitated, then put her hands up to her temples, as if her head was aching.

"I will say good-night to you. You go, I will stay. My brain's all in a whirl. I want to be alone--to steady it."

"I don't like to leave you, in such a place, at such an hour."

"Why not? While I've been abroad I've sometimes spent half the night in wandering alone over the mountains. Why am I not as safe here as there?"

"It's not a question of safety, no doubt you're safe enough. But--it's the idea."

"Be so good as to do as I ask--leave me, please."

"Since you ask me in such a tone. Promise me, at least, that you won't stay half the night out here; that, indeed, you won't stay long."

"I promise, if my doing so affords you any satisfaction. Probably I'll be in my own room in half an hour, only--I must be alone for a few minutes first. Don't you see?"

"I fancy that I do. Good-night. Remember that I'm at least your friend."

"I'll remember."

"By the way, in the morning where, and when, shall I find you?"

"I shall be in the house till lunch."

"Good, then before lunch I'll come to you, as early as I can. Good-night again."

"Good-night. And"--as he was moving off--"you're not to stop about and watch me, playing the part of the unseen protector. I couldn't bear the thought of being watched. I want to be alone."

He laughed.

"All right! All right! Since you've promised me that you'll not stay long I promise you that I'll march straight home."

He strode off, his arms swinging at his sides, his head hanging a little forward on his chest, as his habit was. She followed him with her eyes. When she saw that he vanished among the trees on his own estate, and did not once look back, she was conscious of an illogical little pang. She knew that he wanted her to understand that, in obedience to her wishes, he refused to keep any surveillance over her movements, even to the extent of looking back. Still she felt that he might have given her one backward glance, ere he vanished into the night.

CHAPTER XI
THE MAN ON THE FENCE

Her first feeling, when she knew herself in truth to be alone, was of thankfulness so intense as almost to amount to pain. He knew! As he himself had said, thank goodness! Her relief at the knowledge that her burden was shared, in however slight a degree, was greater than she could have imagined possible. And of all people in the world--by him! Now he understood, and understanding had, in one sense, drawn him closer to her; if in another it had thrust him farther off. Again, to use his own words, he was at least her friend. And, among all persons, he was the one whom-- for every possible reason--she would rather have chosen as a friend. In his hands she knew she would be safe. Whatever he could do, he would do, and more. That ogre who, in a few hours, would again be issuing from the prison gates, would not have her so wholly at his mercy as she had feared. Now, and henceforward, there would be someone else with whom he would have to reckon. One in whom, she was convinced, he would find much more than his match.

Again as he had said--thank goodness!

For some minutes she remained just as he had left her, standing looking after him, where he had vanished among the trees. After a while the restraint which she had placed upon herself throughout that trying interview, began to slacken. The girl that was in her came to the front--nature had its way. All at once she threw herself face downward on the cushioned turf in her own particular nook, and burst into a flood of tears. It was to enable her to do that, perhaps, that she had so wished to be alone. For once in a way, it was a comfort to cry; they were more than half of them tears of happiness. On the grass she lay, in the moonlight, and sobbed out, as it were, her thanks for the promise of help which had so suddenly come to her.

Until all at once she became aware, amidst the tumult of her sobbing, of a disturbing sound. She did not at first move or alter her position. She only tried to calm herself and listen. What was it which had struck upon her consciousness? Footsteps? Yes, approaching footsteps.

Had he played her false, and, despite his promise, kept watch on her? And was he now returning, to intrude upon her privacy? How dare he! The fountain of her tears was all at once dried up; instead, she went hot all over. The steps were drawing nearer. The person who was responsible was climbing the fence, within, it seemed, half a dozen feet of her. She started up in a rage, to find that the intruder was not Hugh Morice.

Seated on the top rail of the fence, on which he appeared to have perched himself, to enable him to observe her more at his ease, was quite a different-looking sort of person, a much more unprepossessing one than Hugh Morice. His coat and trousers were of shepherd's plaid; the open jacket revealing a light blue waistcoat, ornamented with bright brass buttons. For necktie he wore a narrow scarlet ribbon. His brown billycock hat was a little on one side of his head; his face was clean shaven, and between his lips he had an unlighted cigarette. In age he might have been anything between thirty and fifty.

His appearance was so entirely unexpected, and, in truth, so almost incredible, that she stared at him as she might have stared at some frightful apparition. And, indeed, no apparition could have seemed more frightful to her; for the man on the fence was Robert Champion.

For the space of at least a minute neither spoke. It was as if both parties were at a loss for words. At last the man found his tongue.

"Well, Vi, this is a little surprise for both of us."

So far she had been kneeling on the turf, as if the sight of him had paralysed her limbs and prevented her from ascending higher. Now, with a sudden jerky movement, she stood up straight.

"You!" she exclaimed.

"Yes, my dear--me. Taken you a little by surprise, haven't I? You don't seem to have made many preparations for my reception, though of course it's always possible that you've got the fatted calf waiting for me indoors."

"I thought you were in prison."

"Well, it's not a very delicate reminder, is it? on this the occasion of our first meeting. But, strictly between ourselves, I've been in prison, and that's a solid fact; and a nasty, unsociable place I found it."

"But I thought they weren't going to let you out until to-morrow."

"No? Did you? I see. That's why you were crying your heart out on the grass there, because you thought they were going to keep me from you four-and-twenty hours longer. The brutes! I should have thought you'd have found it damp enough without wanting to make it damper; but there's no accounting for tastes; yours always were your own, and I recognise the compliment. As it happens, when a gentleman's time's up on a Sunday, they let him tear himself away from them on the Saturday. Sunday's what they call a dies non; you're a lady of education, so you know what that means. You were right in reckoning that the twelve months for which they tore a husband from his wife wasn't up until tomorrow; but it seems that you didn't reckon for that little peculiarity, on account of which I said goodbye to them this morning. See?"

"But--I don't understand!"

She threw out her arms with a gesture which was eloquent of the confusion--and worse--with which his sudden apparition had filled her.

"No? what don't you understand? It all seems to me clear enough; but, perhaps, you always were a trifle dull."

"I don't understand how you've found me! how it is that you are here!"

"Oh, that's it, is it? Now I begin to catch on. That's the simplest part of the lot. You--the wife of my bosom, the partner of my joys and sorrows--particularly of my sorrows--you never wrote me a line; you never took the slightest interest in my hard fate. For all you cared I might have died. I don't like to think that you really didn't care, but that's what it looked like." He grinned, as if he had said something humorous. "But I had a friend--a true friend--one. That friend met me this morning, where my wife ought to have met me, at the prison gates. From that friend I learned of the surprising things which had happened to you; how you had come into a fortune--a fortune beyond the dreams of avarice. It seems strange that, under the circumstances, you weren't outside the prison, with a coach and four, waiting to bear me away in triumph to your gilded bowers. Ah-h!" He emitted a sound which might have been meant for a sigh. "But I bore up--with the aid of the first bottle of champagne I'd tasted since I saw you last--the gift of my one true friend. So, as you hadn't come to me, I came to you. You might have bungled up the dates or something; there's never any telling. I knew you'd be glad to see me--your loving husband, dear. My late arrival is due to no fault of mine; it's that beastly railway. I couldn't make out which was the proper station for this little shanty of yours! and it seems I took a ticket for the wrong one. Found myself stranded in a God-forsaken hole; no conveyance to be got; no more trains until tomorrow. So I started to walk the distance. They told me it was about five miles. About five miles! I'd like to make 'em cover it as five against the clock; they'd learn! When I'd gone about ten I met an idiot who told me there was a short cut, and set me on it. Short cut! If there's a longer cut anywhere I shouldn't care to strike it. Directly I'd seen the back of him it came on pitch dark; and there was I, in a pathless wilderness, with no more idea of where I was going than the man in the moon. For the last two hours I've been forcing my way through what seemed to me to be a virgin forest. I've had a time! But now I've found you, by what looks very like a miracle; and all's well that ends well. So give us a kiss, like a good girl, and say you're glad to see me. Come and salute your husband."

"You're not my husband!"

"Not--I say! Don't go and throw away your character like that. As my wife, it's precious to me, if it isn't to you."

"What do you suppose you're going to do now?"

"Now?--Do you mean this minute? Well, I did dream of a tender meeting; you know the kind of thing. As a loving wife you ought to, but, perhaps, you'd like to put that off till a little later. Now I suppose we're going up together to the little home of which I've heard, and have come so far to see; and there--well, there we'll have the tender meeting."

"I advise you not to set foot upon my ground!"

"Your ground? Our ground, you mean. Really, how you do mix things up."

"My ground, I mean. You have no more to do with it than--than the jailer who let you out of the prison gate, to prey upon the world again."

She had evidently learnt her lesson from Mr Morice in the nick of time.

"Don't be silly; you don't know what you're talking about. What's yours is mine; what's the wife's the husband's."

"That's a lie, and you know it. I know it's a lie, as you'll discover. This side of that fence is my property. If you trespass on it I'll summon my gamekeepers--there are always plenty of them about--and I'll have you thrown off it. What you do on the other side of the fence is no business of mine. That belongs to someone who is well able to deal with men like you."

"This is a cheerful hearing, upon my word! Can this virago be the loving wife I've come all this way to see? No, it can't be--it must be a delusion. Let me tell you again--don't be silly. Where the wife is the husband's a perfect right to be. That's the law of England and it's the law of God."

"It's neither when the husband is such as you. Let me repeat my advice to you--don't trespass on my ground."

"Where are you going?"

"I'm going to find a gamekeeper; to warn him that bad characters are about, and to instruct him how to deal with them."

"Stop! don't talk nonsense to me like that! Have you forgotten what kind of man I am?"

"Have I forgotten! As if I ever could forget!"

"Then mind it! Come here! Where are you off to? Did you hear me tell you to come here?"

"I repeat, I'm going to find a gamekeeper. I heard you tell me; but I pay no more attention to what you tell me than the trunk of that tree."

"By----! we'll see about that!"

Descending from the fence, he moved towards her. She stopped, turned and faced him.

"What do you think you're going to do?"

"I'm going to see you mind me--that's what I'm going to do."

"Does that mean that you're going to assault me, as you used to?"

He laughed.

"Assault you! Not much! Look here. What's the good of your carrying on like this? Why can't you behave like a reasonable girl, and talk sensibly?" She looked him steadily in the face; then turned on her heel. "You'd better stand still! I'm your husband; you're my wife. It's my duty to see that you obey me, and I'm going to do my duty. So just you mark my words!"

"Husband! Duty! You unutterable thing! Don't touch me! Take your hand from off my shoulder!"

"Then you stand still. I'm not going to have you slip through my fingers, and leave me here, and have the laugh on me; so don't you make any mistake, my girl. You've never had the laugh on me yet, and you never will."

"If you don't take your hand off my shoulder, I'll kill you."

Again he laughed.

"It strikes me that if there's going to be any killing done it's I who'll do it. You're getting my temper up, like you used to; and when you've got it fairly up there'll be trouble. You stand still! Do you hear me? Your eyes-- What's that?" With a sudden, vigorous movement she broke from his retaining grasp. "Would you! I'll teach you!"

He advanced, evidently meaning to renew his grip upon her shoulders. Before he could do so she swung out her right arm with all the strength at her command, and struck him in the face. Not anticipating such violent measures, taken unawares, he staggered blindly backwards. Ere he could recover himself she had sprung round, and was rushing at the top of her speed towards the narrow, winding path along which she had come. As she gained it the moon passed

75

behind the clouds.

CHAPTER XII
WHAT SHE HEARD, SAW AND FOUND

She hurried along as rapidly as she could in the darkness which had followed the eclipse of the moon. Momentarily she expected to hear his footsteps coming after her. But, so far as she was able to tell, there was not a sound which suggested pursuit. Something, possibly, had prevented his giving immediate chase. In the darkness it was impossible to see where she was going, or to make out surrounding objects. What seemed to be the branch of a tree struck her across the face with such force that it brought her to an instant standing. She stood still, trembling from head to foot. The collision had partly stunned her. Her face was smarting, where it had come in contact with the unseen obstacle. For the moment she was demoralised, incapable of moving in any direction. Her breath was coming in great gasps. It would have needed very little to have made her burst into tears.

As she was gradually regaining her equilibrium, her presence of mind, a sound crashed through the darkness, which started her trembling worse than ever. It was a gunshot. Quite close at hand. So close that the flash of it flamed before her eyes. In the air about her was the smell of the powder.

Silence followed, which was the more striking, because it was contrasted with the preceding thunderclap. What had happened? Who had fired? at what? and where? The gun had been fired by someone who was on the left of where she was then standing, possibly within twenty or thirty feet. The direction of the aim, it seemed, had been at something behind her. What was there behind her at which anyone would be likely to fire, in that reckless fashion, at that hour of the night? Robert Champion was behind her; but the idea that anyone--

The silence was broken. Someone was striding through the brushwood towards the place which had been aimed at. She became conscious of another sound, which made her heart stand still. Was not someone groaning, as if in pain? Someone who, also, was behind her? Suddenly there was the sound of voices. The person who had strode through the underwood was speaking to the person who was groaning. Apparently she was farther off than she had supposed, or they were speaking in muffled tones. She could only just distinguish voices. Who were the speakers, and what they said, she had not a notion. The colloquy was but a brief one. Again there was a sound of footsteps, which retreated; then, again, groans.

What did it mean? What had happened? who had come and gone? who had been the speakers? of what had they been talking? The problem was a knotty one. Should she go back and solve it? The groans which continued, and, if anything, increased in vigour, were in themselves a sufficiently strenuous appeal. That someone was in pain was evident--wounded, perhaps seriously. It seemed that whoever was responsible for that gunshot had, with complete callousness, left his victim to his fate. And he might be dying! Whoever it was, she could not let him die without, at least, attempting succour. If she did, she would be a participant in a crime of which--to use an Irishism--she had not only been an unseen, but also an unseeing, witness. If she let this man die without doing something to help him live, his blood would be on her hands also; certainly, she would feel it was. However repugnant the task might be, she must return and proffer aid.

She had just brought herself to the sticking point, and was about to retrace her steps, when, once more, she became conscious of someone being in movement. But, this time, not only did it come from another direction, but it had an entirely different quality. Before, there had been no attempt at concealment. Whoever had gone striding through the underwood, had apparently cared nothing for being either seen nor heard. Whoever was moving now, unless the girl's imagination played her a trick--was desirous of being neither seen nor heard. There was a stealthy quality in the movements, as if someone were stealing softly through the brushwood, taking cautious steps, keenly on the alert against hidden listeners.

In what quarter was the newcomer moving? The girl could not at first decide; indeed, she never was quite clear, but it seemed to her that someone was creeping along the fence which divided Exham Park and Oak Dene. All the while, the wounded man continued to groan.

Suddenly, she could not tell how she knew, but she knew that the newcomer had not only heard the groans, but, in all probability, had detected the quarter from whence they came; possibly had caught sight of the recumbent figure, prostrate on the grass. Because, just then, the moon came out again in undiminished splendour, and, almost simultaneously, the footsteps ceased. To Violet Arnott, the plain inference seemed to be that the returning light had brought the sufferer into instant prominence. Silence again, broken only by groans. Presently, even they ceased.

Then, without the slightest warning, something occurred which was far worse than the gunshot, which affected her with a paralysis of horror, as if death itself had her by the throat.

The footsteps began again, only with a strange, new swiftness, as if whoever was responsible for them had suddenly darted forward. In the same moment there was a noise which might have been made by a man struggling to gain his feet. Then, just for a second, an odd little silence. Then two voices uttering together what seemed to her to be formless ejaculations. While the voices had still not ceased to be audible, there came a dreadful sound; the sound as of a man who was in an agony of fear and pain. Then a thud--an eloquent thud. And, an instant afterwards, someone went crashing, dashing through the underwood, like some maddened wild beast, flying for life.

The runner was passing close to where she stood. She did not dare to move; she could not have moved even had she dared--her limbs had stiffened. But she could manage to move her head, and she did. She turned, and saw, in the moonlight, in headlong flight, forcing aside the brushwood as he went, Hugh Morice.

What happened during the next few moments she never knew. The probability is that, though she retained her footing, consciousness left her. When, once more, she realised just where she was, and what had occurred, all was still, with an awful stillness. She listened for a sound--any sound; those inarticulate sounds which are part and parcel of a wood at night. She could hear nothing--no whisper of the breeze among the leaves; no hum of insect life; no hint of woodland creatures who wake while men are sleeping. A great hush seemed to have fallen on the world--a dreadful hush. Her heart told her that there was horror in the silence.

What should she do? where should she go? what was lying on the ground under the beech tree, on which not so long ago, Hugh Morice had cut their initials with his hunting-knife? She was sure there was something--what?

She would have to go and see. The thought of doing so was hideous--but the idea of remaining in ignorance was not to be borne. Knowledge must be gained at any price; she would have to know. She waited. Perhaps something would happen to tell her; to render it unnecessary that she should go upon that gruesome errand. Perhaps--perhaps he would groan again? If he only would! it would be the gladdest sound she had ever heard.

But he would not--or he did not.

Yet all was still--that awful stillness.

It was no use her playing the coward--putting it off. She would have to go--she must go. She would never know unless she did. The sooner she went, the sooner it would be done.

So she returned along the footpath towards the beech tree. In the moonlight the way was plain enough. Yet she went stumbling along it as she had never stumbled even in the darkness--uncertain upon her feet; reeling from side to side; starting at shadows; stopping half-a-dozen times in as many yards, fearful of she knew not what.

What was that? A sound? No, nothing. Only a trick of her imagination, which was filled with such fantastic imaginings, such shapes and sounds of horror.

She came to the end of the path. Before her was the open space; the favourite nook where she had first met Hugh Morice, which she had come to regard almost as a sanctuary. In front was the saucer-shaped break in the ground which she had found offered such luxurious ease. What was lying in it now?

Nothing? Or--was that something? Well under the shadow of the beech tree, where the moonlight scarcely reached? almost in the darkness, so that at a first glance it was difficult to see? She stood, leaning a little forward, and looked--long, intently. As she looked her heart seemed to become gradually constricted; she became conscious of actual pain--acute, lancinating.

Something was there. A figure--of a man--in light-coloured clothes. He lay on the ground, so far as she could judge from where she stood, a little on his right side, with his hands thrown over his head as if asleep--fast asleep. The recumbent figure had for her an unescapable fascination. She stared and stared, as though its stillness had in it some strange quality.

She called to the sleeper--in a tone which was so unlike her ordinary voice that--even in that awful moment--the sound of it startled her.

"Robert! Robert! Wake up!"

Probably not a dozen times since she had known this man had she called him by his Christian name. It was so singular that she should have done so; the mere singularity of the thing should have roused him from the soundest slumber. But he continued silent. He neither moved nor answered, nor was there any sign to show that he had heard. She called again.

"Robert! Robert! Do you hear me, wake up! Answer me!"

But he did neither--he neither woke nor answered.

The persistent silence was assuming an appalling quality. She could endure it no longer. She suddenly moved forward under the shadow of the beech tree, and bent down to look. What was that upon the front of his jacket? She touched it with her finger.

"Oh--h--h!"

A sound, which was part shriek, part groan, broke from her trembling lips. Her finger-tips were wet. She had not realised what the dark mark might mean--now she understood. All at once she burst out crying, until she saw something shining up at her from the turf almost at her feet. At sight of it she ceased to cry with the same suddenness with which she had begun. She picked the shining thing up. It was a knife--his knife--Hugh Morice's--the one with which he had cut their initials in the trunk of the tree. Its great blade was all wet.

She gave one quick glance round, slipped the blade--still all wet--inside her bodice; then, returning to the winding footpath, ran along it at the top of her speed, neither pausing nor looking back.

CHAPTER XIII
AFTERWARDS

At the foot of the broad flight of steps leading up to her own hall door she stopped for the first time. It was late. What was the exact hour she had no notion. She only knew that, in that part of the world, it would be regarded as abnormal. The hall door was closed, that little fact in itself was eloquent. There were outer and inner doors. It was the custom to leave the outer door wide open until all the household had retired to rest. She would have to knock to gain admission. Her late return could hardly fail to attract attention. She was breathless with the haste she had made, heated, dishevelled. Whoever admitted her would be sure to notice the condition she was in.

It could not be helped. Let them notice. She was certainly not going to fear the scrutiny of her own servants. So she told herself. She declined to admit that they were sufficiently human to dare to criticise her movements. Besides, what did it matter?

She knocked with difficulty, the knocker was so heavy. Instantly the door was opened by old Day, the butler. Day was a person of much importance. He was a survival of her uncle's time, being in occupation of the house while the next owner was being sought for. An excellent servant, with a very clear idea of his own dignity and the responsibility of his position. That he should have opened the door to her with his own hands at that hour, seemed to her to convey a reproof. She marched straight past him, however, without even a word of thanks. He addressed to her an inquiry as she went, in his even, level tones, as if there were nothing strange in her entering in such a condition, immediately after her return from a prolonged absence, at the dead of the night. Again her ardent imagination seemed to scent an unspoken criticism, which she ignored.

"Will anything else be required?"

"Nothing. I am going to bed."

In her bedroom she found Evans dozing in an easy-chair. The woman started up as she entered.

"I beg your pardon, miss, for slipping off, but I was beginning to be afraid that something might be wrong." She stared as she began to realise the peculiarity of her young mistress's appearance. "Why, miss, whatever-- I hope that nothing's happened."

"What should have happened? Why haven't you gone to bed?"

"Well, miss, I thought that you might want me as this was the first night of your coming home."

"What nonsense! Haven't I told you that I won't have you sit up for me when I'm unusually late? I dislike to feel that my movements are being overlooked by my servants, that they are too intimately acquainted with my goings out and comings in. Go to bed at once."

"Is there nothing I can do for you, miss? Are you--I beg your pardon--but are you sure there's nothing wrong? You look so strange!"

"Wrong? What do you mean--wrong? Go!"

Evans went, the imperturbable demeanour of the well-trained servant not being sufficient to conceal the fact that she went unwillingly. When she was gone Miss Arnott looked at the silver clock on the mantel-shelf. It was past two. She had been out more than four hours. Into those four hours had been crowded the events of a lifetime; the girl who had gone out was not the woman who had returned.

For the first time she began to suspect herself of being physically weary. She moved her hand up towards her forehead. As she did so her glance fell on it; it was all smirched with blood. Simultaneously she became aware that stains of the same sort were on the light blue linen costume she was wearing, particularly on the front of the bodice. She moved to a cheval glass. Was it possible? were her eyes playing her a trick? was there something the matter with the light? Not a bit of it, the thing was clear enough, her face was all smeared with blood, probably where it had been touched by her fingers. Why, now that she could see herself plainly, she saw that she looked as if she had come fresh from a butcher's shambles. No wonder Evans had stared at her in such evident perturbation, demanding if she was sure that there was nothing wrong. Old Day must have been an automaton, not a man, to have betrayed no surprise at the spectacle she presented.

She tore open her bodice, took out from it the knife-- his knife, Hugh Morice's. It was drier, but still damp. It was covered with blood all over. It must have been thrust in up to the hilt--even the handle was mired. It had come off on to all her clothes, had penetrated even to her corsets. Seemingly it resembled ink in its capacity to communicate its presence. She stripped herself almost to the skin in the sudden frenzy of her desire to free herself from the contamination of his blood. When she had washed herself she was amazed to see what a sanguine complexion the water had assumed. It seemed to her that she was in an atmosphere of blood--his blood. What was to be done? She sat down on a chair and tried to think.

It was not surprising that she found it hard to bring herself to a condition in which anything like clarity of thought was possible. But, during the last four hours, she had matured unconsciously, had attained to the possession of will power of strength of which she herself was unsuspicious. She had made up her mind that she would think this thing out, and by degrees she did, after a fashion.

Three leading facts became gradually present to her mind to the exclusion of almost all beside. One was that Robert Champion was dead--dead. And so she had obtained release by the only means to which, as it seemed to her, Mr Whitcomb, that eminent authority on the law of marriage, had pointed. But at what a price! The price exceeded the value of the purchase inconceivably. There was the knife--his knife--to show it. When she shut her eyes she could still see him rushing in the moonlight through the brushwood, like some wild creature, mad with the desire to escape. Beyond all doubt the price was excessive. And it had still to be paid. That was the worst of it, very much the worst. The payment--what form would it take?

As that aspect of the position began to penetrate her consciousness, it was all she could do to keep herself from playing the girl. After all, in years, she was only a girl. In simplicity, in ignorance of evil, in essential purity--a child. When she found herself confronted by the inquiry, what form would the payment take? girl-like, her courage began, as it were, to slip through her finger ends. Then there was that other side to the question, from whom would payment be demanded? Suddenly required to furnish an answer to this, for some moments her heart stood still. She looked about her, at the ruddy-hued water in the wash basin, at the clothing torn off because it was stained. Recalled her tell-tale entry, her admission by Day who, in spite of his unnaturally non-committal attitude, must have noticed the state that she was in; Evans's startled face when, attempting no concealment, she blurted out her confession of what she saw. Here, plainly, were all the essentials for a comedy or tragedy of misunderstanding.

If Hugh Morice chose to be silent all the visible evidences pointed at her. They all seemed to cry aloud that it was she who had done this thing. From the ignorant spectator's point of view there could hardly be a stronger example of perfect circumstantial proof.

For some occult reason her lips were wrinkled by a smile at the thought of Hugh Morice keeping silent. As if he would when danger threatened her, for whom he had done this thing. And yet, if he did not keep silent, who would have to pay? Would--? Yes, he would; certainly. At that thought her poor, weak, childish heart seemed to drop in her bosom like a lump of lead. The tears stood in her eyes. She went hot and cold. No--not that. Rather than that, it would be better that he should keep silent. Better--better anything than that. He had done this for her; but, he must not be allowed to do more. He had done enough for her already--more than enough--much more. She must make it her business to see that he did nothing else. Nothing.

Just as she was, all unclothed, she knelt down and prayed. The strangest prayer, a child's prayer, the kind of prayer which, sometimes, coming from the very heart of the child, is uttered in all simplicity. Many strange petitions have been addressed to God; but few stranger than that. She prayed that whoever might have to suffer for what had been done, he might escape scot-free; not only here but also hereafter; in heaven as well as on earth. Although the supplication invoked such an odd confusion of ideas, it was offered up with such intense earnestness and simplicity of purpose, that it had, at anyrate, one unlooked for effect. It calmed her mind. She rose up from her knees feeling more at ease than she had done since ten o'clock. In some vague way, which was incomprehensible to herself, her prayer seemed already to have been answered. Therefore, the future had no perils in store for her; she was at peace with the world.

She collected the garments which she had taken off, arranged them in a neat bundle and placed them in an almost empty drawer which she found at the bottom of a wardrobe. The knife she put under the bundle. Then, locking the drawer, she disposited the key beneath her pillows. In the morning her brain would be clearer. She would be able to decide what to do with the things which, although speechless, were yet so full of eloquence. The water in which she had washed she carried into the apartment which opened out of her bedroom, and, emptying it into the bath, watched it disappear down the waste water pipe. She flushed the bath so as to remove any traces which it might have left behind. Then, arraying herself in her night attire, she put out the lights and got into bed.

She awoke with that sense of pleasant refreshment which comes after calm, uninterrupted slumber. She lay, for some seconds, in a state of blissful indolence. Then, memory beginning to play its part, she raised herself upon her elbow with a sudden start. She looked about the room. All was as she had left it. Although the curtains and the blinds were drawn the presence of the sun was obvious. Through one window a long pencil of sunshine gleamed across the carpet. Evidently a fine night was to be followed by a delightful day. She touched the ivory push piece just above her head. Instantly Evans appeared.

"Get my bath ready. I'm going to get up at once."

She eyed the woman curiously, looking for news upon her face. There were none. Her countenance was again the servant's expressionless mask. When the curtains and blinds were drawn the room was filled with golden light. She had the windows opened wide. The glory of a summer's day came streaming in. The events of the night seemed to have become the phantasmagoria of some transient dream. It was difficult to believe that they were real, that she had not dreamed them. Her spirits were higher than they had been for some time. She sang to herself while she was having her bath. Evans, putting out her clothes in the next room, heard her.

"She seems to be all right now. That's the first time I've heard her singing, and she looks better. Slept well, I suppose. When you're young and healthy a good sleep works wonders. A nice sight she looked when she came in this morning; I never saw anything like it-- never! All covered with blood, my gracious! A queer one she is, the queerest I've ever had to do with, and I've had to do with a few. Seems to me that the more money a woman's got the queerer she is, unless she's got a man to look after her. However, it's no business of mine; I don't want to know what games she's up to. I have found knowing too much brings trouble. But whatever has become of the clothes that she had on? They've vanished, every single thing except the stockings. What can she have done with them? It's queer. I suppose, as she hasn't left them about it's a hint that I'm not to ask questions. I don't want to; I'm sure the less I know the better I'm pleased. Still, I do hope there's nothing wrong. She's a good sort; in spite of all her queernesses, I never want to meet a better. That generous! and simple as a child! Sooner than anything should happen to her I'd--well, I'd do a good deal. If she'd left those clothes of hers about I'd have washed 'em and got 'em up myself, so that no one need have known about the state that they were in. I don't want to speak to her about it. With her ideas about not liking to be overlooked she might think that I was interfering; but, I wish she had."

Somewhat to her surprise Miss Arnott found Mrs Plummer waiting for her at the breakfast-table.

"Why," she exclaimed, "I thought you would have finished long ago--ever so long ago."

"I was a little late myself; so I thought I'd wait for you. What time did you come in?"

"Why do you ask?"

"Nothing. I only wondered. Directly I had finished dinner I went to bed--straight from the table. I was tired; I thought you wouldn't care for me to sit up for you."

"Of course not; what an idea! You never have sat up for me, and I shouldn't advise you to begin. But--you still look tired. Haven't you slept away your fatigue?"

"I don't fancy I have quite. As you say, I'm still a little tired. Yet I slept well, fell asleep as soon as I got into bed directly, and never woke."

"Didn't you dream?"

"Dream? Why should I dream?"

"There's no particular reason that I know of, only when people march straight from dinner to bed dreams do sometimes follow--at least, so I've been told."

"They don't with me; I never dream, never. I don't suppose I've dreamt half-a-dozen times in my life."

"You're lucky."

"I've a clear conscience, my dear; a perfectly clear conscience. People with clear consciences don't dream. Where did you go to?"

"Oh--I strolled about, enjoying the fresh air."

"An odd hour to enjoy it, especially after the quantity of fresh air that you've been enjoying lately. What time did you say it was that you came in?"

"I didn't say. Day will be able to tell you, if you are anxious to know--you appear to be. He let me in." The elder lady was silent, possibly not caring to lay herself open to the charge of being curious. Presently Miss Arnott put the inquiry to the butler on her own account. "Probably, Day, you will be able to supply Mrs Plummer with the information she desires. What time was it when I came in?"

"I'm afraid I don't know. I didn't look at my watch. I've no idea."

The butler kept his eyes turned away as he answered. Something in his tone caused her to look at him-- something which told her that if the man had not been guilty of a positive falsehood, he had at least been a party to the suppression of the truth. She became instantly convinced that his intention was to screen her. She did not like the notion, it gave her an uncomfortable qualm.

CHAPTER XIV
ON THE HIGH ROAD

All that day nothing happened. Miss Arnott went in the morning to church; in the afternoon for a run on her motor, which had been neglected during the whole period of her absence abroad. She continued in a state of expectation. Before she started for church from everyone who approached her she looked for news; being persuaded that, if there were news of the kind she looked for, it would not be hidden from her long. But, plainly, no one had anything to tell.

Mrs Plummer accompanied her to church. Miss Arnott would rather she had refrained. A conviction was forcing itself upon her that, at the back of Mrs Plummer's mind, there was something which she was doing her best to keep to herself, but which now and then would peep out in spite of her--something hostile to herself. A disagreeable feeling was growing on her that the lady knew much more about her movements on the previous night than she was willing to admit. How she knew she did not attempt to guess, or even whether the knowledge really amounted to anything more than a surmise. She had an uncomfortable impression that her companion, who was obviously ill at ease, was watching her with a furtive keenness which she intuitively resented.

When they reached the church she was scarcely in a religious mood. She was conscious that her unexpected appearance made a small sensation. Those who knew her smiled at her across the pews. Only servants were in the Oak Dene pew; the master was absent. She wondered if anything had yet transpired; half expecting some allusion to the matter during the course of the sermon. While the vicar preached her thoughts kept wandering to the mossy nook beneath the beech tree. Surely someone must have been there by now, and seen. She would hear all about it after church--at anyrate, when she reached home.

But no, not a word. Nothing had stirred the tranquil country air. One item of information she did receive on her entering the house-- Hugh Morice had called. She probably appeared more startled than the occasion seemed to warrant. The fact being that she had forgotten the appointment he had made with her the night before. In any case she would not have expected him to keep it. That he should have done so almost took her breath away. He had merely inquired if she was in; on learning that she was not had gone away. He had left no message.

If she had stayed at home and seen him, what would he have said to her?

That was the question which she kept putting to herself throughout the run on her motor; fitting it not with one answer, but a dozen. There were so many things he might have said, so many he might have left unsaid.

She expected to be greeted with the news when she brought the car to a standstill in front of her own hall door. No; still not a word. Not one during the whole of the evening. A new phase seemed to be developing in Mrs Plummer's character--she had all at once grown restless, fidgety. Hitherto, if she had had a tendency, it had been to attach herself too closely to her charge. She was disposed to be too conversational. Now, on a sudden, it was all the other way. Unless the girl's fancy played her a trick she was not only desirous of avoiding her, but when in her society she was taciturn almost to the verge of rudeness. Miss Arnott was anxious neither for her company nor her conversation; but she did not like her apparent unflattering inclination to avoid her altogether.

That night the girl went early to bed. Hardly had she got into her room than she remembered the key; the key of the wardrobe drawer, which, in the small hours of the morning, she had put under her pillow before she got into bed. Until that moment she had forgotten its existence. Now, all at once, it came back to her with a jarring shock. She went to the bed and lifted the pillows--there was nothing there.

"Have you heard anything about a key being found underneath this pillow? I put it there just before I got into bed. I forgot it when I got up."

"No, miss, I haven't. What key was it?"

"It was"--she hesitated--"it was the key of a drawer in this wardrobe. Perhaps it's in it now. No; there's nothing there. Whoever made my bed must have seen it. Who made the bed?"

"Wilson, miss. If she saw a key under your pillow she ought to have given it me at once. I was in the room all the while; but she never said a word. I'll go and ask her at once."

"Do. But I see all the drawers have keys. I suppose any one of them will fit any drawer?"

"No, miss, that's just what they won't do; and very awkward it is sometimes. There's a different lock to every drawer, and only one key which fits it. I'll go and make inquiries of Wilson at once."

While Evans was gone Miss Arnott considered. It would be awkward if the key were lost or mislaid. To gain access to that drawer the lock would have to be forced. Circumstances might very easily arise which would render it necessary that access should be gained, and by her alone. Nor was the idea a pleasant one that, although the drawer was closed to her, it might be accessible to somebody else.

Evans returned to say that the maid, Wilson, denied all knowledge of a key.

"She declares that there was no key there. She says that if there had been she couldn't have helped but see it. I don't see how she could have either. You are sure, miss, that you left it there?"

"Certain."

"Then perhaps it slipped on to the floor when she moved the pillow, without being noticed."

It was not on the floor then--at least, they could discover no signs of it. Evans moved the bed, and went on her knees to see. Nor did it appear to have strayed into the bed itself.

"I will see Wilson myself in the morning," said Miss Arnott, when

Evans's researches proved resultless. "The key can't have vanished into nothing."

But Wilson, even when interviewed by her mistress, afforded no information. She was a raw country girl. A bundle of nerves when she saw that Miss Arnott was dissatisfied. There seemed no possible reason why she should wish to conceal the fact that she had lighted on the key, if she had done so. So far as she knew the key was valueless, certainly it was of no interest to her. Miss Arnott had to console herself with the reflection that if she did not know what had become of the key no one else did either. She gave instructions that if it was found it was to be handed her at once. There, for the moment, the matter rested.

Again on that Monday nothing transpired. It dawned upon the girl, when she began to think things over, that it was well within the range of possibility that nothing would transpire for a considerable period. That mossy nook was in a remote part of the estate. Practically speaking, except the gamekeepers, nobody went there at all. It was certain that whoever did would be trespassing. So far as she knew, thereabouts, trespassers of any sort were few and far between. As for the gamekeepers, there was nothing to take them there.

By degrees her cogitations began to trend in an altogether unexpected direction. If the discovery had not been made already, and might be postponed for weeks, it need never be made at all. The body might quite easily be concealed. If there was time it might even be buried at the foot of the beech tree under which it had been lying, and all traces of the grave be hidden. It only needed a little care and sufficient opportunity. She remembered when a favourite dog had died, how her father had buried it at one side of the lawn in their Cumberland home. He had been careful in cutting out the sods of turf; when replacing them in their former positions, he had done so with such neatness and accuracy that, two or three days after no stranger would have supposed they had ever been moved.

The dead man might be treated as her father had treated Fido. In which case his fate might never become known, unless she spoke. Indeed, for all she could tell, the body might be under the turf by now. If she chose to return to the enjoyment of her favourite lounge there might be nothing to deter her. She might lie, and laze, and dream, and be offended by nothing which could recall unpleasant memories.

As the possibility that this might be so occurred to her she became possessed by a strange, morbid disposition to put it to the test. She was nearly half inclined to stroll once more along that winding path, and see if there was anything to prevent her enjoying another waking dream. This inclination began to be so strong that, fearful lest it should get the better of her, to escape what was becoming a hideous temptation, she went for another run upon her car, and, in returning, met Hugh Morice.

They saw each other's car approaching on the long straight road, while they were yet some distance apart, possibly more than a mile, backed by the usual cloud of dust. She was descending an incline, he was below, far off, where the road first came in sight. For some moments she was not sure that the advancing car was his, then she was undecided what to do; whether to sweep past him, or to halt and speak. Her heart beat faster, her hands were tremulous, her breath came quicker. She had just resolved to go past him with a commonplace salutation, when the matter was taken out of her hands. When he was within a hundred yards of her he stopped his car, with the evident design of claiming her attention for at least a second or two. So she stopped also, when the machines were within a yard of one another.

He was alone. He glanced at her chauffeur with his big grey eyes, as if the sight of him were offensive. Then he looked at her and she at him, and for a while they were silent. It seemed to her that he was devouring her with his eyes. She was vaguely conscious of a curious feeling of satisfaction at being devoured. For her part she could not take her eyes off his face--she loved to look at him.

It was only after some moments had passed that it appeared to occur to him that there might be anything singular in such a fashion of meeting, especially in the presence of her mechanic. When he spoke his voice seemed husky, the manner of his speech was, as usual, curt.

"Why weren't you at home yesterday morning as you promised?"
"I had forgotten that I did promise."
"You had forgotten?"
"Not that it would have made any difference if I had remembered; I should not have stayed in. I did not suppose you would come."
"I told you I should come."
"Yes, you told me."
"What I tell you I will do that I do do. Nothing that may happen will cause me to change my mind." He looked past her along the way she had come, then addressed the chauffeur. "There is something lying on the road. It may be something Miss Arnott has dropped--go and

see."

"I don't think it is anything of mine. I have had nothing to drop."

"Go and see what it is." The man, descending, returned along the road. "I don't choose to have everything you and I may have to say to each other overheard. You knew that I should come, why did you not stay in? of what were you afraid?"

"Afraid? I? Of nothing, There was no reason why I should be afraid."

He searched her face, as if seeking for something which he was amazed to find himself unable to discover.

"You are a strange woman; but then women were always puzzles to me. You may not be stranger than the rest--I don't know. Hadn't you better go away again to-day? Back to the Lake of Como or further?"

"Why should I go away? Of what are you afraid?"

"Of what am I not afraid? I am even afraid to think of what I am afraid--of such different stuff are we two made. I never knew what fear was, before; now, I hardly dare to breathe for fear."

"Don't you trust me?"

"Trust you? What has that to do with it?"

"I see, you think it doesn't matter. I hardly know whether you intend to flatter me or not. Why don't you go away?"

"What's the use? Where should I go where I could be hidden? There is no hiding-place, none. Besides, if I were to hide myself under the sea it might make no difference. Don't you understand?"

"I'm not sure; no, I don't think I do. But, tell me, I want to know! I must know! It was all I could do to keep myself from going to see-- what have you done with him?"

"Done with him?"

"Have you--have you buried him?"

"Buried him? Do you think he could be buried?"

Something came on to his face which frightened her, started her all trembling.

"I--I didn't know. Don't look at me like that. I only wondered."

"You only wondered! Is it possible that you thought it could be hidden like that? My God! that you should be such a woman! Don't speak, here's your chauffeur close upon you; you don't want him to understand. You'll find the dust is worse further on. Good-day!"

He whizzed off, leaving her enveloped in a cloud of the dust of which he had spoken.

CHAPTER XV
COOPER'S SPINNEY

Not till the Friday following was the dead body discovered. And then in somewhat singular fashion.

A young gamekeeper was strolling through the forest with his dog. The dog, a puppy, strayed from his side. He did not notice that it had done so till he heard it barking. When he whistled it came running up to him with something in its mouth--a brown billycock hat. The creature was in a state of excitement. On his taking the hat from it, it ran back in the direction it had come, barking as it went. Puzzled by its behaviour, curious as to how it had found the hat, he followed to where the dead man lay beneath the beech tree.

He thought at first that it was some stranger who, having trespassed and lighted on a piece of open ground, had taken advantage of the springy turf to enjoy a nap. It was only after he had called to him three times, and, in spite, also, of the dog's persistent barking, had received no answer, that he proceeded to examine more closely into the matter. Then he saw not only that the man was dead, but that his clothing was stiff with coagulated blood. There had been a violent thunderstorm the night before. The rain had evidently come drenching down on the silent sleeper, but it had not washed out that blood.

Clarke was a country bumpkin, only just turned eighteen. When it began to break on his rustic intelligence that, in all probability, he was looking down on the victim of some hideous tragedy, he was startled out of his very few wits. He had not the faintest notion what he ought to do. He only remembered that the great house was the nearest human habitation. When he had regained sufficient control of his senses, he ran blindly off to it. A footman, seeing him come staggering up the steps which led to the main entrance, came out to inquire what he meant by such a glaring breach of etiquette.

"What are you doing here? This isn't the place for you. Go round to the proper door. What's the matter with you? Do you hear, what's up?"

"There--there's a man in Cooper's Spinney!"

"Well! what of it? That's none of our business."

"He's--he's dead."

"Dead? Who's dead? What do you mean?"

The hobbledehoy broke into a fit of blubbering.

"They've--they've killed him," he blubbered.

"Killed him? Who's killed him? What are you talking about? Stop that noise. Can't you talk sense?"

Day, the butler, crossing the hall, came out to see what was the cause of the to-do. At any moment people might call. They would please to find this senseless gawk boohooing like a young bull calf. Day and the footman between them tried to make head or tail of the fellow's blundering story. While they were doing so Mrs Plummer appeared in the doorway.

"Day, what is the matter here? What is the meaning of this disturbance?"

"I can't quite make out, but from what this young man says it appears that he's seen someone lying dead in Cooper's Spinney. So far as I can understand the young man seems to think that he's been murdered."

Mrs Plummer started back, trembling so violently that she leaned against the wall, as if in want of its support.

"Murdered? He's not been murdered! It's a lie!"

Day, after one glance at her, seemed to avoid looking in her direction.

"As to that, madam, I can say nothing. The young man doesn't seem to be too clear-headed. I will send someone at once and have inquiries made."

Shortly it was known to all the house that young Clarke's story was not a lie. A horse was put into a trap, the news was conveyed to the village, the one policeman brought upon the scene. When Miss Arnott returned with her motor it was easy enough for her to see that at last the air was stirred.

"Has anything happened?" she inquired of the footman who came to superintend her descent from the motor.

"I am afraid there has--something very unpleasant."

"Unpleasant! How?"

"It appears that a man has been found dead in Cooper's Spinney--murdered, cut to pieces, they do say.

"In Cooper's Spinney? Cut to pieces?" She paused, as if to reflect. "Did you say cut to pieces? Surely there's some mistake."

"I only know what they say, miss. Granger's up there now."

"Granger?"

"The policeman, miss. Now I'm told they've sent for a doctor."

A second footman handed her an envelope as she entered the hall. She saw that "Oak Dene" was impressed in scarlet letters on the flap.

"When did this come?"

"One of Mr Morice's grooms brought it soon after you went out."

She tore the envelope open, and there and then read the note which it contained. It had no preamble, it simply ran,--

"Why have you not acted on my suggestion and gone back to Lake Como or farther?

"At any moment it may be too late! Don't you understand?

"When I think of what may be the consequences of delay I feel as if I were going mad. I shall go mad if you don't go. I don't believe that I have slept an hour since.

"Do as I tell you--go!   H. M."

Then at the bottom two words were added,--

"Burn this."

As she was reading it a second time Mrs Plummer came into the hall, white and shaky.

"Have you heard the dreadful news?"

She asked the question in a kind of divided gasp, as if she were short of breath. Miss Arnott did not answer for a moment. She fixed her glance on the elder lady, as if she were looking not at, but through her. Then she put a question in return.

"Where is Cooper's Spinney?"

Had the girl hauled at her a volley of objurgations Mrs Plummer could not have seemed more distressed.

"Cooper's Spinney!" she exclaimed. "Why do you ask me? How should I know?"

Without stopping for anything further Miss Arnott went up to her bedroom. There she found Evans, waiting to relieve her of her motoring attire. As she performed her accustomed offices her mistress became aware that her hands were trembling.

"What's the matter with you? Aren't you well?"

The woman seemed to be shaking like a leaf, and to be only capable of stammering,--

"I--I don't think, miss, I--I can be well. I--I think that dreadful news has upset me."

"Dreadful news? Oh, I see. By the way, where is Cooper's Spinney?"

"I haven't a notion, miss. I--I only know just about the house."

Miss Arnott put another question as she was leaving the room.

"Has nothing been heard yet of the key of that wardrobe drawer?"

"No, miss, nothing. And, miss--I beg your pardon--but if you want to break it open, you can do it easily, or I will for you; and, if you'll excuse my taking a liberty, if those clothes are in it, I'll wash them for you, and no one shall ever know."

Miss Arnott stared at the speaker in unmistakable surprise.

"It's very good of you. But I don't think I need trouble you to step so far out of the course of your ordinary duties." When she was in her sitting-room she said to herself, "She will wash them for me? What does the woman mean? And what does he mean by writing to me in such a strain?" She referred to Mr Morice's note which she had in her hand. "'Do as I tell you--go.' Why should I go? and how dare he issue his commands to me, as if it were mine merely to obey. Plainly this was written before the news reached Oak Dene; when he hears it, it is possible that he may not stand upon the order of his going, but go at once. I'll answer him. He shall have his reply before he goes, unless his haste's too great. Then, perhaps, he will understand."

On the back leaf of the note signed "H. M." she scribbled.

"Is not the advice you offer me better suited to yourself? Why should I go? It seems to me that it is you who do not understand. Have you heard the news? Possibly understanding will come with it. You do not appear to recognise what kind of person I really am. Believe me, I am to be trusted. But am I the only factor to be reckoned with?

"Had you not better swallow your own prescription?   V. A."

She hesitated before adding the initials, since he knew that they were not actually hers. Then, putting her answer, still attached to his note, into an envelope, she gave instructions that a messenger should ride over with it at once. While she was hesitating whether to go down and learn if any fresh development had occurred, there came a tapping at her sitting-room door. Day entered. To him she promptly put the question she had addressed to others.

"Oh, Day, perhaps you will be able to tell me where is Cooper's Spinney?"

He looked at her until he saw that she was looking at him, then his glance fell.

"Cooper's Spinney is right away to the east, where our land joins Oak Dene. I don't know how it gets its name. It's pretty open there. In one part there's a big beech tree. It was under the tree the--the body was found."

"Thank you, Day. I think I know where you mean." Again the butler's glance rose and fell. Perceiving that he seemed to be at a loss for words she went on. "Is there anything you wish to speak to me about?"

"Yes, Miss Arnott, I'm sorry to say there is. I've come to give you notice."

"To give me notice?"

"Yes, miss, with your permission. I've been in service all my life, good service. I've been in this house a good many years. I've saved a little money. If I'm ever to get any enjoyment out of it, and I've my own ideas, it seems to me that I'd better start doing it. I should like to leave to-day."

"To-day?"

"Yes, miss, to-day. There isn't much to do in the house just now, and there's plenty of people to do it. Bevan's quite capable of taking my place till you get someone else to fill it. Your convenience won't suffer."

"But isn't this a very sudden resolution? What has caused you to arrive at it?"

Day still kept his glance turned down, as if searching for an answer on the carpet. It was apparently only a lame one which he found.

"I'm in an awkward situation, Miss Arnott. I don't want to say anything which can be misconstrued. So much is that my feeling that I thought of going away without saying a word."

"That would not have been nice conduct on your part."

"No, miss; that's what I felt, so I came."

"Come, Day, what is it you are stammering about? Something extraordinary must have happened to make you wish to leave at a moment's notice after your long service. Don't be afraid of misconstruction. What is it, please?"

The man's tone, without being in the least uncivil, became a trifle dogged.

"Well, miss, the truth is, I'm not comfortable in my mind."
"About what?"
"I don't want to be, if I may say so, dragged into this business."
"What business?"
"Of the body they've found in Cooper's Spinney."
"Day, what are you talking about? What possible connection can that have with you?"
"Miss Arnott, I understand that Dr Radcliffe says that that man has been lying dead under that beech tree for at least four or five days. That takes us back to Saturday, the day that you came home. In these sort of things you never know what the police may take it into their heads to do. I do not want to run the risk of being called as a witness at the inquest or--anywhere else, and--asked questions about last Saturday."

Then the man looked his mistress straight in the face, and she understood--or thought she did.

"What you have said, Day, settles the question. Under no circumstances will I permit you to leave my service--or this house--until the matter to which you refer has been finally settled. So resolved am I upon that point that, if I have any further reason to suspect you of any intention of doing so, I shall myself communicate with the police at once. Understand that clearly."

CHAPTER XVI
JIM BAKER

The inquest, which was held at the "Rose and Crown," was productive of one or two pieces of what the local papers were perhaps justified in describing as "Startling Evidence." It was shown that the man had been stabbed to death. Some broad-bladed, sharp-pointed instrument had been driven into his chest with such violence that the point had penetrated to the back. The wall of the chest had been indented by the violence of the blow. Death must have been practically instantaneous. And yet one side of him had been almost riddled by shot. He had received nearly the entire charge of a gun which had been fired at him--as the close pattern showed--within a distance of a very few feet. It was only small shot, and no vital organ had been touched. The discharge had been in no way responsible for his death.

Still, the pain must have been exquisite. The medical witnesses were of opinion that the first attack had come from the gun; that, while he was still smarting from its effects, advantage was taken of his comparative helplessness to inflict the death-wound.

Nothing came out before the coroner to prove motive. There were no signs that the man had been robbed. A common metal watch, attached to a gilt chain, was found on his person, a half-sovereign, six-shillings in silver, and ninepence in copper, a packet of cigarettes, a box of matches, a handkerchief, apparently brand new, and a piece of paper on which was written "Exham Park." As nothing suggested that an attempt had been made to rifle his pockets the probability was that that was all the property he had had on him at the moment of his death. There was no initial or name on any of his clothing, all of which, like his handkerchief, seemed brand new. His identity remained unrevealed by anything which he had about him.

On this point, however, there was evidence of a kind. The police produced witnesses who asserted that, on the preceding Saturday afternoon, he had arrived, by a certain train, at a little roadside station. He had given up a single third-class ticket from London, and had asked to be directed to Exham Park. On being informed that Exham Park was some distance off, he had shown symptoms of disgust. He had endeavoured to hire a conveyance to take him there but had failed. What had happened to him afterwards, or what had been the course of his movements, there was no evidence to show.

The coroner adjourned his court three times to permit of the discovery of such evidence.

During the time the inquiry was in the air the whole countryside was on tip-toe with curiosity, and also with expectation. Tongues wagged, fingers pointed, the wildest tales were told. Exham Park was the centre of a very disagreeable sort of interest. The thing to do was to visit the scene of the murder. Policemen and gamekeepers had to be placed on special duty to keep off trespassers from Cooper's Spinney, particularly on Sundays. The scrap of paper with "Exham Park" written on it, which had been found in the dead man's pocket, was a trifling fact which formed a sufficient basis for a mountain of conjecture.

Why had he been going to Exham Park? Who had he been desirous of seeing there? To furnish answers to these questions, the entire household was subjected by the police--with Miss Arnott's express sanction--to cross-examination. The same set of questions was put to every man, woman and child in the house, about it, and on the estate. Each individual was first of all informed that he or she was not compelled to answer, and was then examined as follows:--

Did you know the deceased? Did you ever see him? Or hear from--or of--him? Had you any knowledge of him of any sort or kind? Have you any reason whatever to suppose that he might have been coming to see you? Have you the least idea of who it was he was coming to see? On what is that idea based?

The house servants were questioned in the dining-room, in Miss Arnott's presence. She sat in the centre of one side of the great dining-table, completely at her ease. On her right was Mrs Plummer, obviously the most uncomfortable person present. She had protested vigorously against any such proceedings being allowed to take place.

"I believe it's illegal, and if it isn't illegal, it's sheer impudence. How dare any common policeman presume to come and ask a lot of impertinent questions, and treat us as if we had a house full of criminals!"

Miss Arnott only laughed.

"As for it's being illegal, I can't see how it can be that, if it's done with my permission. I suppose I can let who I like into my own house. No one's compelled to answer. I'm sure you needn't. You needn't even be questioned if you'd rather not be. As for a house full of criminals, I'm not aware that anyone has suggested that I harbour even one."

But Mrs Plummer was not to be appeased.

"It's all very well for you to say that I needn't be questioned, but if I decline I shall look most conspicuous. Everybody will attribute my refusal to some shameful reason. I dislike the whole affair. I'm sure no good will come of it. But, so far as I'm concerned, I shall answer all their questions without the slightest hesitation."

And she did, with direct negatives, looking Mr Nunn, the detective who had come down specially from London to take the case in charge, straight in the face in a fashion which suggested that she considered his conduct to be in the highest degree impertinent.

Miss Arnott, on the other hand, who proffered herself first, treated the questions lightly, as if they had and could have no application to herself. She said no to everything, denied that she had ever known the dead man, that she had ever seen him, that she had ever heard from, or of, him, that she had any reason to suppose that he was coming to see her, that she had any idea of who he was coming to see, and did it all with an air of careless certainty, as if it must be plain to everyone that the notion of in any way connecting her with him was sheer absurdity.

With the entire household the result was the same. To all the questions each alike said no, some readily enough, some not so readily; but always with sufficient emphasis to make it abundantly clear that the speaker hoped that it was taken for granted that no other answer was even remotely possible.

Thus, to all appearances, that inquiry carried the matter not one hair's breadth further. The explanation of why the dead man had borne those two words--"Exham Park"--about with him was still to seek; since no one could be found who was willing to throw light upon the reasons which had brought him into that part of the world. And as the police, in spite of all their diligence, could produce no further evidence which bore, even remotely, on any part of the business, it looked as if, at anyrate so far as the inquest was concerned, the result would have to be an open verdict. They searched practically the whole country-side for some trace of a weapon with which the deed could have been done; in vain. The coroner had stated that, unless more witnesses were forthcoming, he would have to close the inquiry, and the next meeting of his court would have to be the last, and it was, therefore, with expectations of some such abortive result that, on the appointed day, the villagers crowded into the long room of the "Rose and Crown."

However, the general expectation was not on that occasion destined to be realised. The proceedings were much more lively, and even exciting, than had been anticipated. Instead of the merely formal notes which the reporters had expected to be able to furnish to their various journals, they found themselves provided with ample material, not only to prove a strong attraction for their own papers, but also to serve as appetising matter to the press of the entire kingdom, with contents bills for special editions--"The Cooper's Spinney Murder. Extraordinary Developments."

These "extraordinary developments" came just as the proceedings were drawing to a close. Merely formal evidence had been given by the police. The coroner was explaining to the jury that, as nothing fresh was before them, or, in spite of repeated adjournments, seemed likely to be, all that remained was for them to return their verdict. What that verdict ought to be unfortunately there could be no doubt. The dead man had been foully murdered. No other hypothesis could possibly meet the circumstances of the case. Who had murdered him was another matter. As to that, they were at present able to say nothing. The identity of the miscreant was an unknown quantity. They could point neither in this quarter nor in that. The incidents before them would not permit of it. It seemed probable that the crime had been committed under circumstances of peculiar atrocity. The murderer had first fired at his victim--actually nearly fifty pellets of lead had been found embedded in the corpse. Then, when the poor wretch had been disabled by the pain and shock of the injuries which had been inflicted on him, his assailant had taken advantage of his helplessness to stab him literally right through the body.

The coroner had said so much, and seemed disposed to say much more, in accents which were intended to be impressive, and which, in fact, did cause certain of the more easily affected among his auditors to shiver, when a voice exclaimed from the back of the room,--

"That's a damned lie!"

The assertion, a sufficiently emphatic one in itself, was rendered still more so by the tone of voice in which it was uttered; the speaker was, evidently, not in the least desirous of keeping his opinion to himself. The coroner stopped. Those who were sitting down stood up, those who were already standing turned in the direction from which the voice came.

The coroner inquired, with an air of authority which was meant to convey his righteous indignation,--

"Who said that?"

The speaker did not seem at all abashed. He replied, without a moment's hesitation, still at the top of his voice,--

"I did."

"Who is that man speaking? Bring him here!"

"No one need bring me, and no one hadn't better try. I'm coming, I am; I've got two good legs of my own, and I'm coming as fast as they'll carry me. Now then, get out of the way there. What do you mean by blocking up the floor? It ain't your floor!"

The speaker--as good as his word--was exhibiting in his progress toward the coroner's table a degree of zeal which was not a little inconvenient to whoever chanced to be in his way. Having gained his objective, leaning both hands on the edge of the table he stared at the coroner in a free-and-easy fashion which that official was not slow to resent.

"Take off your cap, sir!"

"All right, governor, all right. Since you've got yours off I don't mind taking mine--just to oblige you."

"Who are you? What's your name?"

"I'm a gamekeeper, that's what I am. And as for my name, everybody knows what my name is. It's Jim Baker, that's what my name is. Is there anybody in this room what don't know Jim Baker? Of course there ain't."

"You're drunk, sir!"

"And that I'm not. If I was drunk I shouldn't be going on like this. You ask 'em. They know Jim Baker when he's drunk. There isn't many men in this parish as could hold him; it would take three or four of some of them."

"At anyrate, you've been drinking."

"Well, and so would you have been drinking if you'd been going through what I have these last weeks."

"How dare you come to my court in this state? and use such language?"

"Language! what language? I ain't used no language. I said it's a damned lie, and so it is."

"You'll get yourself into serious trouble, my man, if you don't take care. I was saying that, having shot the deceased, the murderer proceeded to stab him through the body. Is that the statement to which you object with such ill-timed vigour?"

The answer was somewhat unlooked for. Stretching half-way across the table, Jim Baker shook his fist at the coroner with an amount of vigour which induced that officer to draw his chair a little further back.

"Don't you call me a murderer!"

"What do you mean, sir, by your extraordinary behaviour? I did not call you a murderer; I said nothing of the kind."

"You said that the man who shot him, stabbed him. I say it's a lie; because he didn't!"

"How do you know? Stop! Before you say another word it's my duty to inform you that if you have any evidence to offer, before you do so you must be duly sworn; and, further, in your present condition it becomes essential that I should warn you to be on your guard, lest you should say something which may show a guilty knowledge."

"And what do you call a guilty knowledge? I ask you that."

"As for instance--"

Mr Baker cut the coroner's explanation uncivilly short.

"I don't want none of your talk. I'm here to speak out, that's what I'm here for. I'm going to do it. When you say that the man as shot him knifed him, I say it's a damned lie. How do I know? Because I'm the man as shot him; and, beyond giving him a dose of pepper, I'm ready to take my Bible oath that I never laid my hand on him."

Mr Baker's words were followed by silence--that sort of silence which the newspapers describe by the word "sensation." People pressed further into the room, craning their heads to get a better view of the speaker. The coroner searched him with his eyes, as if to make sure that the man was in possession of at least some of his senses.

"Do you know what it is you are saying?"

"Do I know what I'm saying? Of course I know. I say that I peppered the chap, but beyond that I never done him a mischief; and I tell you again that to that I'm ready to take my Bible oath."

The coroner turned to his clerk.

"Swear this man."

Jim Baker was sworn--unwillingly enough. He handled the Testament which was thrust into his hand as if he would have liked to have thrown it at the clerk's head.

"Now, James Baker, you are on your oath. I presume that you know the nature of an oath?"

"I ought to at my time of life."

There were those that tittered. It was possible that Mr Baker was referring to one kind of oath and the coroner to another.

"And, I take it, you are acquainted with the serious consequences of swearing falsely?"

"Who's swearing falsely! When I swear falsely it will be time for you to talk."

"Very good: so long as you understand. Before proceeding with your examination I would again remind you that you are in no way bound to answer any question which you think would criminate yourself."

"Go on, do. I never see such a one for talking. You'd talk a bull's hind leg off."

Once more there were some who smiled. The coroner kept his temper in a manner which did him credit. He commenced to examine the witness.

"Did you know the dead man?"

"Know him? Not from Adam."

"Did you have any acquaintance with him of any sort or kind?"

"Never heard tell of him in my life; never set eyes on him till that Saturday night. When I see him under the beech tree in Cooper's Spinney I let fly at him."

"Did you quarrel?"

"Not me; there wasn't no time. I let fly directly I see him."

"At a perfect stranger? Why? For what possible reason? Did you suspect him of poaching?"

"I'd been having a glass or two."

"Do you mean to say that because you were drunk you shot this unfortunate man?"

"I made a mistake; that's how it was."

"You made a mistake?"

"I must have been as near drunk as might be, because, when I come upon this here chap sudden like, I thought he was Mr Hugh Morice."

"You thought he was Mr Hugh Morice?"

"I did."

"Remember you are not bound to answer any question if you would rather not. Bearing that well in mind, do you wish me to understand that you intended to shoot Mr Morice?"

"Of course I did."

"But why?"

"He's sitting there; you ask him; he knows."

As a matter of fact Mr Hugh Morice--who had throughout shown a lively interest in the proceedings--was occupying the chair on the coroner's right hand side. The two men exchanged glances; there was an odd look on Mr Morice's face, and in his eyes. Then the coroner returned to the witness.

"If necessary, Mr Morice will be examined later on. At present I want information from you. Why should you have intended to shoot Mr Morice?"

"Obeying orders, that's what I was doing."

"Obeying orders? Whose orders?"

"My old governor's. He says to me--and well Mr Hugh Morice knows it, seeing he was there and heard--'Jim,' he says, 'if ever you see Hugh Morice on our ground you put a charge of lead into him.' So I done it--leastways, I meant to."

The coroner glanced at Mr Morice with an uplifting of his eyebrows which that gentleman chose to regard as an interrogation, and answered,--

"What Baker says is correct; the late Mr Arnott did so instruct him, some seven or eight years ago."

"Was Mr Arnott in earnest?"

Hugh Morice shrugged his shoulders.

"He was in a very bad temper."

"I see. And because of certain words which were uttered in a moment of irritation seven or eight years ago, James Baker meant to shoot Mr Morice, but shot this stranger instead. Is that how it was?"

"That's about what it comes to."

"I would again remind you that you need not answer the question I am about to ask you unless you choose; but, if you do choose, be careful what you say, and remember that you are on your oath. After you had shot this man what did you do?"

"He started squealing. As soon as I heard his voice I thought there was something queer about it. So I went up and had a look at him. Then I saw I'd shot the wrong man."

"Then what did you do?"

"Walked straight off."

"And left that unfortunate man lying helpless on the ground?"

"He wasn't helpless, nor yet he wasn't lying on the ground. He was hopping about like a pig in a fit."

"You know it has been proved that this man was stabbed to death?"

"I've heard tell on it."

"Now--and remember that you are not bound to answer--did you stab him?"

"I did not. I swear to God I didn't. After I pulled the trigger I done nothing to him at all."

"Is it possible that you were so drunk as to have been unconscious of what you did?"

"Not a bit of it. So soon as I see as I'd shot the wrong man that sobered me, I tell you. All I thought about was getting away. I went straight to my own place, two miles off."

"When you last saw this man he was still alive?"

"Very much alive he was."

"He had not been stabbed?"

"He hadn't, so far as I know."

"You must have known if he had been."

"I never touched him, and I asked no questions."

"What was he doing when you saw him last?"

"Hopping about and swearing."

"And you don't know what happened to him afterwards?"

"I see nothing; I'd seen more than enough already. I tell you I walked straight off home."

"And you heard nothing?"

"Nothing out of the way."

"Why haven't you told this story of yours before?"

"Because I didn't want to have any bother, that's why. I knew I hadn't killed him, that was enough for me. Small shot don't hurt no one--at least, not serious. Any man can have a shot at me for a ten-pound note; there's some that's had it for less. But when I heard you saying that the man as shot him stabbed him, then I had to speak--bound to. I wasn't going to have no charge of that kind made against me. And I have spoken, and you've got the truth."

"What time did it happen--all this you have been telling us about?"

Jim Baker answered to the best of his ability. He answered many other questions, also, to the best of his ability. He had a bad time of it. But the worst time was to come when all the questions had been asked and answered.

The coroner announced that, in consequence of the fresh evidence which had been placed before the court, the inquiry would not close that day; but that there would be a further adjournment.

As Mr Baker passed out of the room and down the stairs people drew away from him to let him pass, with an alacrity which was not exactly flattering. When he came out into the street, Granger, the policeman, came forward and laid his hand upon his shoulder, saying, in those squeaky tones which had caused him to be regarded with less respect than was perhaps desirable,--

"James Baker, I arrest you for wilful murder. You needn't say anything, but what you do say will be taken down and used against you. Take my advice and come quiet."

By way of answer Jim Baker stared at Granger and at the London detective at his side and at the people round about him. Then he inquired,--

"What's that you say?"

"I say that I arrest you for wilful murder, and my advice to you is to come quiet."

When Baker saw the policeman taking a pair of handcuffs out of his coat-tail pocket he drew a long breath.

"What's that you've got there?"

"You know what it is very well--it's handcuffs. Hold out your hands and don't let us have no trouble."

Jim Baker held out his hand, his right one. As the policeman advanced, ready to snap them on his wrist, Baker snatched them from him and struck him with them a swinging blow upon the shoulder. Granger, yelling, dropped as if he had been shot. Although he was not tall, his weight was in the neighbourhood of sixteen stone, and he was not of a combative nature.

"If anybody wants some more," announced Mr Baker, "let him come on."

Apparently someone did want more. The words were hardly out of his mouth, before Nunn, the detective, had dodged another blow from the same weapon, and had closed with him in a very ugly grip.

There ensued the finest rough-and-tumble which had been seen in that parish within living memory. Jim Baker fought for all he was worth; when he had a gallon or so of beer inside him his qualifications in that direction were considerable. But numbers on the side of authority prevailed. In the issue he was borne to the lock-up in a cart, not only handcuffed, but with his legs tied together as well. As he went he cursed all and sundry, to the no small amusement of the heterogeneous gathering which accompanied the cart.

CHAPTER XVII
INJURED INNOCENCE

Mr Baker had some uncomfortable experiences. When he was brought before the magistrates it was first of all pointed out--as it were, inferentially--that he was not only a dangerous character, but, also, just the sort of person who might be expected to commit a heinous crime, as his monstrous behaviour when resisting arrest clearly showed. Not content with inflicting severe injuries on the police, he had treated other persons, who had assisted them in their laudable attempts to take him into safe custody, even worse. In proof of this it was shown that one such person was in the cottage hospital, and two more under the doctor's hands; while Granger, the local constable, and Nunn, the detective in charge of the case, appeared in the witness-box, one with his arm in a sling, and the other with plastered face and bandaged head. The fact that the prisoner himself bore unmistakable traces of having lately been engaged in some lively proceedings did not enhance his naturally uncouth appearance. It was felt by more than one who saw him that he looked like the sort of person who was born to be hung.

His own statement in the coroner's court having been produced in evidence against him, it was supplemented by the statements of independent witnesses in a fashion which began to make the case against him look very ugly indeed. Both Miss Arnott and Mr Morice were called to prove that his own assertion--that he had threatened to shoot the master of Oak Dene--was only too true. While they were in the box the prisoner, who was unrepresented by counsel, preserved what, for him, was an unusual silence. He stared at them, indeed, and particularly at the lady, in a way which was almost more eloquent than speech. Then other witnesses were produced who shed a certain amount of light on his proceedings on that memorable Saturday night.

It was shown, for instance, that he was well within the mark in saying that he had had a glass or two. Jenkins, the landlord of the "Rose and Crown," declared that he had had so many glasses that he had to eject him from his premises; he was "fighting drunk." In that condition he had staggered home, provided himself with a gun and gone out with it. A driver of a mail-cart, returning from conveying the mails to be taken by the night express to town, had seen him on a stile leading into Exham Park; had hailed him, but received no answer. A lad, the son of the woman with whom Baker lodged, swore that he had come in between two and three in the morning, seeming "very queer." He kept muttering to himself while endeavouring to remove his boots--muttering out loud. The lad heard him say, "I shot him--well, I shot him. What if I did shoot him? what if I did?" He kept saying this to himself over and over again. After he had gone to bed, the lad, struck by the singularity of his persistent repetition, looked at his gun. It had been discharged. The lad swore that, to his own knowledge, the gun had been loaded when Baker had taken it out with him earlier in the night.

The prisoner did not improve matters by his continual interruptions. He volunteered corroborations of the witnesses' most damaging statements; demanding in truculent tones to be told what was the meaning of all the fuss.

"I shot the man--well, I've said I shot him. But that didn't do him no harm to speak of. I swear to God I didn't do anything else to him. I hadn't no more to do with killing him than an unborn babe."

There were those who heard, however, who were inclined to think that he had had a good deal more to do with killing him than he was inclined to admit.

Miss Arnott, also, was having some experiences of a distinctly unpleasant kind. It was, to begin with, a shock to hear that Jim Baker had been arrested on the capital charge. When she was told what he had said, and read it for herself in the newspapers, she began to understand what had been the meaning of the gunshot and of the groans which had ensued. She, for one, had reason to believe that what the tippling old scoundrel had said was literally true, that he had spoken all the truth. Her blood boiled when she read his appeal to Hugh Morice, and that gentleman's carefully formulated corroboration. The idea that serious consequences might ensue to Baker because of his candour was a frightful one.

It was not pleasant to be called as a witness against him; she felt very keenly the dumb eloquence of the appeal in the blood-shot eyes which were fixed upon her the whole time she was testifying, she observed with something more than amazement. She had a horrible feeling that he was deliberately endeavouring to fit a halter round the neck of the drink-sodden wretch who, he had the best reason for knowing, was innocent of the crime of which he was charged.

A brief encounter which took place between them, as they were leaving the court, filled her with a tumult of emotions which it was altogether beyond her power to analyse. He came out of the door as she was getting into her car. Immediately advancing to her side he addressed her without any sort of preamble.

"I congratulate you upon the clearness with which you gave your evidence, and on the touch of feminine sympathy which it betrayed for the prisoner. I fear, however, that that touch of sympathy may do him more harm than you probably intended."

There was something in the words themselves, and still more in the tone in which they were uttered, which sent the blood surging up into her face. She stared at him in genuine amazement.

"You speak to me like that?--you? Certainly you betrayed no touch of sympathy. I can exonerate you from the charge of injuring him by exhibiting anything of that kind."

"I was in rather a difficult position. Don't you think I was? Unluckily I was not at my ease, which apparently you were."

"I never saw anyone more at his ease than you seemed to be. I wondered how it was possible."

"Did you? Really? What a curious character yours is. And am I to take it that you were uneasy?"

"Uneasy? I--I loathed myself."

"Not actually? I can only assure you that you concealed the fact with admirable skill."

"And--I loathed you."

"Under the circumstances, that I don't wonder at at all. You would. I even go further. Please listen to me carefully, Miss Arnott, and read, as you very well can, the meaning which is between the lines. If a certain matter goes as, judging from present appearances, it very easily may go, I may have to take certain action which may cause you to regard me with even greater loathing than you are doing now. Do not mistake me on that point, I beg of you."

"If I understand you correctly, and I suppose I do, you are quite right in supposing that I shall regard you with feelings to which no mere words are capable of doing justice. I had not thought you were that kind of man."

Events marched quickly. Jim Baker was brought up before the magistrates three times, and then, to Miss Arnott's horror, he was committed for trial on the capital charge. She could hardly have appeared more affected if she herself had been committed. When the news was brought to her by Day, the butler, who still remained in her service, she received it with a point-blank contradiction.

"It's not true. It can't be true. They can't have done anything so ridiculous."

The old man looked at his young mistress with curious eyes, he himself seemed to be considerably disturbed.

"It's quite true, miss. They've sent him to take his trial at the assizes."

"I never heard of anything so monstrous. But, Day, it isn't possible that they can find him guilty?"

"As for that, I can't tell. They wouldn't, if I was on the jury, I do know that."

"Of course not, and they wouldn't if I was."

"No, miss, I suppose not."

Day moved off, Miss Arnott following him with her eyes, as if something in his last remark had struck her strangely.

A little later, when talking over the subject with Mrs Plummer, the elder lady displayed a spirit which seemed to be beyond the younger one's comprehension. Miss Arnott was pouring forth scorn upon the magistrates.

"I have heard a great deal of the stupidity of the Great Unpaid, but I had never conceived that it could go so far as this. There is not one jot or tittle of evidence to justify them in charging that man with murder."

Mrs Plummer's manner as she replied was grim.

"I wonder to hear you talk like that."

"Why should you wonder?"

"I do wonder." Mrs Plummer looked her charge straight in the face oddly. Miss Arnott had been for some time conscious of a continual oddity in the glances with which the other favoured her. Without being aware of it she was beginning to entertain a very real dislike for Mrs Plummer; she herself could scarcely have said why. "For my part I have no hesitation in saying that I think it a very good thing they have sent the man for trial; it would have been nothing short of a public scandal if they hadn't. On his own confession the man's an utterly worthless vagabond, and I hope they'll hang him.

"Mrs Plummer!"

"I do; and you ought to hope so."

"Why ought I to hope so?"

"Because then there'll be an end of the whole affair."

"But if the man is innocent?"

"Innocent!" The lady emitted a sound which might have been meant to typify scorn. "A nice innocent he is. Why you are standing up for the creature I can't see; you might have special reason. I say let them hang him, and the sooner the better, because then there'll be an end of the whole disgusting business, and we shall have a little peace and quietude."

"I for one should have no peace if I thought that an innocent man had been hanged, merely for the sake of providing me with it. But it is evidently no use our discussing the matter. I can only say that I don't understand your point of view, and I may add that there has been a good deal about you lately which I have not understood."

Mrs Plummer's words occasioned her more concern than she would have cared to admit; especially as she had a sort of vague feeling that they were representative of the state of public opinion, as it existed around her. Rightly or wrongly she was conscious of a very distinct suspicion that most of the people with whom she came into daily and hourly contact would have been quite willing to let Jim Baker hang, not only on general principles, but also with a confused notion--as Mrs Plummer had plainly put it--of putting an end to a very disagreeable condition of affairs.

In her trouble, not knowing where else to turn for advice or help, she sent for Mr Stacey. After dinner she invited him to a tête-à-tête interview in her own sitting-room, and then and there plunged into the matter which so occupied her thoughts.

"Do you know why I have sent for you, Mr Stacey?"

"I was hoping, my dear young lady, that it was partly for the purpose of affording me the inexpressible pleasure of seeing you again."

She had always found his urbanity a little trying, it seemed particularly out of place just now. Possibly she did not give sufficient consideration to the fact that the old gentleman had been brought out of town at no small personal inconvenience, and that he had just enjoyed a very good dinner.

"Of course there was that; but I am afraid that the principal reason why I sent for you is because of this trouble about Jim Baker."

"Jim Baker?"

"The man who is charged with committing the murder in Cooper's Spinney."

"I see, or, rather, I do not see what connection you imagine can exist between Mr Baker and myself."

"He is innocent--as innocent as I am."

"You know that of your own knowledge?"

"I am sure of it."

"What he has to do is to inspire the judge and jury with a similar conviction."

"But he is helpless. He is an ignorant man and has no one to defend him. That's what I want you to do--I want you to defend him."

"Me! Miss Arnott!" Mr Stacey put up his glasses the better to enable him to survey this astonishing young woman. He smiled benignly. "I may as well confess, since we are on the subject of confessions"--they were not, but that was by the way--"that there are one or two remarks which I should like to make to you, since you have been so kind as to ask me to pay you this flying visit; but, before coming to them, let us first finish with Mr Baker. Had you done me the honour to hint at the subject on which you wished to consult me, I should at once have informed you that I am no better qualified to deal with it than you are. We--that is the firm with which I am associated--

do no criminal business; we never have done, and, I think I am safe in assuring you, we never shall do. May I ask if you propose to defray any expenses which may be incurred on Mr Baker's behalf? or is he prepared to be his own chancellor of the exchequer?"

"He has no money; he is a gamekeeper on a pound a week. I am willing to pay anything, I don't care what."

"Then, in that case, the matter is simplicity itself. Before I go I will give you the name of a gentleman whose reputation in the conduct of criminal cases is second to none; but I warn you that you may find him an expensive luxury."

"I don't care how much it costs."

Mr Stacey paused before he spoke again; he pressed the tips of his fingers together; he surveyed the lady through his glasses.

"Miss Arnott, will you permit me to speak to you quite frankly?"

"Of course, that's what I want you to do."

"Then take my very strong advice and don't have anything to do with Mr Baker. Don't interfere between him and the course of justice, don't intrude yourself in the matter at all. Keep yourself rigidly outside it."

"Mr Stacey! Why?"

"If you will allow me to make the remarks to which I just now alluded, possibly, by the time I have finished, you will apprehend some of my reasons. But before I commence you must promise that you will not be offended at whatever I may say. If you think that, for any cause whatever, you may be disposed to resent complete candour from an old fellow who has seen something of the world and who has your best interests very much at heart, please say so and I will not say a word."

"I shall not be offended."

"Miss Arnott, you are a very rich young lady."

"Well?"

"You are also a very young lady."

"Well again?"

"From such a young lady the world would--not unnaturally--expect a certain course of action."

"How do you mean?"

"Why don't you take up that position in the world to which you are on all accounts entitled?"

"Still I don't quite understand."

"Then I will be quite plain--why do you shut yourself up as if, to use a catch phrase, you were a woman with a past?"

113

Miss Arnott started perceptibly--the question was wholly unexpected. Rising from her chair she began to re-arrange some flowers in a vase on a table which was scarcely in need of her attentions.

"I was not aware that I did."

"Do you mean that seriously?"

"I imagined that I was entitled to live the sort of life I preferred to live without incurring the risk of criticism--that is what I mean."

"Already you are beginning to be offended. Let us talk of the garden. How is it looking? Your uncle was very proud of his garden. I certainly never saw anything finer than his roseries. Do you still keep them up?"

"Never mind the roseries, or the garden either. Why do you advise me not to move a finger in defence of an innocent man, merely because I choose to live my own life?"

"You put the question in a form of your own; which is not mine. To the question as you put it I have no answer."

"How would you put it?"

"Miss Arnott, in this world no one can escape criticism;--least of all unattached young ladies;--particularly young ladies in your very unusual position. I happen to know that nothing would have pleased your uncle better than that you should be presented at Court. Why don't you go to Court? Why don't you take your proper place in Society?"

"Because I don't choose."

"May I humbly entreat you to furnish me with your reasons?"

"Nor do I choose to give you my reasons."

"I am sorry to hear it, since your manner forces me to assume that you have what you hold to be very sufficient reasons. Already I hear you spoken of as the 'Peculiar Miss Arnott.' I am bound to admit not wholly without cause. Although you are a very rich woman you are living as if you were, relatively, a very poor one. Your income remains practically untouched. It is accumulating in what, under the circumstances, I am constrained to call almost criminal fashion. All sorts of unpleasant stories are being connected with your name--lies, all of them, no doubt; but still, there they are. You ought to do something which would be equivalent to nailing them to the counter. Now there is this most unfortunate affair upon your own estate. I am bound to tell you that if you go out of your way to associate yourself with this man Baker, who, in spite of what you suggest, is certainly guilty in some degree, and who, in any case, is an irredeemable scoundrel; if you persist in pouring out money like water in his defence, although you will do him no manner of good, you may do yourself very grave and lasting injury."

"That is your opinion?"

"It is."

"I thank you for expressing it so clearly. Now may I ask you for the name of the gentleman--the expert criminal lawyer--to whom you referred? and then we will change the subject."

He gave her the name, and, later, in the seclusion of his own chamber, criticised her mentally, as Mr Whitcomb once had done.

"That girl's a character of an unusual kind. I shouldn't be surprised if she knows more about that lamentable business in Cooper's Spinney than she is willing to admit, and, what's more, if she isn't extremely careful she may get herself into very serious trouble."

CHAPTER XVIII
AT THE FOUR CROSS-ROADS

The next morning Miss Arnott sent a groom over to Oak Dene with this curt note:--

"I shall be at the Wycke Cross--at the four crossroads--this afternoon at half-past three, alone. I shall be glad if you will make it convenient to be there also. There is something which it is essential I should say to you.   V. A."

The groom brought back, in an envelope, Mr Hugh Morice's visiting card. On the back of it were four words,--

"I will be there."

And Mr Hugh Morice was there before the lady. Miss Arnott saw his car drawn up by the roadside, long before she reached it. She slackened her pace as she approached. When she came abreast of it she saw that its owner was sitting on a stile, enjoying a pipe. Taking his pipe out of his mouth, his cap off his head, he advanced to her in silence.

"Am I late?" she asked.

"No, it is I who am early."

They exchanged glances--as it were, neutral glances--as if each were desirous, as a preliminary, of making a study of the other. She saw--she could not help seeing--that he was not looking well. The insouciance with which, mentally, she had always associated him, had fled. The touch of the daredevil, of the man who looks out on to the world without fear and with something of humorous scorn, that also had gone. She did not know how old he was, but he struck her, all at once, as being older than she had supposed. The upper part of his face was seamed with deep lines which had not always, she fancied, been so apparent. There were crow's-feet in the corners of his eyes, the eyes themselves seemed sunken. The light in them was dimmed, or perhaps she only fancied it. It was certain that he stooped more than he had used to do. His head hung forward between his broad shoulders, as if the whole man were tired, body, soul and spirit. There was something in his looks, in his bearing, a suggestion of puzzlement, of bewilderment, of pain, which might come from continuous wrestling with an insistent problem which defied solution, which touched her to the heart, made her feel conscious of a feeling she had not meant to feel. And because she had not intended to harbour anything even remotely approaching such a feeling, she resented its intrusion, and fought against herself so that she might appear to this man to be even harder than she had proposed to be.

On his part he saw, seated in her motor car, a woman whom he would have given all that he possessed to have taken in his arms and kept there. His acumen was greater, perhaps, than hers; he saw with a clearness which frightened him, her dire distress, the weight of trouble which bore her down. She might think that she hid it from the world, but, to him, it was as though the flesh had been stripped from her nerves, and he saw them quivering. He knew something of this girl's story; this woman whose childhood should have been scarcely yet behind her, and he knew that it had brought that upon her face which had no right to be there even though her years had attained to the Psalmist's span. And because his whole nature burned within him with a desire that she might be to him as never woman had been before, he was unmanned. He was possessed by so many emotions, all warring with each other, that, for the moment, he was like a helmless ship, borne this way and that, he knew not why or whither.

Then she was so hard, looked at him out of eyes which were so cold, spoke to him as if it were only because she was compelled that she spoke to him at all. How could he dare to hint--though only in a whisper--at sympathy, or comfort? He knew that she would resent it as bitterly as though he had lashed her with a whip. And, deeming herself the victim of an outrage, the probabilities were that she would snatch the supposititious weapon out of his hand and strike him with all her force with the butt of it.

So that, in the end, her trouble would be worse at the end than it had been at the beginning. He felt that this was a woman who would dree her own weird, and that from him, of all men in the world, she would brook only such interference, either by deed word, as she herself might choose to demand.

When they had done studying one another she put her hand up to her face, as if to brush away cobwebs which might have been spun before her eyes, and she asked,--

"Shall we talk here?"

His tone was as stiff and formal as hers had been.

"As you please. It depends upon the length to which our conversation is likely to extend. As I think it possible that what you have to say may not be capable of compression within the limits of a dozen words, I would, suggest that you should draw your car a little to one side here, where it would not be possible for the most imaginative policeman to regard it as an obstruction to the traffic which seldom or never comes this way; and that you should then descend from it, and say what you have to say under the shade of these trees, and in the neighbourhood of this stile."

She acted on his suggestion, and took off the long dust cloak which she was wearing, and tossed it on the seat of her car. Going to the stile she leaned one hand on the cross bar. He held out his pipe towards her.

"May I smoke?"

"Certainly, why not? I think it possible that you may require its soothing influence before we have gone very far."

There was something in her voice which seemed as if it had been meant to sting him; it only made him smile.

"I also think that possible."

She watched him as, having refilled and relighted his pipe, he puffed at it, as if he found in the flavour of the tobacco that consolation at which she had hinted. Perceiving that he continued to smoke in silence she spoke again, as if she resented being constrained to speak.

"I presume that you have some idea of what it is I wish to say to you?"

He shook his head.

"I haven't."

"Really?"

"Absolutely. If you will forgive my saying so, and I fear that you are in an unforgiving mood, I have ceased attempting to forecast what, under any stated set of circumstances, you may either say or do. You are to me what mathematicians call an unknown quantity; you may stand for something or for nothing. One never knows."

"I have not the honour to understand you, Mr Morice."

"Don't imagine that I am even hinting at a contradiction; but I hope, for both our sakes, that you understand me better than I do you."

"I think that's very possible."

"I think so also; alas! that it should be so."

"You may well say, alas!"

"You are right; I may."

She was silent, her lips twitching, as if with impatience or scorn.

"My acquaintance with the world is but a slight one, Mr Morice; and, unfortunately, in one respect it has been of an almost uniform kind. I have learned to associate with the idea of a man something not agreeable. I hoped, at one time, that you would prove to be a variation; but you haven't. That is why, in admitting that I did understand you a little, I think that you were justified in saying, alas!"

"That, however, is not why I said it, as I should have imagined you would have surmised; although I admire the ingenuity with which you present your point of view. But, may I ask if you have ordered me to present myself at Wyche Cross with the intention of favouring me with neatly turned remarks on the subject of men in general and of myself in particular?"

"You know I haven't."

"I am waiting to know it."

"I had not thought that anyone fashioned in God's image could play so consummately the hypocrite."

"Of all the astounding observations! Is it possible that you can have overlooked your own record?"

As he spoke the blood dyed her face; she swerved so suddenly that one felt that if it had not been for the support of the stile she might have fallen. On the instant he was penitent.

"I beg your pardon; but you use me in such a fashion; you say such things, that you force me to use my tongue."

"Thank you, you need not apologise. The taunt was deserved. I have played the hypocrite; I know it--none know it better. But let me assure you that, latterly, I have continued to play the hypocrite for your sake."

"For my sake?"

"For your sake and for yours only, and you know it."

"I know it? This transcends everything! The courage of such a suggestion, even coming from you, startles me almost into speechlessness. May I ask you to explain?"

"I will explain, if an explanation is necessary, which we both know it is not!"

He waved his pipe with an odd little gesture in the air.

"Good heavens!" he exclaimed.

CHAPTER XIX
THE BUTTONS OFF THE FOILS

Outwardly she was the calmer of the two. She stood upright and motionless; he was restless and fidgety, as if uneasy both in mind and body. She kept her eyes fixed steadily upon his face; he showed a disposition to elude her searching glance. When she spoke her tone was cool and even.

"You have accused me of playing the hypocrite. It is true, I have. I have allowed the world to regard me as a spinster, when I was a married woman; as free when I was bound. I have told you that I should have ceased before this to play the hypocrite, if it had not been for you. You have--pretended--to doubt it. Well, you are that kind of man. And it is because you are that kind of man that I am constrained to ask if you wish me now to cease to play the hypocrite and save Jim Baker's life?"

"Is not that a question for your consideration rather than for mine?"

"You propose to place the responsibility upon my shoulders!"

"Would you rather it were on mine?"

"That is where it properly belongs."

"In dealing with you I am at a serious disadvantage, since you are a woman and I am a man. The accident of our being of different sexes prevents my expressing myself with adequate precision."

"You appear to be anxious to take refuge even when there is nothing behind which you can hide. The difference in our sexes has never prevented you from saying to me exactly what you pleased, how you pleased--you know it. Nor do I intend to allow your manhood to shelter you. Mr Morice, the time for fencing's past. When life and death are hanging in the balance, words are weightless. I ask you again, do you intend to save Jim Baker's life?"

"I have yet to learn that it is in imminent peril."

"Then acquire that knowledge now from me. I am informed that if someone is not discovered, on whom the onus of guilt can be indubitably fixed, the probabilities are that Jim Baker will be hanged for murder."

"And you suggest that I should discover that--unhappy person?"

"I ask you if you do not think the discovery ought to be made, to save that wretched creature?"

"What I am anxious to get at, before I commit myself to an answer is this--presuming that I think the discovery should be made, do you suggest that it should be made by you or by me?"

"Mr Morice, I will make my meaning plainer, if the thing be possible. When--that night--in the wood it happened, I thought that it was done for me. I still think that might have been the motive; partly, I confess, because I cannot conceive of any other, though the misapprehension was as complete as it was curious. I did not require that kind of service--God forbid! And, therefore, thinking this--that I was, though remotely, the actual cause--it appears to me that I was, and am, unable to speak, lest it would seem that I was betraying one whose intention was to render me a service."

"For all I understand of what you're saying you might be talking in an unknown tongue. You speak of the futility of fencing, when you do nothing else but fence! To the point, if you please. What service do you suppose was intended to be rendered you that night in Cooper's Spinney?"

There was a perceptible pause before she answered, as if she were endeavouring to summon all her courage to her aid.

"Mr Morice, when you killed my husband, did you not do it for me?"

His countenance, as she put this question, would have afforded an excellent subject for a study in expression. His jaw dropped open, his pipe falling unnoticed to the ground; his eyes seemed to increase in magnitude; the muscles of his face became suddenly rigid--indeed the rigidity of his whole bearing suggested a paralytic seizure. For some seconds he seemed to have even ceased to breathe. Then he gave a long gasping breath, and with in his attitude still some of that unnatural rigidity, he gave her question for question.

"Why do you ask me such a monstrous thing? You! you!"

Something in his manner and appearance seemed to disturb her more than anything which had gone before. She drew farther away from him, and closer to the stile.

"You forced me to ask you."

"I forced you to ask me--that!"

"Why do you look at me so? Do you wish to frighten me?"

"Do you think I didn't see? Have you forgotten?"

"See? Forgotten? What do you mean?"

"Oh, woman! that you should be so young and yet so old; so ignorant and yet so full of knowledge; that you should seem a shrine of all the virtues, and be a thing all evil!"

"Mr Morice, why do you look at me like that! you make me afraid!"

"Would I could make you afraid--of being the thing you are!"

"It's not fair of you to speak to me like that I--it's not fair! I'm not so wicked! When I married--"

"When you married! No more of that old wife's tale. Stick to the point, please--to the point! You whited sepulchre! is it possible that, having shown one face to the world, you now propose to show another one to me, and that you think I'll let you? At anyrate, I'll have you know that I do know you for what you are! Till now I have believed that that dead man, your husband, Mrs Champion, was as you painted him--an unspeakable hound; but now, for the first time, I doubt, since you dared to ask me that monstrous thing, knowing that I saw you kill him!"

She looked at him as if she were searching his face for something she could not find on it.

"Is it possible that you wish me to understand that you are speaking seriously?"

"What an actress you are to your finger-tips! Do you think I don't know you understand?"

"Then you know more than I do, for I myself am not so sure. My wish is to understand, and--I am beginning to be afraid I do."

He waved his hand with an impatient gesture.

"Come, no more of that! Let me beg you to believe that I am not quite the fool that you suppose. You asked me just now if I intend to save Jim Baker's life? Well, that's where I'm puzzled. At present it's not clear to me that it's in any serious danger. I think that the very frankness of his story may prove to be his salvation; I doubt if they'll be able to establish anything beyond it. But should the contrary happen, and he finds himself confronted by the gallows, then the problem will have to be fairly faced. I shall have to decide what I am prepared to do. Of course my action would be to some extent guided by yours, that is why I'm so anxious to learn what, under those circumstances, you would do."

"Shall I tell you?"

"If you would be so very kind."

"I should send for Granger and save Jim Baker's life."

"By giving yourself up?"

She stood straighter.

"No, Mr Morice, by giving you up."

"But again I don't understand."

"You have had ample warning and ample opportunity. You might have hidden yourself on the other side of the world if you chose. If you did not choose the fault was yours."

"But why should I hide?"

"If you forced me, I should tell Granger that it was you who killed Robert Champion, and that I had proofs of it, and so Jim Baker would be saved."

Again he threw out his arms with the gesture which suggested not only impatience, but also lack of comprehension.

"Then am I to take it that you propose to add another item to your list of crimes?"

"It is not a crime to save the innocent by punishing the guilty."

"The guilty, yes; but in that case where would you be?"

"I, however unwillingly, should be witness against you."

"You would, would you? A pleasant vista your words open to one's view."

"You could relieve me of the obligation--easily."

"I don't see how--but that is by the way. Do you know it begins to occur to me that the singularity of your attitude may be induced by what is certainly the remote possibility that you are ignorant of how exactly the matter stands. Is it possible that you are not aware that I saw you--actually saw you--kill that man."

"What story are you attempting to use as a cover? Are you a liar

122

as well as that thing?"

"Don't fence! Are you denying that I saw you kill him, and that when you ran away I tried to catch you?"

"Of course I deny it! That you should dare to ask me such a question!"

"This is a wonderful woman!"

"You appear to be something much worse than a wonderful man--something altogether beyond any conception I had formed of you. Your suppositional contingency may be applied to you; it is just possible that you don't know how the matter stands, and that that explains your attitude. It is true that I did not see you kill that man."

"That certainly is true."

"But I heard you kill him."

"You heard me?"

"I heard you--I was only a little way off. First I heard the shot--Baker's shot. Then I heard him go. Then I heard you come."

"You heard me come?"

"I heard you strike him; I heard him fall. Then I saw you running from the thing that you had done."

"You saw me running?"

"I saw you running. The moon was out; I saw you clearly running among the bushes and the trees. I did not know who it was had come until I saw you, then I knew. After you had gone I was afraid to go or stay. Then I went to see what you had done. I saw your knife lying on the ground. I picked it up and took it home with me."

"I can easily believe you took it home with you."

"I have it now--to be produced, if need be in evidence."

"Of what?"

"Of your guilt! of what else?"

"She asks me such a question! Now let me tell you my story. If it lacks something of the air of verisimilitude which gives yours such a finish, let me remind you that there are those who lie like truth. After we had parted I discovered that I had left my knife behind--the one with which I had cut our initials on the tree. It was a knife I prized--never mind why. When I had allowed sufficient time to enable you to have reached home I returned to look for it. To my surprise, as I approached our trysting-place I heard voices--yours and a man's. You were neither of you speaking in a whisper. At night in the open air sound travels far. When I came a little nearer I saw you and a man. So I withdrew till I was out of sight again, and could only hear the faint sound of distant voices. Presently a gun was fired. I rushed forward to see by whom, and at what. When I came near enough there was a man staggering about underneath the tree. I saw you come out from among the bushes and look at him. You picked up a knife from the ground--my knife. I saw you drive it into his chest. As he fell--for ever--you ran off into the forest and I ran after you."

"You ran after me! after me?"

"After you; but you ran so quickly, or you knew your way so well, or I blundered, or something, because, after you had once disappeared in the wood, I never caught sight of you."

"And have you invented this story--which you tell extremely well--to save your neck at the expense of mine?"

"What an odd inquiry! Referring to your own tale, may I ask what motive you would ascribe to me, if you were asked what you suppose induced me, a peaceful, law-abiding citizen, to kill at sight--under circumstances of peculiar cowardice--an inoffensive stranger?"

"I imagined that you knew he was my husband, and that you killed him to relieve me. You see I credited you with something like chivalry."

"Did you indeed. And you would prostitute the English language by calling conduct of that sort chivalry! However, it is plainly no use our pushing the discussion further. We appear to understand each other now if we never did before. Each proposes to save Jim Baker's life--at a pinch--by sacrificing the other. Good! I must hold myself prepared. I had dreamt of discovering means of saving you from the consequences of your crime, but I had scarcely intended to go the lengths which you suggest--to offer myself instead of you. But then I did not credit you with the qualifications which you evidently possess. In the future I shall have to realise that, even if I save your life, I cannot save your soul, because, plainly, you intend to perjure that lightheartedly, and to stain it with the blood of two men instead of only one. Let me give you one warning. I see the strength of the case which your ingenious--and tortuous--brain may fabricate against me. Still, I think that it may fail; and that you may yourself fall into the pit which you have digged for me, for this reason. They know me, hereabouts and elsewhere; my record's open to all the world. They don't know you, as yet; when they do they'll open their eyes and yours. Already some unpleasant tales are travelling round the country. I myself have been forced to listen to one or two, and keep still. When my story is told, and yours, I am afraid that your story will prove to be your own destruction; it will hang you, unless there comes a reprieve in time. I saw you kill your husband. You know I saw you; you know that I can prove I saw you. Therefore, take the advice I have already tendered, go back to Lake Como and further. Lest, peradventure, by staying you lose your life to save Jim Baker's. Henceforward, Mrs Champion, the buttons are off our foils; we fight with serious weapons--I against you and you against me. At least we have arrived at that understanding; to have a clear understanding of any sort is always something, and so, good-day."

CHAPTER XX
THE SOLICITOR'S CLERK

Hugh Morice was the first to leave the four crossroads; Miss Arnott stood some time after he had gone, thinking. Life had had for her some queer phases--none queerer than that which confronted her, as she stood thinking by the stile.

That Hugh Morice should have done the thing she knew he had done, was bad enough. That he should have denied it to her face in such explicit terms and coupled with his denial such a monstrous accusation, was inconceivable. He had not gone very far before she told herself that, after all, she had misunderstood him, she must have done. For some minutes she was half disposed to jump into her car, follow him and insist on a clearer explanation. He could not have meant what he had appeared to do, not seriously and in earnest.

But she refrained from putting her idea into execution as she recalled the almost savage fashion in which he had hurled opprobrium at her. He had meant it; he must have meant it, or he would not have spoken to her in such a strain. At the thought she shivered.

Because, if this were the case, if she really had to regard his words as seriously intended, then she would have to rearrange her whole outlook on to life, particularly that portion of it which was pressing so hardly on her now. In her blackest moments she had not credited Hugh Morice with being a scoundrel. He had been guilty of a crime, but she could have forgiven him for that. By what he had done he had separated himself from her for ever and for ever. Still, she could have looked at him across the dividing chasm with something tenderer than pity.

This new attitude he had taken up altered the position altogether. If it meant anything it meant that he had killed Robert Champion for some recondite reason of his own--one with which she had no sort of connection. Obviously, if he had done it for her sake, he would not be so strenuous in denial; still less would he charge her with his crime.

Thus the whole business assumed a different complexion. The inference seemed to be that Hugh Morice and Robert Champion had not been strangers to each other. There had been that between them which induced the one to make away with the other when opportunity offered. The whole thing had been the action of a coward. In imagination the girl could see it all. Hugh Morice coming suddenly on the man he least expected--or desired--to meet; the great rush of his astonishment; the instant consciousness that his enemy was helpless; the sight of the knife; the irresistible, wild temptation; the yielding to it; the immediate after-pangs of conscience-stricken terror; the frantic flight through the moon-lit forest from the place of the shedding of blood.

And this was the man whom, almost without herself being aware of it, she had been making a hero of. This sordid wretch, who, not content with having slain a helpless man for some, probably wholly unworthy, purpose of his own, in his hideous anxiety to save his own miserable skin was willing, nay, eager, to sacrifice her. Possibly his desire to do so was all the greater because he was haunted by the voice of conscience crying out to him that this girl would not only be a continual danger, but that he would never be able to come into her presence without being racked by the knowledge that she knew him-- no matter how gallantly he bore himself--to be the thing he really was.

So it was plain to her that here was a new danger sprung up all at once out of the ground, threatening more serious ills than any she had known. If Jim Baker was found guilty of this man's crime, and she moved a finger to save him from his unmerited fate, then it might be that she would find herself in imminent peril of the gallows. For it needed but momentary consideration to enable her to perceive that what he had suggested was true enough, that if they began to accuse each other it would be easier, if he were set on playing the perjurer, to prove her guilt than his. And so quite possibly it might come about that, in order to save Jim Baker, it would be necessary she should hang. And life was yet young in her veins, and, though she had in it such sorry usage, still the world was very fair, and, consciously, in all her life she had never done an evil thing.

And then it was not strange that, there in the sunshine by the roadside, at the bare thought that it was even remotely possible that such a fate might be in store for her, she sat down on the stile, clinging to the rail, trembling from head to foot.

She would have sat there longer had she not been roused by a familiar, unescapable sound--the panting of a motor. Along the road was approaching a motor bicyclist. At sight of her, and of the waiting car, he stopped, raising his cap.

"I beg your pardon, but is there anything wrong with the car?"

She stood up, still feeling that, at anyrate, there was something wrong with the world, or with her.

"No, thank you, the car's all right; I was only resting."

"I beg your pardon once more, but aren't you Miss Arnott of Exham Park?"

She looked at the speaker, which hitherto she had avoided doing. He was a young man of four or five and twenty, with a not unpleasing countenance; so far as she knew, a stranger to her.

"I am, but I don't know you."

"That is very possible--I am a person of no importance. My name is Adams--Charles Adams. I am clerk to Mr Parsloe, solicitor, of Winchester. We had a communication from a man who is in Winchester Gaol, waiting his trial for murder, a man named Baker. Possibly you have heard of him."

"Oh yes, I have heard of Jim Baker; he is a gamekeeper on my own estate."

"So he gave me to understand. Mr Parsloe sent me to see him. I did see him, in private. He gave me a note, which he was extremely anxious that I should give into your own hands. I was just coming on to Exham Park on the off-chance of finding you in. Perhaps you won't mind my giving it to you now?"

"By all means. Why not?"

He had taken out of a leather case a piece of folded paper.

"You see it is rather a rough-and-ready affair, but I should like to give you my assurance that I have no idea what it contains."

"I don't suppose it would matter much if you did. Jim Baker is hardly likely to have a communication of a private nature to make to me."

"As to that I know nothing. I can only say that Baker was not satisfied till I had sworn that I would not attempt to even so much as peep at the contents of his note, or let it go out of my hands until it reached yours."

"Really?"

"Really! I never saw a man more desperately in earnest on a point of the kind."

"Jim Baker is a character."

"He certainly is. You will see that the note is written on a piece of rough paper. Where he got it from I don't know, and was careful not to ask; but it looks suspiciously like a fly-leaf which had been torn out of a book. You are possibly aware that in prison, in the ordinary way, they are allowed neither paper, pen nor ink. I fancy you'll find that this is written with a pencil. When I first saw it it had been simply folded, and one end slipped into the other. I happened to have some sealing-wax in my pocket. Baker insisted on my sealing it, in his presence, in three places, as you perceive, so that it was impossible to get at the contents without breaking the seals. I say all this because Baker himself was emphatically of opinion that this note contained matter of an extremely confidential nature, to which I should like you clearly to understand that I have had no sort of access. I may add another fact, of which you are also possibly aware, and that is that the whole transaction was irregular. He had no right to give me the note, and I had no right to convey it out of the prison; but he did the one, and I did the other, and here it is."

Mr Adams handed the lady the scrap of paper, she asking him a question as he did so,--

"To whom did you say that you were clerk?"

"To Mr Parsloe, a well-known and highly-esteemed Winchester solicitor."

"Why did Baker, as you put it, communicate with Mr Parsloe?"

"He wanted us to undertake his defence."

"And are you going to do so?"

Mr Adams smiled.

"As matters are, I am afraid not. Baker appears to be penniless, he is not even able to keep himself while awaiting trial, but is on the ordinary prison fare. It is necessary that a client should not only have his solicitor's sympathy, but also the wherewithal with which to pay his fees."

"Then it is only a question of money. I see. At what address shall I find Mr Parsloe if I wish to do so?"

The gentleman gave the lady a card.

"That is Mr Parsloe's address. You will find my name in the corner as representing him. I may mention that I also am an admitted solicitor."

"It is possible that you will hear from me. In the meantime, thank you very much for taking so much trouble in bringing me this note. Any expenses which may have been incurred I shall be happy to defray."

"At present no expenses have been incurred. I need hardly say that any instructions with which you may honour us will receive our instant and most careful attention."

Again Mr Adams's cap came off. He turned his bicycle round, and presently was speeding back the way he had come. Miss Arnott stood looking after him, the "note" in her hand.

Jim Baker's "note," as the solicitor's clerk had more than hinted, was distinctly unusual as to form. It was represented by an oblong scrap of paper, perhaps two inches long by an inch broad. Nothing was written on the outside; on the exterior there was nothing whatever to show for what destination it was designed. As Mr Adams had said, where one end had been slipped into the other three seals had been affixed. On each seal was a distinct impression of what probably purported to be Mr Adams's own crest; with, under the circumstances, a sufficiently apposite motto--for once in a way in plain English--"Fear Nothing."

CHAPTER XXI
THE "NOTE"

Miss Arnott displayed somewhat singular unwillingness to break the seals. She watched Mr Adams retreating on his bicycle; not only till the machine itself was out of sight, but the cloud of dust which marked its progress had vanished also. Then she turned the scrap of paper over and over in her fingers, possessed by an instinctive reluctance to learn what it contained. It seemed ridiculous to suppose that Jim Baker could have anything to cause her disturbance, yet she had an eerie feeling that there was something disagreeable inside his "note," something which she would much rather not come into contact with. Had she followed her own inclination she would have shredded it into pieces, and scattered the pieces over the roadway. In some indescribable fashion she was actually afraid of the scrap of paper which she held between her fingers.

It was the sudden realisation that this was so which stung her into action. Afraid of anything Jim Baker might have to say? She? Nonsense! The idea! Could anything be more absurd!

There and then she broke the seals, unfolded the sheet of paper. But when she had got so far again she hesitated. The thing was fresh from a prison; had about it, she fancied, a prison atmosphere, a whiff of something sordid which it had borne with it out of gaol. It was that, she told herself, which she did not relish. Why should she read the scrawl? What interest could it have for her? Better instruct Mr Parsloe, or that eminent practitioner in the conduct of criminal cases with whose name Mr Stacey had furnished her, to undertake Baker's defence, and spare no expense in doing so, and so have done with it. Let her keep her own fingers out of the mire; leave the whole thing to the lawyers; that would be better for everyone concerned. So it would not be necessary for her to spell her way through the man's ill-written scribble.

And then she read Jim Baker's "note."

As Mr Adams had surmised it was written in pencil; apparently with a blunt stump of pencil used by unaccustomed fingers, probably under circumstances in which a skilful writer would have been uneasy. Here and there it seemed that the pencil had refused to write; possibly only by dint of pressure had it been induced to write at all. The letters were blurred and indistinct, ill-formed, irregular, disjoined--in general, mere hieroglyphics. And yet, despite the crabbed writing, the eccentric spelling, the clumsy wording, Jim Baker's "note" made a stronger impression on Miss Arnott than the most eloquent epistle with which she had ever been favoured.

"Miss Arnott I see you done it but I wouldnt say nuthink about it if it wasnt that from what I ear they are going to hang me for what I se you doing and I wont say nuthin about it now if you se I have a loryer and all regular so as to get me out of this were it aint rite I should be sein I saw you they may cutt my tung out before Ill speak unless they make out I dun it so if you dont se I have a loryer and all regular Ill have to speke Jim Baker."

That was Mr Baker's note; unpunctuated, formless, badly put together, ill-spelt, but alive and eloquent in spite of its obvious deficiencies. It was plain why he was so anxious that Mr Adams should not peep at the contents, why he had insisted on the three seals, why he had stipulated on its being given into Miss Arnott's own hands. From his point of view the "note" was a messenger of life and death, with hanging matter in every line.

The lady read it once and again and then again. As she crumpled it up in her hand it seemed to her that the country round about had assumed a different appearance, the cloudless sky had become dimmed, a grey tint had settled upon everything; for her the sunlight had gone out of the world.

Here was Jim Baker calling to her out of his prison cell that he was where she ought to be, because he had seen her do it, warning her, if she did not provide him with a lawyer "and all regular" to get him "out of this," that he would have to speak. What hallucination was this which all at once possessed men's minds? Could it be possible that the hallucination was actually hers? Could what, first Hugh Morice, now Jim Baker, said be true, and that they had seen her do it? What condition could she have been in at the time? Was it conceivable that a person could do such a deed unwittingly? During what part of her sojourn in the wood had she been in her sober senses? When had she ceased to be responsible for her own actions? and how? and why? Which of those awful happenings had been plain material fact and which nightmare imaginings?

She re-read Jim Baker's opening words,--"Miss Arnott I see you done it." The accusation was bold enough, plain enough, conclusive enough. It staggered her; forced her to wonder if she was, unknowingly, this dreadful thing.

But, by degrees, her common sense regained the upper-hand, and she began to put two and two together in an attempt to solve the mystery of Jim Baker's words. The man was drunk; so much was admitted. He had probably seen her, hazily enough, bearing away the blood-stained knife; and had, therefore, jumped to an erroneous conclusion. Then she remembered that he had sworn that, after firing the shot, he had gone straight home; then, how came he to see her? More, he had sworn that on his homeward way he had seen nothing; so, somewhere, there was a lie. At the very worst, Jim Baker was labouring under a misapprehension; the statement in his note was capable of no other explanation.

Still, it was awkward that he should be under such a misapprehension, in view of the attitude which Hugh Morice had just been taking up. The problem of saving Jim Baker's life became involved. If freeing him meant that Mr Morice would prefer against her such a charge, and that Baker himself would support it; then it behoved her to be careful how she went. In any case it was not agreeable to think that that ancient but muddle-headed family retainer believed--with some considerable foundation in truth--that she was willing--to say no more--that he should suffer for her offences.

Her thoughts were not pleasant companions on her homeward journey. Nor was her peace of mind heightened by a brief interview which she had with Mrs Plummer almost immediately on her return. The lady, waylaying her on the landing, followed her into her sitting-room. She was evidently in a state of considerable agitation.

"My dear, there is something which I must say to you at once--at once!"

Miss Arnott looked at her with that mixture of amusement and resentment with which she had been conscious that, of late, Mrs Plummer's near neighbourhood was wont to fill her.

"Then by all means speak, especially if refraining from doing so would occasion you inconvenience."

"Mrs Forrester called; you are never in when people come."

"I am not sorry that I was out when Mrs Forrester came; she bores me."

"You ought to fix a regular day, so that people might know when to find you."

"You have made that remark before. Is that all you have to say?"

"No, it is not; and let me tell you that this flippant way you have of treating everything I say may have the most serious and unlooked-for consequences."

Miss Arnott laughed, which caused Mrs Plummer to resort to a trick she had--when at all put out--of rubbing the palms of her hands briskly together.

"Oh, you may laugh; but I can assure you that if things go on like this much longer I don't know what will be the end of it."

"The end of what?"

"Do you know what Mrs Forrester has been saying? She tells me that there is a story going about the place that that evening you were out in the woods till all hours of the night; and she wanted to know if she should contradict it."

"That's as she pleases."

"But don't you see how serious it is? Won't you understand? I understand; if you don't. Violet, I insist upon your telling me what time it was when you came in that night; where you went, and what you did. I insist! I insist!"

At each repetition Mrs Plummer brought her hands together with quite a smart clap. Miss Arnott looked down at the excited little woman as if she was still divided between two moods.

"You insist? Mrs Plummer, aren't you--rather forgetting yourself?"

"Of course I am prepared for you to adopt that tone. You always adopt it when I ask you a question, and I am ready to leave the house this moment if you wish it; but I can only assure you that if you won't give me an answer you may have to give one to somebody else before very long."

"What do you mean by that?"

"I mean exactly what I say. Won't you see?"

"I can see that you are in a state of excitement which is not warranted by anything I understand."

It was odd what a disinclination the elder lady showed to meet the young one's eyes. She moved hither and thither, as if possessed by a spirit of restlessness; but, though Miss Arnott kept her gaze fixed on her unfalteringly wherever she went, she herself never glanced in the girl's direction.

"Excited! I can't help being excited! How you can keep so cool is what I don't know! Everyone is pointing a finger and saying that you were out in the woods at the very time that--that wretched man was--was being murdered"--Mrs Plummer cast furtive looks about her as if the deed was being enacted that very moment before her eyes--"and asking where you were and what you were doing all alone in the woods at that hour, and how it was that you knew nothing at all of what was taking place, possibly quite close by you; and you let them ask, and say and do nothing to stop their tongues; and if they are not stopped heaven only knows where they'll lead them. My dear, won't you tell me where you went? and what it was that you were doing?"

"No, Mrs Plummer, I won't--so now your question is answered. And as I have some letters to write may I ask you to leave me?"

Mrs Plummer did glance at Miss Arnott for one moment; but for only one. Then, as if she did not dare to trust herself to speak again, she hurried from the room. Left alone, the young lady indulged in some possibly ironical comments on her companion's deportment.

"Really, to judge from Mrs Plummer's behaviour, one would

imagine that this business worried her more than it does me. If she doesn't exercise a little more self-control I shouldn't be surprised if it ends in making her actually ill."

CHAPTER XXII
MR ERNEST GILBERT

Miss Arnott wrote to Mr Ernest Gilbert--the famous lawyer whose name Mr Stacey had given her--asking him to make all necessary arrangements for Jim Baker's defence. She expressed her own personal conviction in the man's innocence, desiring him to leave no stone unturned to make it plain, and to spare no expense in doing so. In proof of her willingness to pay any costs which might be incurred she enclosed a cheque for £500, and assured him that she would at once forward any further sum which might be required. Mr Gilbert furnished himself with a copy of the depositions given before the committing justices, and also before the coroner; and, having mastered them, went down to see his client in Winchester Gaol.

He found Mr Baker in very poor plight. The gamekeeper, who probably had gipsy blood in his veins, had been accustomed from childhood to an open air life. Often in fine weather he did not resort to the shelter of a roof for either sleeping or eating. Crabbed and taciturn by constitution he loved the solitude and freedom of the woods. On a summer's night the turf at the foot of a tree was couch enough for him, the sky sufficient roof. Had he been able to give adequate expression to his point of view, his definition of the torments of hell would have been confinement within four walls. In gaol--cribbed, cabined and confined--he seemed to slough his manhood like a skin. His nature changed. When Mr Gilbert went to see him, the dogged heart of the man had lost half its doggedness. He pined for freedom--for God's air, and the breath of the woods--with such desperate longing that, if he could, he would have made an end of every soul in Winchester Gaol to get at it.

Mr Gilbert summed him up--or thought he did--at sight. He made it a rule in these sort of cases to leap at an instant conclusion, even though afterwards it might turn out to be erroneous. Experience had taught him that, in first interviews with clients of a certain kind, quickness of speech--and of decision--was a trick which often paid. So that the door had hardly been closed which left the pair together than--

metaphorically--he sprang at Mr Baker like a bull terrier at a rat.

"Now, my man, do you want to hang?"

"Hang? me? No, I don't. Who does?"

"Then you'll tell me who stuck a knife into that fellow in Cooper's Spinney."

"Me tell you? What do you mean?"

"You know what I mean, and you know who handled that knife; and it's only by telling me that you'll save your neck from the gallows."

Baker stared with tightened lips and frowning brows. This spruce little gentleman was beyond him altogether.

"Here! you go too fast for me. I don't know who you are, not from Adam. Who might you be?"

"My name's Gilbert--I'm a lawyer--and I'm going to save you from the gallows, if I can."

"A lawyer?" Baker put up a gnarled hand to rasp his stubbly chin. He looked at the other with eyes which trouble had dimmed. "Has she sent you?"

"She? Who?"

"You know who I mean."

"I shall know if you tell me. How can I know if you don't tell me?"

"Has Miss Arnott sent you?"

"Miss Arnott? Why should Miss Arnott send me?"

"She knows if you don't."

"Do you think Miss Arnott cares if you were strung up to the top of the tallest tree to-morrow?"

"She mightn't care if I was strung up, but I ain't going to be strung up; and that she does know."

The lawyer looked keenly at the countryman. All at once he changed his tone, he became urbanity itself.

"Now, Baker, let's understand each other, you and I. I flatter myself that I've saved more than one poor chap from a hempen collar, and I'd like to save you. You never put that knife into that man."

"Of course I didn't; ain't I kept on saying so?"

"Then why should you hang?"

"I ain't going to hang. Don't you make any mistake about it, and don't let nobody else make any mistake about it neither. I ain't going to hang."

"But, my good fellow, in these kind of affairs they generally hang someone; if they can't find anyone else, it will probably be you. How are you going to help it?"

Baker opened and closed his mouth like a trap, once, twice, thrice, and nothing came out of it. There was a perceptible pause; he was possibly revolving something in his sluggish brain. Then he asked a question,--

"Is that all you've got to say?"

"Of course it's not. My stock of language isn't quite so limited. Only I want you to see just where you're standing, and just what the danger is that's threatening. And I want you to know that I know that you know who handled that knife; and that probably the only way of saving you from the gallows is to let me know. You understand that it doesn't necessarily follow that I'm going to tell everyone; the secret will be as safe with me as with you. Only this is a case in which, if I'm to do any good, I must know where we are. Now, Baker, tell me, who was it who used the knife?"

Again Baker's jaws opened and shut, as if automatically; then, after another interval, again he asked a question.

"You ain't yet told me if it was Miss Arnott as sent you?"

"And you haven't yet told me why Miss Arnott should send me?"

"That's my business. Did she? Do you hear me ask you--did she?"

Baker brought his fist down with a bang on to the wooden table by which he was standing. Mr Gilbert eyed him in his eager, terrier-like fashion, as if he were seeking for a weak point on which to make an attack. Then, suddenly, again his manner altered. Ignoring Baker's question as completely as if it had never been asked, he diverted the man's attention from the expected answer by all at once plunging into entirely different matters. Before he knew what was happening Baker found himself subjected to a stringent examination of a kind for which he was wholly unprepared. The solicitor slipped from point to point in a fashion which so confused his client's stupid senses that, by the time the interview was over, Jim Baker had but the vaguest notion of what he had said or left unsaid.

Mr Gilbert went straight from the gaol to a post-office from which he dispatched this reply-paid telegram:--

"To Hugh Morice, Oak Dene.

"When I was once able to do you a service you said that, if ever the chance offered, you would do me one in return. You can do me such a service by giving me some dinner and a bed for to-night.

"Ernest Gilbert.
"George Hotel, Winchester."

He lunched at the George Hotel. While he was smoking an after-luncheon cigar an answer came. Hugh Morice wired to say that if he arrived by a certain train he would meet him at the station. Mr Gilbert travelled by that train, and was met. It was only after a tête-à-tête dinner that anything was said as to the reason why the lawyer had invited himself to be the other's guest.

"I suppose you're wondering why I've forced myself upon your hospitality?"

"I hope that nothing in my manner has caused you to think anything of the kind. I assure you that I'm very glad to see you."

"It's very nice of you to say so. Still, considering how I've thrown myself at you out of the clouds you can hardly help but wonder."

"Well, I have taken it a little for granted that you have some reason for wishing to pay me a visit at this particular moment."

"Exactly. I have. It's because I find myself in rather a singular situation."

"As how?"

The lawyer considered. He looked at his host across the little table, on which were their cups of coffee, with his bright eyes and the intensely inquisitive stare, which seemed to suggest that curiosity was his devouring passion. His host looked back at him lazily, indifferently, as if he were interested in nothing and in no one. The two men were in acute contrast. The one so tall and broad; the other so small and wiry--in the scales possibly not half Hugh Morice's size. The solicitor glanced round the room, inquiringly.

"I suppose we're private here?"

They were in the billiard-room. The doors were shut, windows closed, blinds drawn--the question seemed superfluous.

"Perfectly. No one would hear you if you shouted."

"It's just as well to be sure; because what I have to say to you is of a particularly private nature."

"At your leisure."

"You and I have had dealings before--you will probably remember that, under certain circumstances, I'm not a stickler for professional etiquette."

"I remember it very well indeed."

"That's fortunate. Because, on the present occasion, I'm going to outrage every standard of propriety which is supposed--professionally-- to hedge me round. Now listen to me attentively; because I don't wish to use plainer speech than I can help; I don't want to dot my 'i's,' and I want you, at a hint from me, to read between the lines. This is a ticklish matter I'm going to talk about."

"I'm all attention."

"That's good; then here's what I've come to say."

CHAPTER XXIII
THE TWO MEN

Yet Mr Gilbert hesitated. He took his cigar from between his lips, carefully removed the ash, sipped at his coffee, and all the time kept his glance on Hugh Morice, as if he were desirous of gleaning from his face indications as to the exact line which his remarks should take. When he did speak he still continued to stare at his host.

"I have been retained to defend James Baker."

"James Baker?"

"The man who is to stand his trial for the murder in Cooper's Spinney."

"Oh, Jim Baker. Hereabouts he is known as Jim. When you spoke of him as James, for the moment I didn't know who you meant."

"This morning I saw him in Winchester Gaol."

"That is what you were doing in Winchester? Now I understand. How is he?"

"In a bad way. They may as well hang him as keep him jailed. He's not at home in there."

"So I should imagine. Jim Baker!"

Hugh Morice smiled sardonically, as if the idea of Jim Baker being in gaol was grimly humorous.

"That interview has resulted in placing me in a very curious quandary."

"I should imagine that interviews with your clients did occasionally have results of that kind."

"That's so; but I don't recall one which had just this result, and--I don't like it. That's why I've come to you."

"I don't see the sequitur. What have I to do with your quandaries?--that is, mind you, with your professional quandaries;

because, outside your profession, as you're perfectly well aware, I'm willing enough to help you in any kind of a hole."

"This is both professional and unprofessional--that's the trouble. Anyhow, I'm going to make you my confidant, and I shall expect you to give me some sort of a pointer."

"What might you happen to be driving at? I take it that you don't credit me with the capacity to read between lines which are non-existent."

"I'll tell you in a sentence. James--or, as you call him--Jim Baker has left the impression on my mind that it was Miss Arnott, of Exham Park, who killed that man in Cooper's Spinney."

"The scoundrel!"

"Generally speaking, perhaps, in this particular instance--I doubt it."

"Do you mean to say that he formulated the charge in so many words?"

"He never formulated it at all. On the contrary, he didn't even begin to make it. I fancy that if you were to go to him now, he'd say that he never so much as hinted at anything of the sort. But all the same it was so present in his mind that it got into mine. I have a knack, occasionally, of studying my clients' minds rather than their words."

"My good sir, if A is charged with a crime he quite constantly--sometimes unconsciously--tries to shift the guilt on to B."

"As if I didn't know it! Talk sense! There are times when I am able to detect the real from the counterfeit, and this is one. I tell you that Jim Baker is convinced that Miss Arnott stabbed that man in the wood, and that, if he chose, he could advance substantial reasons for the faith that is in him."

"Good God! You--you shock me!"

"Are you sure I shock you?"

"What the devil do you mean by that? Look here, Gilbert, if you've come here to make yourself disagreeable you'll have to excuse me if I go to bed."

"My dear chap, why this sudden explosion! So far from wishing to make myself disagreeable my desire is all the other way; but you haven't yet let me explain to you the nature of the quandary I am in."

"I know Jim Baker better than you do. I've thrashed him within an inch of his life before to-day, and, by George! if what you say is true, I'd like to do it again. If you've come to retail any cock and bull stories emanating from that source I don't want to listen to them--that's plain."

"Perfectly plain. I've come to retail cock and bull stories emanating from no source. If you'll grant me thirty seconds I'll tell you what the trouble is. The trouble is that I've been retained by Miss Arnott to defend Jim Baker."

"The deuce!"

"Yes, as you observe, it is the deuce. She has behaved--in a pecuniary sense--very handsomely, and is apparently prepared--in that sense--to continue to behave very handsomely."

"Then where's the trouble if you're well paid for the work you're asked to do?"

"Supposing, for the sake of argument, that Miss Arnott is guilty, and that Jim Baker knows it, that, from one point of view, would be a sufficient reason why she should spend money like water in his defence, and I should be placed in a very awkward situation."

"Are you taking it for granted that what that blackguard says--"

"Baker has said nothing."

"That what he hints is true? Do you know Miss Arnott?"

"I don't; do you?"

"Of course, she's my neighbour."

"But you're some distance apart."

"Nothing as we count it in the country."

"Is she an old woman?"

"Old! She's a girl!"

"A girl? Oh! now I perceive that we are getting upon delicate ground."

"Gilbert, may I ask you to be extremely careful what you allow yourself to say."

"I will be--extremely careful. May I take it that you are of opinion that there is no foundation for what Jim Baker believes?"

"What on earth have I to do with what Jim Baker believes or with what he chooses to make you think he believes?"

"Precisely; I am not connecting you with his belief in any way whatever. What I am asking is, are you of opinion that he has no ground for his belief?"

"How should I know what ground he has or thinks he has? That fellow's mind--what he has of it--is like a rabbit warren, all twists and turns."

The speaker had risen from his chair. Possibly with some intention of showing that he did not find the theme a pleasant one, he had taken down a billiard cue. The lawyer watched him as he prepared to make a shot.

"Morice, do you know to what conclusion you are driving me?"

"I don't know, and I don't care. Come and have a game."

"Thank you, I don't mind. But first, I should like to tell you what that conclusion is. You are forcing me to think that Jim Baker's belief is yours."

Mr Morice did not make his shot. Instead, he stood up straight, gripping his cue almost as if he meant to use it as a weapon.

"Gilbert!"

"It's no use glaring at me like that. I'm impervious to threats. I've been the object of too many. Let me tell you something else. A faint suspicion, which I had before I came here, has become almost a certainty. I believe that Baker saw what that young woman did and I believe you saw her also."

"You hound! Damn you! I'd like to throw you out of the house!"

"Oh no, you wouldn't; that's only a momentary impulse. An instant's reflection will show you that this is a position in which the one thing wanted is common sense, and you've got plenty of common sense if you choose to give it a chance. Don't you see that we shall, all of us-- Miss Arnott, Jim Baker, you and me--find ourselves in a very uncomfortable situation, if we don't arrive at some common understanding. If Jim Baker saw that girl committing murder, and if you saw her--"

"You have not the faintest right to make such a monstrous insinuation."

"I have invited contradiction and none has come."

"I do contradict you--utterly."

"What, exactly, do you contradict?"

"Everything you have said."

"To descend from the general to the particular. Do you say that you did not see what that girl did?"

"I decline to be cross-examined. I'm your host, sir, I'm not in the witness-box."

"No, but at a word from me you very soon will be. That's the point you keep on missing."

"Gilbert, I'll wring your neck!"

"Not you, if only because you know that it would make bad worse. It's no good your throwing things at me. I'm as fairly in a cleft stick as you are. If I throw up Jim Baker's case, Miss Arnott, who has sent me a cheque for £500, will naturally want to know why. What shall I tell her? I shall have to tell her something. If, on the other hand, I stick to Baker, my first and only duty will be towards him. I shall have to remember that his life is at stake, and leave no stone unturned to save it. But, being employed by Miss Arnott, I don't want to take advantage of that employment and of her money to charge her with the crime, nor do I want to have to put you into the witness-box to prove it. What I want to know is which course am I to follow? And to get that knowledge I've come to you. Now, you've got the whole thing in a nutshell."

Mr Morice, perhaps unconsciously, was still gripping the billiard cue as if it were a bludgeon. Plainly, he was ill at ease.

"I wish you'd been kept out of the affair. I'd have kept you out if I'd had a chance. I should have known you'd make yourself a nuisance."

"Having a clear perception of the lines on which I should be likely to make myself a nuisance, I see. Shall I tell you what I do wish? I'm inclined to wish that I'd been retained by Miss Arnott on her own account."

"What do you mean by that?"

"You will make me dot my i's. However, I'll dot them if you like. Here are two men who know the truth. Isn't it probable that there are other persons who suspect it? So far the affair's been bungled. Baker himself put the police on the wrong scent. They've followed it blindly. But when the right man's put on the job I'm prepared to wager that he'll find the whole air is full of the lady's name. Then she'll want assistance."

Hugh Morice returned the cue to its place with almost ostentatious precision, keeping his back towards his guest as he did so. Then, turning, he took up his stand before the fireplace. His manner had all at once become almost unnaturally calm.

"There are two or three points, Mr Gilbert, on which I should like to arrive at that understanding which you pretend to desiderate. When you suggest, as you do, that I have any guilty knowledge of the crime with which Jim Baker stands charged, you not only suggest what is wholly false, but you do so without the slightest shadow of an excuse, under circumstances which make your conduct peculiarly monstrous. I have no such knowledge. It, therefore, necessarily follows that I know nothing of Miss Arnott's alleged complicity in the matter. More, I believe from my heart that she had no more to do with it than you had; she is certainly as innocent as you are. You yourself admit that Baker has said nothing. I fancy you may have jumped at an erroneous conclusion; your fault is over-cleverness. I know him to be a thorough-paced coward and rascal. If he ever does say outright, anything of the nature you have hinted at, there will be no difficulty whatever in proving him to be a liar. Now, sir, have I given you all the information which you require?"

Mr Gilbert looked at the fresh cigar, which he had just lighted, with the first smile in which he had permitted himself to indulge during the course of the discussion.

"Then I am to defend Jim Baker and do my best for him?"

It was a second or two before Hugh Morice answered.

"I think that, feeling as you do, you had better withdraw from the case."

"And what shall I tell Miss Arnott?"

"You need tell her nothing. I will tell her all that is necessary."

"I see. I thought you would probably feel like that."

"For once in a way you thought correctly."

"The cheque shall be returned to her. Shall I return it through you?"

"I think that perhaps you had better."

"I think so also."

Mr Gilbert rose from his chair.

"Before I go to bed, with your permission, I will finish this excellent cigar upstairs, and I'm afraid that game of billiards will have to be postponed. Will you allow me to say, without prejudice, that if, later, Miss Arnott finds herself in need of legal aid I shall esteem myself fortunate to be allowed to render her any assistance in my power. I can make my presence felt in a certain kind of case, and this is going to be a very pretty one, though that mayn't be your feeling just now. I should like to add that I feel sure I could defend her much better than I could Jim Baker."

"There will not be the slightest necessity for you to do anything of the kind."

"Of course not. I am merely putting a suppositious case. May I take it that you are the lady's friend?"

"You may."

"And that you would be willing to do her a service?"

"I would do her any service in my power."

"Then shall I tell you what is the best service you could do her?"

"I am listening."

"Start for the most inaccessible part of the globe you can think of at the very earliest opportunity, and stay there."

"Why should I do that?"

"Because if they can't find you, they can't put you in the witness-box, and, if I were acting for Miss Arnott, I would much rather, for her sake, that you kept out. Good-night, Mr Morice. I have to thank you for your generous hospitality."

When the solicitor was in his bedroom he said to himself.

"I'm glad I came. But what a tangle! Unless I err they'll have my lady under lock and key before the assizes begin; or, at anyrate, under police observation. And my host loves her. What a prospect? When a man, who is not a constitutional liar, does lie, he's apt to give his lie too artistic a finish; still, as an example of the lie cumulative and absolute, that lie of his was fair, very fair indeed."

Hugh Morice had his thoughts also.

"If she'd only let me know that she proposed to call in Ernest Gilbert I'd have stopped her somehow. There's no more dangerous man in England. Now it's too late. We shall have to face the music. If I am subpœnaed I'll go into the witness-box and swear I did it. She charged me with having done it. She shall go into the witness-box and give evidence against me. We'll dish Ernest Gilbert. 'Greater love hath no man than this, that a man lay down his life for his friend.' And she's my friend, since I love her. At anyrate, I'll be her friend, if the thing may be."

CHAPTER XXIV
THE SOMNAMBULIST

Miss Arnott was not happy. Money had not brought her anything worth having. In her case, fortune had been synonymous with misfortune. Young, rich "beyond the dreams of avarice," good-looking; all those papers which deal with what are ironically called "personal topics," held her up to public admiration as one of the persons in the world who were most to be envied. In plain truth she was one of the most miserable. In her penniless days she was not unhappier. Then her trouble was simple, now it was compound. Not the least of her disasters was the fact that health was failing. That robust habit of mind and body which had, so far, stood her in good stead, was being sapped by the continuous strain. Her imagination was assuming a morbid tinge. Her nights were sleepless, or dream-haunted, which was as bad. She was becoming obsessed by an unhealthy feeling that she lived in a tainted atmosphere. That all the air about her was impregnated with suspicion. That she was becoming the centre of doubting eyes, whispering tongues, furtively pointing fingers.

While she was more or less unconsciously drifting into this physically and mentally unhealthy condition she received a visit from a Mrs Forrester, in the course of which that lady insisted on dwelling on topics of a distinctly disagreeable kind.

Mrs Forrester was a widow, childless, well-to-do. She had two occupations--one was acting as secretary to the local branch of the Primrose League, and the other was minding other people's business. She so managed that the first was of material assistance to her in the second. She was a person for whom Miss Arnott had no liking. Had she had a chance she would have denied herself. But Mrs Forrester came sailing in through the hall just as she was going out of it.

"Oh, my dear Miss Arnott, this is an unexpected pleasure! I am so fortunate in finding you at home, I so seldom do! And there is something of the first importance which I must speak to you about at once--of the very first importance, I do assure you."

The motor was at the door. Miss Arnott's inclination was to fib, to invent a pressing engagement--say, twenty miles off--and so shunt the lady off on to Mrs Plummer. It seemed as if the visitor saw what was in her mind. She promptly gave utterance to her intention not to be shunted.

"Now you mustn't say you're engaged, because I sha'n't keep you a minute, or at most but five. That motor of yours can wait, and you simply must stop and listen to what I have to say. It's in your own interest, your own urgent interest, so I can't let you go."

Miss Arnott stopped, perforce. She led the way into the red drawing-room. Mrs Forrester burst into the middle of the subject, which had brought her there, in her own peculiar fashion.

"Now, before I say a single word, I want you to understand most clearly that the only reason which has brought me here, the one thing I have come for, is to obtain your permission, your authority, to contradict the whole story."

"What story?"

The visitor held up her hands.

"What story! You don't mean to say you haven't heard? It simply shows how often we ourselves are the last persons to hear of matters in which we are most intimately concerned. My dear, the whole world is talking about it, the entire parish! And you say, what story?"

"I say again, what story? I've no doubt that my concerns do interest a large number of persons, even more than they do me, but I've not the vaguest idea to which one of them you're now referring."

"Is it possible? My dear, I was told no longer ago than this morning that you walk every night through the woods in--well, in your nightdress."

"What's that?"

"Of course it's nonsense. No one knows better than I do that such an idea's ridiculous. But there's the story. And, as I've said, I've come on purpose to ask you to allow me to offer an authoritative contradiction."

"But what is the story? I should be obliged to you, Mrs Forrester, if you could manage to make it a little clearer."

"I will make it clear. To me it has been made painfully clear--painfully. I may tell you that I've heard the story, in different forms, from various sources. Indeed I believe it's no exaggeration to say that it's on everybody's tongue, and, on the whole, no wonder. My informant this morning was Briggs, the postman. You know him?"

"I can't claim the honour. However, I'm willing to take your statement as proof of his existence."

"A most respectable man, most respectable. His wife has fifteen children--twins only last March,--but perhaps I oughtn't to speak of it to you. He used to be night watchman at Oak Dene in old Mr Morice's time. Sometimes he takes the letter-bags to and from the mail train, which goes through at half-past one in the morning. He did so last night. He assures me with his own lips that, coming home, as he was passing your place, he heard something moving, and on looking round saw you among the trees in your nightdress. Of course it couldn't have been you. But, at the same time, it is most singular. He is such a respectable man, and his story was most circumstantial. Could it have been you?"

"I was not out last night at all, and it never is my custom to wander about the grounds in the costume you refer to, if that is what you mean, Mrs Forrester--at least, not consciously."

"Exactly, that is the very point, of course--not consciously. But do you do it unconsciously?"

"Unconsciously! What do you mean?"

"My dear, it is my duty to tell you that all sorts of people claim to have seen you wandering--sometimes actually running--through the woods of Exham Park at the most extraordinary hours, clad only in your nightdress. The suggestion is that you are walking in your sleep."

"Walking in my sleep? Mrs Forrester!"

"Yes, my dear, walking in your sleep. It is strange that the story should not have reached you; it is on everybody's tongue. But when, as I tell you, Briggs made that positive statement to me with his own lips, I felt it my bounden duty to come and see you about it at the earliest possible moment. Because, if there is any truth in the tale at all--and they can't all be liars--it is absolutely essential for your own protection that you should have someone to sleep with you--at any rate, in the same room. Somnambulism is a most serious thing. If you are a somnambulist--and if you aren't, what are you?--proper precautions ought to be taken, or goodness only knows what may happen."

"If I am a somnambulist, Mrs Forrester. But am I? In all my life I have never heard it hinted that I am anything of the kind, and I myself have never had any reason to suspect it."

"Still, my dear, there are all those stories told by all sorts of people."

"They may have imagined they saw something. I very much doubt if they saw me."

"But there is Briggs's positive assertion. I have such faith in Briggs. And why should he invent a tale of the sort?"

"Did he see my face?"

"No; he says you were walking quickly from him, almost running, but he is positive it was you. He wanted to come and tell you so himself; but I dissuaded him, feeling that it was a matter about which you would prefer that I should come and speak to you first."

"What time was it when he supposes himself to have seen me?"

"Somewhere about two o'clock."

Miss Arnott reflected.

"To the best of my knowledge and belief I was in bed at two o'clock, and never stirred from it till Evans called me to get into my bath. If, as you suggest, I was out in the woods in my nightdress--delightful notion!--surely I should have brought back with me some traces of my excursion. I believe it rained last night."

"It did; Briggs says it was raining at the time he saw you."

"Then that settles the question; he didn't see me. Was I

147

barefooted?"

"He couldn't see."

"The presumption is that, if I choose to wander about in such an airy costume as a nightgown, it is hardly likely that I should think it necessary to go through the form of putting on either shoes or stockings. Anyhow, I should have been soaked to the skin. When I woke up this morning my nightgown would have shown traces at least of the soaking it had undergone. But not a bit of it; it was as clean as a new pin. Ask Evans! My feet were stainless. My bedroom slippers--the only footwear within reach, were unsoiled. No; I fancy, Mrs Forrester, that those friends of yours have ardent imaginations, and that even the respectable Briggs is not always to be trusted."

"Then you authorise me to contradict the story in toto?"

"Yes, Mrs Forrester; I give you the fullest authority to inform anyone and everyone that I never, in the whole course of my life, went out for a stroll in my nightgown, either asleep or waking. Thank you very much indeed for giving me the opportunity of furnishing you with the necessary power."

Mrs Forrester rose from her chair solemnly.

"I felt that I should only be doing my duty if I came."

"Of course you did, and you never miss an opportunity of doing your duty. Do you?"

Before the lady had a chance of replying a door opened. Miss Arnott turned to find that it had admitted Mr Morice. The sight of him was so unexpected, and took her so wholly by surprise that, at a momentary loss for a suitable greeting, she repeated, inanely enough, almost the identical words which she had just been uttering to Mrs Forrester.

"Mr Morice! This is--this is a surprise. I--I was just telling Mrs Forrester, who has been good enough to bring me rather a curious story, that if anyone mentions, in her hearing, that they saw me strolling through the woods in the middle of the night in a state of considerable undress, I shall be obliged if she gives such a statement a point-blank contradiction."

Mr Morice inclined his head gravely, as if he understood precisely what the lady was talking about.

"Certainly. Always advise Mrs Forrester to contradict everything she hears. Mrs Forrester hears such singular things."

CHAPTER XXV
HUGH MORICE EXPLAINS

So soon as Mrs Forrester had gone Mr Morice asked a question.

"What tale has that woman been telling you?"

"She actually says that people have seen me walking about the woods in the middle of the night in my nightdress. That a postman, named Briggs, saw me doing so last night. I believe I am supposed to have been walking in my sleep. Of course it is only some nonsensical rigmarole. I won't say the whole thing is an invention of Mrs Forrester's own brain, but it's the sort of thing she's fond of."

"That's true enough. It is the sort of tale she's fond of; but, for once in a way, she is justified by fact. Since we are on the subject I may as well inform you that, four nights or rather mornings, ago I myself saw you, at two o'clock in the morning, in Cooper's Spinney, in some such costume as that which you describe."

"Mr Morice!"

"I do not know that I should have told you if it had not been for Mrs Forrester; but, since she has intervened, I do so. In any case, it is perhaps as well that you should be on your guard."

"Are you sure you saw me?"

"I am not likely to make a mistake in a matter of that sort."

"But are you sure it was me?"

"Certain."

"What was I doing?"

"You were under the beech tree--our beech tree. You appeared to me to be looking for something on the ground--something which you could not find."

"But four nights ago? I remember it quite well. I was reading and writing till ever so late. Then I fell asleep directly I got into bed. I certainly never woke again until Evans called me."

"The probability is that you got out of bed directly you were asleep. It struck me that there was something singular about your whole proceedings. A doubt crossed my mind at the time as to whether you could possibly be in a somnambulistic condition. As I approached you retreated so rapidly that I never caught sight of you again."

"Do you mean to say I was in my nightdress?"

"As to that I cannot be certain. You had on something white; but it struck me that it was some sort of a dressing-gown."

"I have no white dressing-gown."

"On that point I cannot speak positively. You understand that I only saw you for a few seconds, just long enough to make sure that it was you."

She put her hands up to her face, shuddering.

"This is dreadful! that I should walk in my sleep--in the woods--and everyone see me--and I know nothing! What shall I do?"

"There is one thing I should recommend. Have someone to sleep in your room--someone who is quickly roused."

"That is what Mrs Forrester advised. I will certainly have that done. A bed shall be put in my room, and Evans shall sleep in it tonight. Is it to make this communication that you have favoured me with the very unexpected honour of your presence here, Mr Morice?"

"No, Mrs--I beg your pardon, Miss Arnott--it is not." As she noticed the slip she flushed. "The errand which has brought me here is of a different nature, though not, I regret to say, of a more pleasant one."

"Nothing pleasant comes my way. Do not let unpleasantness deter you, Mr Morice. As you are aware I am used to it."

There was a bitterness in her tone which hurt him. He turned aside, searching for words to serve him as a coating of sugar, and failing to find them.

"Why," he presently asked, "did you instruct Ernest Gilbert to defend Jim Baker?"

She stared in amazement; evidently that was not what she expected.

"Why? Why shouldn't I?"

"For the simple but sufficient reason that he was the very last man whose interference you should have invited in a matter of this particular kind."

"Mr Stacey was of a different opinion. It was he who gave me his name. He said he was the very man I wanted."

"Mr Stacey? Mr Stacey was not acquainted with all the circumstances of the case, Miss Arnott. Had you consulted me--"

"I should not have dreamt of consulting you."

"Possibly not. Still, I happen to know something of Mr Gilbert personally, and had you consulted me I should have warned you that, in all human probability, the result would be exactly what it has turned out to be."

"Result? Has anything resulted?"

"Something has--Mr Gilbert has withdrawn from the case."

"Withdrawn from the case! What do you mean?"

"Here is the £500 which you sent him. He has requested me to hand it back to you."

"A cheque for £500? Mr Morice, I don't understand! Why has Mr Gilbert returned me this?"

"I will tell you plainly. We are, both of us, in a position in which plainness is the only possible course."

"Well, tell me--don't stand choosing your words--tell me plainly! Why has Mr Gilbert sent me back my cheque through you?"

"Because Jim Baker conveyed the impression to his mind that he--Jim--saw you commit the crime with which he stands charged."

"I don't understand."

"I think you do. Gilbert's position is that he finds himself unable to retain your money when his duty to Baker may necessitate his putting you in the dock on the capital charge."

"Mr Morice! It's--it's not true!"

"Unfortunately, it is true. Lest, however, you should think the position worse than it actually is, part of my business here is to reassure your mind on at least one point."

"Reassure my mind! Nothing will ever do that--ever! ever! And reassurance from you!--from you!"

"If matters reach a certain point--before they go too far--it is my intention to surrender myself--say, to Granger--our local representative of law and order--as having been guilty of killing that man in Cooper's Spinney."

"Mr Morice! Do you--do you mean it?"

"Certainly I mean it. Then you will have an opportunity of going into the witness-box and giving that testimony of which you have spoken. That in itself ought to be sufficient to hang me."

"Mr Morice!"

"What we have principally to do is to render it impossible that the case against me shall fail. A very trifling accident may bring the whole business to an end; especially if Ernest Gilbert puts ever such a distant finger in the pie. Against the possibility of such an accident we shall have to guard. For instance, by way of a beginning, where's that knife?"

"Knife?"

"The knife."

"I've lost the key."

"Lost the key? of what?"

"I put it in a wardrobe drawer with my--my things, and locked it, and, somehow, I lost the key."

"I don't quite follow. Do you mean that, having locked up my knife in a drawer with some other articles, you have mislaid the key of the lock?"

"Yes, that's what I mean."

"Then in that case, you had better break that lock open at the earliest possible moment."

"Why?"

"The answer's obvious, in order that you may hand me back my knife. If I'm to be the criminal it will never do for my knife to be found in your possession. It would involve all sorts of difficulties which we might neither of us find it easy to get over. Give me the knife. I will hide it somewhere on my own premises, where I'll take care that, at the proper moment, it is found. Properly managed, that knife ought to make my guilt as plain as the noonday sun; mismanaged, the affair might assume quite a different complexion."

For the first time a doubt entered the girl's mind.

"Mr Morice, do you wish me to understand that you propose to surrender merely to save me?"

"I wish you to understand nothing of the sort. The position is--in its essence--melodrama; but do let us make it as little melodramatic as we conveniently can. Someone must suffer for the--blunder. It may as well be me. Why not?"

"Do you wish me--seriously--to believe that it was not you who--blundered?"

"Of course I blundered--and I've kept on blundering ever since. One blunder generally does lead to another, don't you know. Come--Miss Arnott"--each time, as she noticed, there was a perceptible pause before he pronounced the name to which she still adhered--"matters have reached a stage when, at any moment, events may be expected to move quickly. Your first business must be to get that drawer open--key or no key--and let me have that knife. You may send it by parcel post if you like. Anyhow, only let me have it. And, at latest, by tomorrow night. Believe me, moments are becoming precious. By the way, I hope it hasn't been--cleaned."

"No, it hasn't been cleaned."

"That would have been to commit a cardinal error. In an affair of this sort blood-stains are the things we want; the pièces de conviction which judge and jury most desire. Give me the knife--my knife--that did the deed, with the virginal blood-stains thick upon it. Let it be properly discovered by a keen-nosed constable in an ostentatious hiding-place, and the odds are a hundred to one as to what the verdict will be. A hundred? a million! I assure you that I already feel the cravat about my neck." Hugh Morice put his hand up to his throat with a gesture which made Miss Arnott shiver. "Only, I do beg of you, lose no time. Get that drawer open within the hour, and let me have my hunting-knife before you have your dinner. Let me entreat you to grasp this fact clearly. At any moment Jim Baker may be out of Winchester Gaol; someone will have to take his place. That someone must be me."

CHAPTER XXVI
THE TWO MAIDS

After Hugh Morice had left her, Miss Arnott had what was possibly the worst of all her bad half hours. The conviction of his guilt had been so deeply rooted in her mind that it required something like a cataclysm to disturb its foundations. She had thought that nothing could have shaken it; yet it had been shaken, and by the man himself. As she had listened to what he had been saying, an impression had been taking hold of her, more and more, that she had misjudged him. If so, where was she herself standing? A dreadful feeling had been stealing on her that he genuinely believed of her what she had believed of him. If such was the case, what actually was her position.

Could she have done the thing which he believed her to have done? It was not only, moreover, what he believed; there were others. An array of witnesses was gathering round her, pointing with outstretched fingers. There was Jim Baker--it seemed that he was honestly persuaded that, with his own eyes, he had seen her kill her husband. So transparent was his honesty that he had succeeded-- whether intentionally or not she did not clearly understand--in imparting his faith to the indurated lawyer to such a degree, that he had actually thrown her money back at her, as if it had been the price of blood. She had little doubt that if her own retainers were polled, and forced to vote in accordance with the dictates of their consciences, merely on the strength of the evidence they believed themselves to be already in possession of, they would bring her in as guilty. She had had this feeling dimly for some time--she had it very clearly then.

And now she was walking in her sleep. That thing of which she had read and heard, but never dreamt to be--a somnambulist. It seemed that her conscience drove her out at dead of night to revisit--unwittingly--the scene of the crime which stained her soul.

Could that be the interpretation of the stories which Mrs Forrester had told her? and Hugh Morice? She had been seen, it would appear, by half the countryside, clad--how? wandering--conscience-driven--on what errand?

The more she thought, however, of the tale which Briggs the postman had retailed to Mrs Forrester, not to speak of Hugh Morice's strange narrative--the more she doubted--the more she had to doubt. They might have the evidence of their own eyes, but it seemed to her that she had evidence which was at least equally conclusive. It was incredible--impossible that she could have tramped through the rain and the mire, among the trees and the bushes, in the fashion described, and yet have found no traces of her eccentric journeyings either on her clothes or on her person. But in that matter measures could--and should--be taken. She would soon learn if there was any truth in the tales so far as they had reference to her. Evans should be installed in her room that night as watchman. Then, if she attempted to get out of bed while fast asleep, the question would be settled on the spot. The question of the knife--Hugh Morice's knife--was a graver one. But as regards that also steps should be promptly taken. Whether it should be returned to its owner as he suggested, or retained in her possession, or disposed of otherwise. These were problems which required consideration. In the meanwhile, she would have it out of its hiding-place at once. She went upstairs to force open that wardrobe drawer. So soon as she entered her bedroom she perceived that she had been forestalled, and that, in consequence, a lively argument was going on. The disputants were two--her own maid, Evans, and Wilson, the housemaid, who had been supposed to have been in part responsible for the disappearance of the key. Miss Arnott was made immediately conscious--even before she opened the door--that the pair were talking at the top of their voices. Evans's was particularly audible. She was pouring forth on to her fellow-servant a flood of language which was distinctly the reverse of complimentary. So occupied, indeed, were they by the subject under discussion that, until Miss Arnott announced her presence, they were not conscious that she had come into the room.

Their young mistress paused on the threshold, listening, with feelings which she would have found it difficult to analyse, to some of the heated observations which the disputants thought proper to fling at each other. She interrupted Evans in the middle of a very warmly coloured harangue.

"Evans, what is the meaning of this disturbance? and of the extraordinary language you are using?"

The maid, though evidently taken by surprise by the advent of her mistress, showed very few of the signs of shame and confusion which some might have considered would have become a person in her position. Apparently she was much too warm to concern herself, at anyrate for the moment, with matters of etiquette. She turned to Miss Arnott a flushed and angry face, looking very unlike the staid and decorous servant with whom that young lady was accustomed to deal. Hot words burst from her lips,--

"That there Wilson had the key all the time. I knew she had."

To which Wilson rejoined with equal disregard of ceremonial usages,--

"I tell you I hadn't! Don't I tell you I hadn't! At least, I didn't know that I had, not till five minutes ago."

Evans went on, wholly ignoring her colleague's somewhat singular disclaimer,--

"Then if she didn't use it to unlock your drawer with--your private drawer--and to take liberties with everything that was inside it. I daresay if I hadn't come and caught her she'd have walked off with the lot. And then to have the face to brazen it out!"

To which Wilson, in a flame of fury,--

"Don't you dare to say I'd have taken a single thing, because I won't have it. I'm no more a thief than you are, nor perhaps half so much, and so I'll have you know. You're a great deal too fond of calling names, you are; but if you call me a thief I'll pay you for it. You see!"

Evans turned again to her adversary, eager for a continuance of the fray.

"If you weren't going to take them what did you go to the drawer for?"

"I tell you I went to the drawer to see if it was the key."

"Why didn't you bring the key to me?"

"I would have brought it, if you'd given me a chance."

"You would have brought it! Didn't I catch you--"

Miss Arnott thought she had heard enough; she interposed.

"Will you be so good as to be still, both of you, and let me understand what is the cause of this disgraceful scene. Evans, has the key of the drawer been found?"

"Yes, miss, it has. It was never lost; she had it all the time, as I suspected."

"I didn't have it, miss--leastways, if I did, I didn't know it, not till just now."

"Explain yourself, Wilson. Has or has not the key been in your possession?"

"It's like this, miss; it must somehow have slipped inside my dress that morning when I was making your bed."

"She'll explain anything!"

This was the resentful Evans.

"I'll tell the truth anyhow, which is more than you do."

Again their mistress interposed.

"Evans, will you allow Wilson to tell her story in her own way. Wilson, you forget yourself. On the face of it, your story is a lame one. What do you mean by saying that the key of my wardrobe drawer slipped into your dress? Where was it that it was capable of such a singular proceeding?"

"That's more than I can tell you, miss. I can only say that just now when I was taking down a skirt which I haven't worn since I don't know when, it felt heavy, and there in the hem on one side--it's a broad hem, miss, and only tacked--there was a key, though how it got there I haven't a notion."

"Of course not!"

This was Evans. Miss Arnott was in time to prevent a retort.

"Evans! Well, Wilson, what did you do then?"

"I came with it to Evans."

The lady's-maid was not to be denied.

"That's a falsehood, anyhow. You came with it to me! I do like that!"

The housemaid was equal to the requirements of the occasion.

"I did come with it to you. I came with it straight to this bedroom. They told me you were here; it wasn't my fault if you weren't."

"Oh dear no! And, I suppose, it wasn't your fault if, finding I wasn't here, you unlocked the drawer!"

"I only wanted to see if it was the lost key I had found; I meant no harm."

Again Miss Arnott.

"Now, Evans, will you be silent! Well, Wilson, I don't see that, so far, you have been guilty of anything very reprehensible. It's quite possible that, somehow, the key may have slipped into the hem of your skirt; such accidents have been known. When you had tried the key and found that it was the one which had been mislaid; when you had opened the drawer with it, what did you do then?"

Again the lady's-maid was not to be denied. Orders or no orders, she refused to be silent.

"Yes, what did she do? I'll tell you what she did; don't you listen to anything she says, miss. She took liberties with everything that was inside that drawer, just as if the things was her own. She turned all the things out that was in it; you can see for yourself that it's empty! and she's got some of them now. Though I've asked her for them she won't give them up; yet she has the face to say she didn't mean to steal 'em!"

This time the housemaid was silent. Miss Arnott became conscious that not only had she been all the time holding herself very upright, but, also, that she was keeping her hands behind her back--in short, that her attitude more than suggested defiance.

"Wilson, is this true?"

The answer was wholly unlooked for.

"My mother is Jim Baker's cousin, miss."

"Your mother--" Miss Arnott stopped short to stare. "And what has that to do with your having in your possession property which is not your own?"

Her next answer was equally unexpected.

"And Mr Granger, he's my uncle, miss."

"Mr Granger? What Mr Granger?"

"The policeman down in the village, miss."

"Apparently, Wilson, you are to be congratulated on your relations, but I don't see what they have to do with what Evans was saying."

"I can't help that, miss."

"You can't help what? Your manner is very strange. What do you mean?" The girl was silent. Miss Arnott turned to the lady's-maid. "Evans, what does she mean?"

"Don't ask me, miss; she don't know herself. The girl's wrong in her head, that's what's the matter with her. She'll get herself into hot water, if she don't look out; and that before very long. Now, then, you give me what you've got there!"

"Don't you lay your hands on me, Mrs Evans, or you'll be sorry."

"Evans!--Wilson!"

Kit had not been for Miss Arnott's presence it looked very much as if the two would have indulged in a scrimmage then and there. The lady's-maid showed a strong inclination to resort to physical force, which the other evinced an equal willingness to resent.

"Wilson, what is it which you are holding behind your back? I insist upon your showing me at once."

"This, miss--and this."

CHAPTER XXVII
A CONFIDANT

In her right hand Wilson held a knife--the knife. Miss Arnott needed no second glance to convince her of its identity. In her left a dainty feminine garment--a camisole, compact of lace and filmy lawn. The instant she disclosed them Evans moved forward, as if to snatch from her at least the knife. But Wilson was as quick as she was--quicker. Whipping her hands behind her back again she retreated out of reach.

"No, you don't! hands off! you try to snatch, you do!"

The baffled lady's-maid turned to her mistress.

"You see, miss, what she's like! and yet she wants to make out that she's no thief!"

Miss Arnott was endeavouring to see through the situation in her mind, finding herself suddenly confronted by the unforeseen. It was impossible that the girl could mean what she seemed to mean; a raw country wench in her teens!

"Wilson, you seem to be behaving in a very strange manner, and to be forgetting yourself altogether. It is not strange that Evans has her doubts of you. Give me those things which you have in your hands at once."

"Begging your pardon, miss, I can't."

"They're not yours."

"No, miss, I know they're not."

"Then, if you're an honest girl, as you pretend, what possible reason can you have for refusing to give me my own property, which you have taken out of my drawer in a manner which is at least suspicious?"

"Because Jim Baker, he's my mother's cousin; and Mr Granger he's my uncle."

"What possible justification can that be for your trying to steal what belongs to me?"

Then it came out.

"My uncle he says to me, 'I don't believe Jim Baker done it--I don't believe he did anything to the chap beyond peppering him. Jim's no liar. 'Twill be a shame if they hang him. No, my girl,' Mr Granger says, 'it's my belief that they know more over at Exham Park than they pretend, or, at least, someone does. You keep your eyes wide open. We don't want to have no one hung in our family, specially for just peppering a chap. If you come across anything suspicious, you let me know and you let me have a look at it, if so be you can. Your mother don't want to have Jim Baker hung, nor more don't I.' Miss Arnott, you put them things in the drawer the time that you came home, the time that chap was murdered, the time that you was out in the woods till all hours. They haven't found the knife what did it yet, and this knife's all covered with blood; so's the things. I'm going to let Mr Granger see what I've got here, and tell him where I found them. If there's nothing wrong about them I'll have to suffer, but show them to him I will."

Miss Arnott, perceiving that here was an emergency in which prompt action was the one thing needful, glanced at Evans, who was quick to take the hint. She advanced towards Wilson with designs which that young woman considered sufficiently obvious. To evade her, still holding her booty behind her to secure it from Evans, she turned her back to Miss Arnott who was not slow to avail herself of the opportunity to grip her wrists and tear the knife and camisole away from her. The wench, finding herself outwitted, sprang at her mistress, screaming,--

"Give them to me! give them to me! You give them back to me!"

But Miss Arnott had already dropped them into the open wardrobe drawer, shut the drawer and turned the key. While she kept the girl at arms' length, to prevent her wresting from her the key, Miss Arnott issued her instructions to the lady's-maid.

"Evans, ring the bell, keep on ringing."

There was a lively minute or so. Then Bevan, Mr Day's

understudy, appeared in the doorway, to stare at the proceedings open-eyed. Miss Arnott had succeeded in retaining possession of the key, though she had not found the excited girl easy to manage. Bevan, striding forward, spun the housemaid round on her feet as if she were a teetotum.

"Now, then," he demanded, "what do you think you're doing? Are you mad?"

"Bevan," exclaimed Miss Arnott, "Wilson has been misbehaving herself. See that she is paid her wages and sent about her business at once."

Wilson, who by now was more than half hysterical, shrieked defiance.

"Mr Bevan, you make her give me that knife! you make her. I believe she killed that chap in Cooper's Spinney. She's got the knife she killed him with shut up in that drawer there! You make her give it me! I'm going to show it to my uncle!"

Bevan was unsympathetic.

"Now, then, out you go!" was the only answer he made to her appeal.

But Mr Granger's niece was not disposed to go in compliance with his mere request. When he essayed persuasion of a more active kind she began to fight him tooth and nail. Reinforcements had to be brought upon the scene. When, finally, she was borne from the room, she was kicking and struggling like some wild cat. A pretty tumult she managed to create as they conveyed her down the stairs.

Miss Arnott and her maid, left alone together, surveyed each other with startled looks. The plumage of both had been something more than ruffled; a tress of hair which was hanging down Miss Arnott's back was proof of the housemaid's earnestness. Evans was the first to speak.

"I wish you'd let me do as I said, miss--break that drawer open, and let me wash those things."

"But who would have thought she was such a creature! Is she mad?"

"Oh, she's sane enough after her own fashion; though, if she's one of that Baker and Granger set, she's mad enough for anything. I can't abide that village lot, and they know it. I wish you'd let me do as I said!"

"I wish I had. As for my clothes, you can wash them now--if you don't mind, that is."

"I'll wash them fast enough. I've done some washing in my time. Though, after those stains have been in them all this time, they'll want some soaking. What are you going to do about that knife, miss? If I had known it was there I'd have broken open that drawer first and asked your permission afterwards."

"I'll see to that."

"You'll see to it! But, miss, you'll never get these stains out, never! not now! They're eaten into the steel! Nothing will get them out except re-burnishing. If that Wilson gets down to that fool of a Granger it's quite likely that we'll have him here with a search warrant, and then Heaven help us! No, miss, you'll give me that knife, if you please. I'll make it safe enough."

Miss Arnott was struck by the singularity of the woman's manner; she yielded to a sudden impulse.

"Evans, I fancy you are under a misapprehension. If so, let me remove it from your mind, if it can be removed. I believe you think that I am responsible for what happened to that man in Cooper's Spinney. I'm not. I had no hand in it whatever."

"You didn't kill him?"

"Emphatically, no. I had nothing to do with killing him; nothing."

"Miss, are you sure?"

"I am quite sure; quite."

"I believe you, miss, I believe you. But--I don't understand--the stains upon your things; the knife? If you didn't kill him yourself you know who did."

"I thought I did; that is why the knife is in my possession. Bringing it home--inside my bodice--caused the stains."

"Whose knife is it? Did it belong to the--man who was killed?"

"No; it did not. I would rather not tell you to whom it did belong--at least, not now."

"You know?"

"Oh, yes, I know. Evans, I believe you're disposed to be my friend, and I'm in need of a friend."

"You are, miss, in more need than you have perhaps a notion of. I don't want to use any big words, but there's nothing I wouldn't do for you, and be glad to do it, as, maybe, before all's done, I'll prove. But I wish you'd trust me, miss--trust me all the way. I wish you'd tell me whose knife that is and how you came to have it."

"I'd rather not, and for this reason. I was convinced that the owner of that knife was the murderer. That is why, when I found it, I brought it home with me."

"To screen him?"

"You must not ask me that. Quite lately I have begun to think that I was wrong, that the owner of that knife is as innocent as I am. It's a tangle. I was quite close when it happened; I heard it all happening; yet now I am conscious that I have no more real knowledge of who did it than you have. You mustn't ask me any questions; I may tell you more some other time--I may have to--not now! not now! I want to think! But, Evans, there is one thing I wish to say to you--do you believe that I'm a somnambulist?"

"A somnambulist? A sleep-walker do you mean? Whatever has put that idea into your head?"

"Have you heard the tales they're telling--about my having been seen in the woods at night in my nightdress?"

"I've heard some stuff; it's all a pack of nonsense! What next?"

"Do you know Briggs the postman? What sort of man is he?"

"He's got his head screwed on right enough for a countryman."

"Well, Mrs Forrester called this afternoon for the express purpose of informing me that Briggs the postman saw me in the woods at two o'clock this morning in my nightdress."

"But, miss, it's impossible! Did you ever walk in your sleep?"

"Never to my knowledge. Have you ever had occasion to suspect me of anything of the kind?"

"That I certainly have not."

"This time it seems peculiarly incredible, because it was pouring cats and dogs. If I had done anything of the sort there must have been traces on my nightdress, or on something. This is a question I mean to have settled one way or the other. I'm going to have a bed put up in this room, and I'm going to ask you to sleep in it, if you conveniently can, with one eye open. You'll soon find out what my habits are when fast asleep. Between ourselves I believe that this is going to be an opportunity for me to play that favourite character in fiction--the detective--on lines of my own."

"I'll sleep here, miss, and be pleased to do it. But as for your walking in your sleep, I should have found it out long ago if you'd been given that way. I don't believe a word of it; that's all nonsense."

Miss Arnott seemed to reflect before she spoke again.

"I'm not so sure of that--that it's all nonsense, Evans. I'm going to tell you something; at present it's a secret, but I think I can trust you to keep it. You're not the only person who has suspected me of having killed that man."

"Lor' bless you, miss, as if I didn't know that! That's no secret! I don't believe you've any idea yourself of what a dangerous place it is in which you're standing."

"I'll be ready for the danger--when it comes. I'll not be afraid. What I meant was that I have been actually supposed to have been seen killing that man. Someone was seen to kill him, and that someone was a woman."

"You're quite sure, miss, that it wasn't you? You're quite sure?"

"Quite, Evans; don't you be afraid."

"Then if that's so, miss, I don't mind. If you're innocent I don't care what they do; let them do their worst."

"That's what I feel--exactly. But I wish you'd let me make my meaning clear to you! If a woman did do it, then--though I confess I don't understand how--we must all of us be on the wrong scent, and the woman who has been seen wandering through the woods at dead of night--and that such an one has been seen I have good reasons for knowing--is the one we want. So what we have to do is to identify that somnambulist."

"But how are we going to do it?"

"That, as yet, I own is more than I can tell you. The first step is to make sure it isn't me."

"Don't you fret about that, miss; I'm sure it isn't. I'll take these things away and get 'em in soak at once." She gathered up the various garments which her mistress had worn on that fateful night. "I wish you'd let me take that knife; I'd feel safer if you would."

"Thank you, Evans; but at present I'd rather you left the knife with me."

As Evans left the room Mrs Plummer came in, in the state of fluster which, of late, was her chronic condition.

"My dear," she began, "what is this I hear about Wilson? What is this shocking story?"

"Wilson has misbehaved herself and is therefore no longer in my service. I imagine, Mrs Plummer, that that is what you hear. I am sorry you should find it so shocking. It is not such a very unusual thing for a servant to forget herself, is it?"

"I don't know, my dear, when it comes to fighting Bevan and positively assaulting you. But everything seems to be at sixes and sevens; nothing seems to go right, either indoors or out. It makes me most unhappy. And now there's an extraordinary person downstairs who insists on seeing you."

"An extraordinary person? What do you call an extraordinary person? Do you know, Mrs Plummer, that a good deal of your language lately has seemed to me to have had a flavour of exaggeration."

"Exaggeration? You call it exaggeration? I should have thought it would have been impossible to exaggerate some of the things which have happened in this neighbourhood in the last few weeks. But there's no accounting for people. I can only tell you that I should call the person who is below an extraordinary person. Here is her card; she herself thrust it into my hand."

"Mrs Darcy Sutherland? I don't know anyone of that name."

"She knows you, or she pretends she does. I met her on the steps as I was coming in. When I told her you were out--because I thought you had gone on your motor, you said you were going--she replied that she would wait till you came back, if she had to wait a week. That I call an extraordinary remark to make."

"It is rather an unusual one. I will go down and see Mrs Darcy Sutherland."

CHAPTER XXVIII
MRS DARCY SUTHERLAND

As Miss Arnott went to her visitor she had premonitions that more disagreeables were at hand. No one whom she was desirous of seeing would have uttered such a speech as that which Mrs Plummer had repeated. Her premonitions were realised to the full. As she entered the sitting-room, into which the caller had been shown, a big, blowsy, over-dressed woman rose from a chair, whom the girl instantly acknowledged that Mrs Plummer had been perfectly justified in calling an extraordinary person. She was painted, and powdered, and pencilled, and generally got up in a style which made it only too plain what kind of character she was. With a sinking heart Miss Arnott recognised Sarah Stevens, her quondam associate as a model in that costume department of that Regent Street draper's where, once upon a time--it seemed centuries ago--she had earned her daily bread, the woman who had introduced her to Robert Champion, who had urged her to marry him, to whom she owed all the trouble which had come upon her, and whose real character she had learned too late.

She had not expected, as she had asked herself what awaited her now, that it was anything so bad as this.

"You!" she stammered.

"Yes, my dear, me! A nice little surprise for you, isn't it?" The woman advanced towards her with the apparent intention of greeting her with a kiss. Miss Arnott showed by her manner, as much as by the way in which she drew back, that she did not intend to submit to anything of that sort. The visitor was not at all abashed. She continued to smile the hard, mechanical smile of the woman of her class. "You didn't expect to see me, I'll be bound. Perhaps you'd forgotten me, and you thought, perhaps, that I'd forgotten you, but you see I haven't. I've got a very good memory, I have. Well, my love, and how are you? You're not looking so well as I expected; quite peaked, you seem, nothing like so well filled out as you used to be."

"What do you mean by coming here? And by calling yourself Mrs Darcy Sutherland?"

"My dear Vi!"

"Have the goodness not to address me by my Christian name."

"It used to be Vi and Sally in the days gone by. But I suppose circumstances are changed, that sometimes makes a difference. I don't mind, it's all the same to me. I'll call you whatever you choose--Miss Arnott if you like. I'm surprised to find that they all do seem to call you that round here."

"You haven't answered my questions. Why have you come here? And why do you call yourself Mrs Sutherland?"

"As to why I've come here, I'll tell you in half a minute, though there's some who wouldn't ask such a thing of an old friend. Let me get my breath, my love; that rotten old fly shook me all to pieces. As to why I call myself Mrs Sutherland--that does seem an unpleasant remark to make to a lady, let alone an old friend. But I'm not one that's quick to take offence. I call myself Mrs Sutherland because I am Mrs Sutherland. I've married since I saw you last."

"You've married?"

"Yes, why shouldn't I? And, unlike you, I'm not ashamed of my married name, or of my husband's. By the way, my love, you must remember my husband."

"Remember him?"

"Of course you must. He remembers you quite well. He was a

friend of your husband's."

"A friend of my husband?"

"Rather. They were pals--thick as thieves. Darcy knew Robert Champion long before you did."

"Darcy?"

"That's my husband's Christian name. You can call him by it if you like, though you don't want me to call you by yours. But then I'm more open-minded, perhaps, than you are, and open-hearted too."

"Be so good as to tell me why you have come here."

The woman took a handkerchief from the bag made of steel beads which was suspended from her waist; opening it out she twiddled it between the white-gloved fingers of either hand. Miss Arnott immediately became conscious of the odour of some strong perfume.

"Can't you guess?"

"I cannot."

"Sure?"

"I am quite sure that I am unable to think of any plausible excuse for your presence in my house. You never were a friend of mine. Nor are you a person whose acquaintance I desire to renew. You are perfectly well aware that I know what kind of character you are. You did me all the harm you could. It was only by the mercy of God that you did not do me more. I do not intend to allow my house to be sullied by your presence one moment longer than I can help."

The girl crossed the room.

"What are you going to do?"

"I am going to ring to have you shown to the door."

"You had better hear first what I've come for, unless you want me to tell you in front of your servants."

"As to that, I am indifferent. If you have anything to say to me say it at once."

"Oh, I'll tell you fast enough, don't you worry. It won't take me long to say it. I can say it in just one sentence. Mrs Champion, I've come to see your husband."

The girl started, perceiving that trouble was threatening from still another quarter. She was conscious that her visitor noticed her start, but in spite of it she could not prevent her pulses throbbing unpleasantly.

"My husband? What do you mean?"

"Oh, you know what I mean well enough, don't try acting the stupid with me. You're not so dull as all that, nor yet so simple; and I'm

166

not if you are. Mrs Champion, I've come to see your husband, Mr Robert Champion, my old friend Bob."

"He's not here, you know he's not here."

"How do I know he's not here? I know he came here."

"How do you know he came here?"

"Because me and my husband met him outside the gate of Wandsworth Prison the Saturday morning he came out of it from doing his sentence. His wife ought to have been there--that's you! but you wasn't! I suppose you were on your couch of rose-leaves and didn't want to be disturbed. Nice idea of a wife's duties you seem to have, and a pretty sort you are to want to look down on me. Poor fellow! he was in sad trouble, without a penny in his pocket, or a chance of getting one, and him with the richest woman in England for his wife. When we told him of the luck you'd had--"

"So it was you who told him, was it?"

"Yes, it was, and I daresay you'd have rather we hadn't; you'd have rather he'd starved and got into trouble again, and rotted out his life in gaol. But Darcy and me were his true friends, if his own wife wasn't. We weren't going to see him hungry in the gutter while you were gorging yourself on the fat of the land. We gave him a good meal, he wanted it, poor chap; nothing but skin and bone he was. We told him all about you, and where you lived, put him inside a new suit of clothes, clothed him in new things from head to foot, we did, so that you shouldn't think he disgraced you by his appearance, and gave him the money to come down here; and he came."

"Well?"

For Mrs Darcy Sutherland had paused.

"Well? You think it's well, do you? Then all I can say is, I don't. Mrs Champion, I've come to see your husband."

"He's not here."

"He's not here? Then where is he?"

"It is sufficient for you to be informed that he's not here."

"Oh, no, it isn't; and don't you think it, my love. It's not sufficient by a long way. He promised to let us hear from him directly he got down here; we've heard nothing from that day to this, and that's some time ago, you know."

"If that is all you have to say I'll ring the bell."

"But it's not all I've got to say. Still, you can ring the bell if you like, it's not my bell. Though, if you take my advice, you'll hear me out before you do."

"Go on."

"Oh, I'll go on, as I told you before, don't you worry, and don't you try to bully me, because I'm not to be bullied, threatening me with your bells! Mrs Champion," the woman repeated the name with a curious gusto, enjoying the discomfort the sound of it occasioned the girl in front of her, "Mr Sutherland and me, we're not rich. Your husband promised to give us back that money we let him have, and since it seems that I can't see him I should like to see the colour of the money."

"That's what you want, is it? I begin to understand. How much was it?"

"Well, we'll say a thousand pounds."

"A thousand pounds!"

"A thousand pounds."

"Do you dare to pretend that you gave him a thousand pounds?"

"I don't pretend anything of the kind. I pretend nothing. What I say is this. If I can see Mr Robert Champion and enjoy the pleasure of a little chat with him I shall be content to receive back the cash we lent him. If I can't do that I want a thousand pounds. Don't you understand, my love?"

Miss Arnott did understand at last. She realised that the purport of this woman's errand was blackmail. When comprehension burst upon her she was silent; she was trying to collect her thoughts, to think--a process which the increasing pressure of "the slings and arrows of outrageous fortune" made difficult. Mrs Darcy Sutherland observed her obvious discomposure with smiling amusement, as the proverbial child might observe the movements of the fly which it has impaled with a pin.

Miss Arnott was saying to herself, or rather, endeavouring to say to herself--for her distress of mind was blurring her capacity for exact expression--that a thousand pounds was but a trifling sum to her, and that if by the expenditure of such an amount she could free herself from this new peril it would be money well spent. She did not stop to reflect, although, all the while, the idea was vaguely present in her mind that, by yielding to this woman's demand, she would be delivering herself to her body and soul. Her one feeling was the desire to get this woman out of the house without a scene--another scene such as she had had with Wilson, probably a much worse one than that. If she could only be relieved of the odious oppression born of her near neighbourhood, breathe purer air uncontaminated by this creature's presence, if she could only do this for a time it would be something. She would have a chance to look round her, to gather together her forces, her scattered senses. If she could only do that she might be more than a match for Mrs Darcy Sutherland yet. But she must have that chance, she must not have exposure--in its worst form--thrust upon her now, in her present state--she was becoming more and more conscious of shaky nerves--that might be more than she was able to bear. The chance was well worth a thousand pounds, which to her was nothing.

She was all at once seized with an overwhelming longing to take instant advantage of the chance the woman offered her. She resolved to give her what she asked.

"If I let you have what you want will you promise to go away immediately--right away?"

"I'll walk out of this house without speaking a word to a creature in it, or to anyone out of it for the matter of that, and I'll take the next train back to town, if that's what you mean."

"That's what I do mean. If I give you a cheque for a thousand pounds will that do?"

"If you leave it open, and make it payable to bearer, I don't know that I'd mind taking it. I suppose there's money enough at the bank to meet it; and that you won't try to stop its being paid."

"There's plenty of money to meet it, and I certainly shall not try to stop its being paid."

"Then I'll tell you what; you give me all the ready money you have got in the house, and an open cheque to bearer for the balance--that'll be more satisfactory for both parties--then I'll take myself off as fast as you like."

"Very well. I'll go and see what money I've got and I'll bring you a cheque for the rest."

Miss Arnott moved towards the door, intending to perpetrate what was perhaps the worst folly of which she had been guilty yet. Just as she reached the door it opened. Mr Stacey entered, followed by a dark, dapper gentleman--Ernest Gilbert.

CHAPTER XXIX
SOME PASSAGES OF ARMS

Mr Stacey held out both hands to her in the effusive fashion which, when he chose, he could manage very well.

"My dear Miss Arnott, I think I'm unexpected." He was; so unexpected that, in the first flush of her surprise, the girl was oblivious of his outstretched hands. He went on, ignoring her confusion. "But I trust I am not unwelcome because I happen to come unheralded." Looking about him he noticed Mrs Sutherland. "But you are not alone. I hope that our unannounced entrance has not been an intrusion. May I ask you to make me known to your"--something caused him not to use the word which was already on the tip of his tongue--"to this lady."

"This is Mrs Darcy Sutherland."

"Mrs Darcy Sutherland?" In spite of his mellifluous tones there was something in the way in which he repeated the name which hardly suggested a compliment. "And what might Mrs Darcy Sutherland want with you?"

Mrs Sutherland took it upon herself to answer.

"Well, I never! the impudence of that! Who are you, pray? and what business is it of yours?"

The lawyer was blandness itself.

"I beg your pardon. Were you speaking to me?"

"Yes, I was speaking to you, and you know I was." She turned to Miss Arnott. "I think, my dear, it would be better if you were to ask these two gentlemen to leave us alone together till you and I have finished our little business."

"Business?" At the sound of the word Mr Stacey pricked up his ears. He addressed Miss Arnott. "As in all matters of business I have the honour to represent you, don't you think that, perhaps, you had better leave me to deal with this--lady in a matter of business?"

The lady referred to resented the suggestion hotly.

"What next, I wonder? You'll do nothing of the kind, my dear, not if I know it you won't. And as I'm in rather a hurry, perhaps you'll go and do what you said you would."

Mr Stacey put to Miss Arnott a question.

"What was it you said that you would do for this lady?"

Again the lady showed signs of heat.

"I never saw the equal of you for meddling. Don't you go poking your nose into other people's affairs, or you'll be sorry. If you take my advice, my dear, you won't tell him a single thing. I sha'n't, if you won't, you may trust me for that. You'll keep your own business to yourself, especially when it's business of such a very particular kind--interfering old party!"

"If you take my advice, Miss Arnott, and I think you have reason to know that in general my advice is to be trusted, you will tell me in the fewest, and also in the plainest, possible words what this person wants with you. It is evidently something of which she is ashamed, or she would not be so anxious for concealment."

"Don't you call me a person, because I won't have it; and don't you interfere in what's my business, because I won't have that either." The indignant Mrs Darcy Sutherland rose to her feet. "Now, look here, and don't let there be any mistake about it, I'm not going to have this impudent old man humbugging about with me, so don't let anyone think it. So you'll please to understand, Miss Arnott, that if you're going to get what you promised to get, you'd better be quick about it, because I've had about as much as I care to put up with. I'm not going to let any man trample on me, I don't care who he is, especially when I don't know him from Adam."

"Surely there can be no objection to my putting a simple question. What is it you promised to get for this--lady about which she betrays so much anxiety?"

Miss Arnott replied.

"If you don't mind, I'd rather not have any bother. I've had some trouble already."

"I know you have; it is because of that that we are here. Believe me, my dear young lady, you will be quite safe if you trust yourself in my hands."

"I don't want to have any more trouble, so, as it wasn't a sum which was of much consequence to me, I was just going to get some money which Mrs Sutherland wanted when you came in."

"Money?"

"Yes, money!--money she owes me!--so now you know!"

"Do you owe this--lady money?"

"Well, it isn't exactly that I owe it, but money is owing to her, I believe."

"How much?"

"A thousand pounds."

"A thousand pounds! Is it possible that you were thinking of giving this woman a thousand pounds?"

At this point Mrs Darcy Sutherland thought proper to give her passion reins, with results which were hardly becoming.

"Look here, don't you call me a woman, you white-headed old rooster, as if I wasn't a lady! I'm as much a lady as she is, and a good deal more. The next time you give me any more of your sauce, I'll smack your face; I've done it to better men than you before to-day, so don't you say that I didn't warn you!" She turned to Miss Arnott. "As for you--how much longer are you going to be tommy-rotting about? Are you going to give me that thousand pounds, or aren't you? You know what the consequences will be if you don't! Don't you think, in spite of his smooth tongue, that he can save you from them, because he can't, as you shall very soon see. Now, am I going to have that money or not?"

Mr Gilbert, asserting himself for the first time, interfered.

"Stacey, I should like to say a few words to Mrs Darcy Sutherland. Mrs Darcy Sutherland, I believe my name is not unknown to you--Ernest Gilbert."

"Ernest Gilbert?" The woman changed countenance. "Not the Ernest Gilbert?"

"Yes, the Ernest Gilbert. And I see you are the Mrs Darcy Sutherland; thank you very much. I have been favoured with instructions to proceed against a gang of long firm swindlers, the ringleader of whom is a man who calls himself Darcy Sutherland. There's a warrant out for his arrest, but for the moment he's slipped through our fingers. There has been some talk as to whether your name should be included in that warrant; at present, it isn't. When you leave here I'll have you followed. The probability is that you'll make for the man you call your husband. If you do so, we'll have him; if you don't, we'll have you--see?"

On hearing this the woman flung all remnants of decency from her.

"That's the time of day, is it? You think you've got me, do you? Fancy you've only got to snap your fingers and I'm done for? That's where you're wrong, as I'll soon show you. If I'm in a bit of a hole, what about her? Who do you think she is? What do you think she's been doing? I'll tell you if you don't know, and then we shall know where we are!--and she'll know too!--by----! she will!"

Mr Ernest Gilbert glanced round towards Mr Stacey.

"Take Miss Arnott out of the room."

Inside thirty seconds Mr Stacey had whisked the girl out of the room and vanished with her. Mrs Darcy Sutherland, realising the trick which was being played, rushed to the door. But Mr Gilbert was there first; with the key turned, he stood with his back to the door and faced her.

"You get away from in front of that door! What do you mean by turning that key? You open that door and let me out this instant!"

The lawyer's reply did not breathe the spirit of conciliation.

"I'll see you hung first."

"Don't you speak to me like that! Who do you think you're talking to?"

"To you. Now, you foul-mouthed judy, I'm going to take off the gloves to deal with you. I've not had the dregs of the criminal population pass through my hands all these years without knowing how to deal with a woman of your type, as I'm going to show you. What were you going to say to Miss Arnott?--out with it!"

"Never mind what I was going to say to Miss Arnott; I'm going to say nothing to you; don't you think it! Who do you think you're trying to bounce?"

"You're going to say exactly what you would have said if that young lady had remained in the room, or when you do go it will be in the charge of a policeman."

"Oh, shall I? We'll see! Don't you make any mistake!"

"Don't you."

"You must think I'm a simple-minded innocent, to come trying to play your confidence tricks off on me. What do you want me to think I'll be in the charge of a policemen for, I'd like to know?"

"Blackmail."

"Blackmail! What do you mean?"

"You know perfectly well what I mean. You have just been trying to blackmail that girl to the tune of a thousand pounds. No offence more severely punished. I'll have you jugged on one charge, and the blackguard you call your husband on another."

"I wasn't trying to do anything of the sort; don't fancy you can bluff me! I was only telling the truth."

"Makes it worse. Suppose you believed her to have committed murder, and said you'd out with what you knew if she didn't give you a thousand pounds--that would be blackmail in its most heinous form; you'd get a lifer as sure as you're alive. My time's valuable. Which is it going to be--the policeman or what you call the truth?"

"If I do tell you what use will you make of it?"

"No questions answered. Which is it going to be?"

"If I tell you, will you let me go right straight off? No shadowing or anything of that kind?"

"The only promise I'll make is that I won't let you go if you don't. Out with it!"

"You're very hard on a girl! I don't know what I've done to you!"

"No snivelling; put away that evil-smelling rag; I'm going to have that policeman."

He was standing by the bell.

"Don't! I'll tell you!"

"Then tell!"

"I don't know what it is you want me to tell you--I really don't!"

"I want you to tell me what's the pull you've got, or think you've got, over Miss Arnott."

"It's about that chap who was killed in the woods here."

"What about him?"

"He was her husband."

"How do you know?"

"I ought to. He was an old friend of mine, and I was her bridesmaid when she married him."

"Why did she keep him dark?"

"Well, he got into a bit of trouble."

"Go on! out with it all! and don't you stammer!"

"I'm not stammering, and I'm going on as fast as ever I can! I never saw anyone like you. He got into prison, that's what he did, and of course she wasn't proud of it. He only came out the morning of the day he came down here; my husband and me lent him the money to come with, and we want our money back again--we can't afford to lose it."

"I see. His object in coming was blackmail--like yours. Is that all the pull?"

"All! I should think it's enough, considering. But, as it happens, it isn't all."

"What else is there?"

"Why, she killed him."

"How do you know?"

"It stands to reason. Why didn't she let out he was her husband and that she knew all about him? Isn't it plain enough why? Because they met in the woods, and had a bit of a quarrel, and she knifed him, that's why. And she'll swing for it in spite of all her money. And it's because she knows it that she was so willing to give me that thousand pounds. What do you think?"

"You evil-speaking, black-hearted cat! Now I'll have that policeman, and for what you've said to me you shall have a lifer!"

He moved towards the bell.

"Don't! you promised you'd let me go!"

"I promised nothing of the kind, you---! I tell you what I will do. I'll unlock that door and let you through it. You shall have six hours' start, and then I'll have a warrant out for you, and if I catch you I promise I'll do my best to get you penal servitude for life. As we've a shrewd idea of your husband's whereabouts, if you take my advice you'll keep away from him. Now, out you go!"

Unlocking the door he threw it open.

"Six hours mind, honest!"

"Six hours, by my watch. After that, if I can catch you I will, you can bet on it. Take yourself outside this house before I change my mind. You'd better!"

Apparently Mrs Darcy Sutherland was of his opinion; she was out of the house with a swiftness which did credit to her agility. Almost as soon as she had gone Mr Stacey appeared in the doorway of the room she had just quitted.

CHAPTER XXX
MISS ARNOTT IS EXAMINED

Mr Stacey put a question to Mr Gilbert.

"Have you got rid of her?"

"Very much so. Stacey, I must see Miss Arnott at once, the sooner the safer. I'm afraid she did it."

"Do you mean that she killed that fellow in Cooper's Spinney? I don't believe a word of it. What's that woman been saying?"

"It's not a question of belief but of fact. I'll tell you afterwards what she's been saying. What we want to do is to get at the truth. I fancy we shall do it if you let me have a few minutes' conversation with your young friend. If she didn't do it I'll do my level best to prevent a hair of her head from being injured, and if she did I may be able to save her. This is one of those cases in which, before I'm able to move, I must know just where I am standing."

"You seem to have an ethical standard of your own."

"A man in my line of business must have. Where's Miss Arnott?"

"I'll take you to her. She's expecting you. I told her you'd like to have a little talk with her. But, mind this, she's anything but well, poor girl! I believe she's been worried half out of her mind."

"I shouldn't wonder."

"I didn't bring you down here to subject her to a hostile cross-examination. I won't let you do it--especially in her present condition."

"When you've finished perhaps you'll take me to her; you don't want her to hang."

"Hang! Gilbert! God forbid! Whatever she may have done she's only a child, and I'm persuaded that at heart she's as innocent as you or me."

"If she isn't more innocent than I am I'm sorry for her. Will you take me to see this paragon of all the feminine virtues?"

"You wear your cynicism like a cloak; it's not such an essential part as you choose to imagine."

Ernest Gilbert smiled as if he would show his teeth.

Mr Stacey led the way to an apartment which was called the red drawing-room, where already that afternoon Miss Arnott had interviewed Hugh Morice and Mrs Forrester. It was a pleasant, well-lighted room, three windows ran up one side of it almost from floor to ceiling. The girl was standing in front of one of these as the two men entered, looking out on to the Italian garden, which was a blaze of sunshine and of flowers. Mr Stacey crossed to her with his somewhat exuberant, old-fashioned courtesy.

"Permit me, my dear young lady, to offer you a chair. I think you will find this a comfortable one. There, how is that?" She had seated herself, at his invitation, in a large, straight-backed armchair covered with a fine brocade, gold on a crimson background, whose age only enhanced its beauty. "As I was telling you just now, I have heard, to my great distress, that several things have happened recently, hereabouts, which could hardly tend to an increase of your comfort."

"No, indeed."

"Part of my information came from my very good friend here, and he will be your very good friend also if you will let him. Let me introduce you to Mr Ernest Gilbert."

In acknowledgment of the introduction the girl inclined her head. Mr Gilbert gave his a perfunctory little shake, as if he had a stiff neck.

"I am glad to meet you, Mr Gilbert. I was sorry to learn from Mr Morice that you have sent me back my money and refused to defend

Jim Baker."

Mr Stacey interposed before the other had a chance to answer.

"Quite so, my dear young lady, quite so; we will come to that presently. Mr Gilbert came to see me this morning on that very subject. It is in consequence of certain communications which he then made to me that we are here. You instructed him, from what I understand, to defend this unfortunate man."

"Which he at first consented, and then declined to do."

This time it was Mr Gilbert who interposed, before Mr Stacey was ready with his reply.

"Stacey, if you don't mind, I'll speak. I think it's possible that Miss Arnott and I may understand each other in half a dozen sentences."

Mr Gilbert was leaning over the back of a chair, right in front of her. The girl eyed him steadily. There was a perceptible interval, during which neither spoke, as if each was taking the other's measure. Then the girl smiled, naturally, easily, as if amused by some quality which she discerned either in the lawyer's terrier-like countenance or in the keenness of his scrutiny. It was she who was the first to speak, still with an air of amusement.

"I will try to understand you, and I should like you to understand me. At present I'm afraid you don't."

"I'm beginning to."

"Are you? That's good news."

"Your nerves are strong."

"I've always flattered myself that they weren't weak."

"You like plain speaking."

"I do--that is, when occasion requires."

"This is such an occasion."

"I think it is."

"Then you won't mind my asking you a plain question."

"Not at all."

"Who killed that man in Cooper's Spinney?"

"I don't know."

"You are sure?"

"Quite."

"Are you aware that Jim Baker thinks you killed him?"

"I am."

"And that Hugh Morice thinks so also?"

"I know he did think so; I fancy that now he has his doubts--at least, I hope he has."

"How do you explain the fact of two such very different men being under the same erroneous impression?"

"I can't explain it; I can explain nothing. I don't know if you are aware that until quite recently I thought it was Mr Morice himself who killed that man."

"What made you think that?"

"Two or three things, but as I am now of a different opinion it doesn't matter what they were."

"But it does matter--it matters very much. What made you think that Hugh Morice killed that man?"

The girl turned to Mr Stacey.

"Shall I answer him? It's like this. I don't know where Mr Gilbert's questions may be landing me, and I don't want to have more trouble than I have had already--especially on this particular point."

"My dear young lady, if your own conscience acquits you--and I am sure it does--my strongest advice to you is, tell all you have to tell. The more light we have thrown on the matter the better. I grieve to learn that the finger of scandal has been pointed at you, and that, if we are not very careful, very serious and disagreeable consequences may presently ensue. I implore you to hide nothing from us which may enable us to afford you more than adequate protection from any danger which may threaten. This may prove to be a very grave business."

"I'm not afraid of what may happen to me, not one bit. Pray don't either of you be under any delusion on that point. What I don't want is to have something happen to anyone else because of me." She addressed Mr Gilbert. "What use will you make of any information which I may give you with regard to Mr Morice?"

"If it will relieve your mind, Miss Arnott, and enable you to answer my question, let me inform you that I am sure--whatever you may suppose to the contrary--that Hugh Morice is not the guilty person."

"Why are you sure?"

"First, because I know him; and he's not that kind of man. And second, because in the course of a lengthy interview I had with him I should have perceived something to cause me to suspect his guilt, instead of which I was struck by his conviction of yours."

"Now I also believe he is innocent--but I had reasons for my doubts; better ones than he had for his doubts of me."

"May I ask what those reasons were?"

"I was within a very short distance of where the murder was committed, and though I was not an actual witness, I heard. A moment afterwards I saw Mr Morice come running from--the place where it was done, as if for his life. Then--by the dead man I found the knife with which he had been killed. It was Mr Morice's knife; a few minutes before I had seen him with it in his hand."

"You found Hugh Morice's knife? What did you do with it?"

"It is still in my possession. You see, I thought that he was guilty, and--for reasons of my own--I did not wish to have the fact made public."

"This is a curious tangle into which you have managed to get things between you. Have you any idea of what it is Mrs Darcy Sutherland has just been telling me?"

"I can guess. She has probably told you that the dead man was my husband--Robert Champion."

"Your husband! My dear young lady!"

This was Mr Stacey.

"Yes, my husband, who had that morning been released from gaol." Mr Stacey would, probably, have pursued the subject further, but with a gesture Mr Gilbert prevented him. The girl went on. "Mr Morice knew he was my husband. I thought he had killed him to save me from him; he thought I had done so to save myself. It is a puzzle. There is only one thing that seems clear."

"And that is?"

"That it was a woman who killed my husband."

"I see what you mean. I have been trying to splice the threads. That person who has just been here--Mrs Darcy Sutherland--do you think it possible that she could have been that woman?"

"I should say that it was impossible."

CHAPTER XXXI
THE TWO POLICEMEN

Mr William Granger, of the County Police, was just finishing tea in his official residence when there came a rap at the door leading into the street. Mr Granger was not in the best of tempers. The county policeman has not quite such a rosy time as his urban colleague is apt to suppose. Theoretically he is never off duty; his armlet is never off his sleeve. It is true that he has not so much to do as his city brother in the way of placing law-breakers under lock and key; but then he has to do a deal of walking exercise. For instance, Mr Granger had a twelve-mile beat to go over every day of his life, hot or cold, rain or shine, besides various local perambulations before or after his main round was finished. Not infrequently he walked twenty miles a day, occasionally more.

One would have thought that so much pedestrianism would have kept Mr Granger thin; he himself sincerely wished that it had had that effect. As a matter of fact he was the stoutest man in the village, which was galling. First, because he was conscious that his bulk did not tend to an increase of personal dignity. Second, because, when the inspector came from the neighbouring town, he was apt to make unpleasant remarks about his getting plumper every time he saw him; hinting that it was a very snug and easy billet for which he drew his pay; adding a hope that it was not because he was neglecting his duty that he was putting on weight so fast. Third, because when one is fat walking is apt to result in considerable physical discomfort, and twenty miles on a hot summer's day for a man under five foot ten who turns the scale at seventeen stone!

Mr Granger, who had come back hot and tired, had scarcely flung his helmet into one corner of the room, and his tunic into the other, when his inspector entered. That inspector was fond of paying surprise visits; he surprised Mr Granger very much just then. The policeman had a bad time. His official superior more than hinted that not only had he cut his round unduly short on that particular day, but that he was in the habit of curtailing it, owing to physical incapacity. Then he took him for another little stroll, insisting on his accompanying him to the station and seeing him off in the train which took him back to headquarters, which entailed another walk of a good six miles--three there and three back--along the glaring, dusty road.

By the time Mr Granger was home again he was as bad-tempered a policeman as you would have cared to encounter. Tea, which had been postponed to an unholy hour, did but little to improve either his temper or his spirits. He scarcely opened his mouth except to swallow his food and snap at his wife; and when, just as she was clearing away the tea-things, there came that rap at the door, there proceeded from his lips certain expletives which were very unbecoming to a constable, as his wife was not slow to point out.

"William! what are you saying? I will not have you use such language in my presence. I should like to know what Mr Giles would say if he heard you."

Mr Giles was the inspector with whom Mr Granger had just such an agreeable interview; the allusion was unfortunate.

"Mr Giles be----"

"William!"

"Then you shouldn't exasperate me; you only do it on purpose; as if I hadn't enough to put up with as it is. Don't stand there trying to put me in a bad temper, but just open that door and see who's knocking."

Possibly Mr Granger spoke in louder tones than he supposed, because before his helpmate could reach the door in question it was opened and someone put his head inside.

"All right, Mr Granger, I'm sure that good lady of yours has enough to do without bothering about opening doors; it's only yours very truly."

The newcomer spoke in a tone of voice which suggested complete confidence that he would be welcome; a confidence, however, which was by no means justified by the manner of his reception. The constable stared at him as if he would almost sooner have seen Inspector Giles again.

"You! What brings you here at this time of day? I thought you were in London."

"Ah, that's where you thought wrong. Mrs Granger, what's that you've got there--tea? I'm just about feeling equal to a sup of tea, if it's only what's left at the bottom of the pot."

The speaker was a tall, loose-limbed man with a red face, and hair just turning grey. From his appearance he might have been a grazier, or a farmer, or something to do with cattle; only it happened that he was Mr Thomas Nunn, the detective from London who had been specially detailed for duty in connection with the murder in Cooper's Spinney. As Mr Granger had learned to associate his presence with worries of more kinds than one, it was small wonder-- especially in the frame of mind in which he then was--that he did not receive him with open arms. Mr Nunn seemed to notice nothing, not even the doubtful glances with which Mrs Granger looked into her teapot.

"There isn't a drop in here, and I don't know that it will bear more water."

"Put in another half-spoonful and fill it up out of the kettle; anything'll do for me so long as there's plenty of it and it's moist, as you'd know if you saw the inside of my throat. Talk about dust!"

Mr Granger was eyeing him askance.

"You never come down from London. I saw the train come in, and you weren't in it."

"No, I haven't come from London."

"The last train back to London's gone--how are you going to manage?"

"Well, if it does come to the pinch I thought that you might give me a shake-down somewhere."

The policeman glanced at his wife.

"I don't know about that. I ain't been paid for the last time you were here. They don't seem too anxious to pay your bills--your people don't."

"That's their red tape. You'll get your money. This time, however, I'm going to pay for what I have down on the nail."

"What's brought you? You know, Mr Nunn, this ain't an inn. My wife and me don't pretend to find quarters for all the members of the force."

"Of course you don't. But I think you'll be interested when you hear what has brought me. I may be wrong, but I think you will. I've come from Winchester."

"From Winchester?"

Husband and wife both started.

"Yes, from Winchester. I've been to see that chap Baker. By the way, I hear he's a relation of yours."

"Most of the people is related hereabouts, somehow; but he's only distant. He's only a sort of a cousin, and I've never had much truck with him though I ain't saying he's not a relation. What's up with him now?"

"He made a communication to the governor, and the governor made a communication to headquarters, and headquarters made a communication to me. In consequence of that communication I've been paying him a call."

"What's the last thing he's been saying?"

"Well, he's been making a confession."

At this point Mrs Granger--who was lingering with the tea-tray--interposed.

"A confession, Mr Nunn! You don't mean for to tell that after all he owns up 'twas he who killed he man?"

"No, I can't say exactly that I do. It's not that sort of confession he's been making. What he's been confessing is that he knows who did kill him."

"Who was it, Mr Nunn?"

"Supposing, Mrs Granger, you were to get me that sup of tea. If you were to know what my throat felt like you wouldn't expect to get much through it till it had had a good rinsing."

The constable issued his marital orders.

"Now then, Susan, hurry up with that tea for Mr Nunn. What are you standing there gaping for? If you were to know what the dust is like you'd move a little quicker."

Mrs Granger proceeded to hurry. Mr Nunn seated himself comfortably at the table and waited, showing no sign of a desire to continue the conversation till the tea appeared. His host dropped a hint or two, pointing out that to him, in his official capacity, the matter was of capital importance. But Mr Nunn declined to take them. When the tea did appear he showed more reticence than seemed altogether necessary. He was certainly slower in coming to the point than his hearers relished. Mr Granger did his best to prompt him.

"Well, Mr Nunn, now that you've had three cups of tea perhaps you wouldn't mind mentioning what Jim Baker's been saying that's brought you here."

Mr Nunn helped himself to a fourth.

"I'm in rather a difficult position."

"I daresay. It might make it easier perhaps if you were to tell me just what it is."

"I'm not so sure, Granger, I'm not so sure. That relative of yours is a queer fish."

"Maybe I know what sort of a fish he is better than you do, seeing I've known him all my life."

"What I've got to ask myself is--What reliance is to be placed on what he says?"

"Perhaps I might be able to tell you if you were to let me know what he does say."

"Oh, that's the point." Mr Nunn stirred what remained of his fourth cup of tea with a meditative air. "Mr Granger, I don't want to say anything that sounds unfriendly or that's calculated to hurt your feelings, but I'm beginning to be afraid that you've muddled this case."

"Me muddled it! Seeing that you've had the handling of it from the first, if anyone's muddled it, it's you."

"I don't see how you make that out, Mr Granger, seeing that you're on the spot and I'm not."

"What's the good of being on the spot if I'm not allowed to move a finger except by your instructions?"

"Have there been rumours, Mr Granger? and by that I mean rumours which a man who had his professional advancement at heart might have laid his hand on."

"Of course there have been rumours! there's been nothing else but rumours! But every time I mentioned one of them to you all I got was a wigging for my pains."

"That's because the ones you mentioned to me were only will-o'-the-wisps. According to the information I've received the real clues you've let slip through your fingers."

Mr Granger stood up. He was again uncomfortably hot. His manner was hardly deferential.

"Excuse me, Mr Nunn, but if you've come here to lecture me while drinking of my wife's tea, since I've had a long and a hard day's work, perhaps you'll let me go and clean myself and have a bit of rest."

"If there's anything in what Jim Baker says there's plenty for you to do, Mr Granger, before you think of resting."

"What the devil does he say?"

"You needn't swear at me, Mr Granger, thank you all the same. I've come here for the express purpose of telling you what he says."

"Then you're a long time doing it."

"Don't you speak to me like that, Granger, because I won't have it. I conduct the cases which are placed in my hands in my own way, and I don't want no teaching from you. Jim Baker says that although he didn't kill the chap himself he saw him being killed, and who it was that killed him."

"Who does he say it was?"

"Why, the young woman up at Exham Park--Miss Arnott."

CHAPTER XXXII
THE HOUSEMAID'S TALE

Mr And Mrs Granger looked at each other. Then the husband dropped down into the chair which he had just vacated with a sound which might be described as a snort; it was perhaps because he was a man of such plethoric habit that the slightest occasion for surprise caused him to emit strange noises. His wife caught at the edge of the table with both her hands.

"Lawk-a-mussy!" she exclaimed. "To think of Jim Baker saying that!"

"It seems to me," observed Mr Nunn, with an air of what he perhaps meant to be rhadamanthine severity, "that if there's anything in what that chap says somebody ought to have had their suspicions before now. I don't say who."

This with a very meaning glance at Mr Granger.

"Suspicions!" cried the lady. "Why, Mr Nunn, there ain't been nothing but suspicions! I shouldn't think there was a soul for ten miles round that hasn't been suspected by someone else of having done it. You wouldn't have had my husband lock 'em all up! Do you believe Jim Baker?"

"That's not the question. It's evidence I want, and it's for evidence, Mr Granger, I've come to you."

"Evidence of what?" gasped the policeman. "I don't know if you think I keep evidence on tap as if it was beer. All the evidence I have you've got--and more."

His wife persisted in her inquiry.

"What I ask you, Mr Nunn, is--Are you going to lock up that young lady because of what Jim Baker says?"

"And I repeat, Mrs Granger, that that's not the question, though you must allow me to remark, ma'am, that I don't see what is your locus standi in the matter."

"Aren't you drinking my tea?"

"I don't see what my drinking your tea has got to do with it anyhow. At the same time, since it'll all soon enough be public property, I don't know that it's of much consequence. Of course a man hasn't been at the game all the years I have without becoming aware that nothing's more common than for A, when he's accused of a crime, to try to lay the blame of it on B; and that, therefore, if for that reason only, what that chap in Winchester Gaol says smells fishy. But at the same time the statement he has made is of such a specific nature, and should be so open to corroboration, or the reverse, that I'm bound to admit that if anything did turn up to give it colour I should feel it my duty to act on it at once."

"Do you mean that you'd have her arrested?"

"I do--that is if, as I say, I obtain anything in the nature of corroborative evidence, and for that I look to Mr Granger."

There was no necessity for him to do that, fortunately for the peace of mind and body of the active and intelligent officer referred to. Evidence of the kind of which he spoke was coming from an altogether different quarter. Indeed, it was already at the door.

Hardly had he done speaking than a modest tap was heard. Opening, Mrs Granger found a small urchin standing in the dusk without, who slipped an envelope into her hand, with which she returned into the room, peering at the address.

"What's this? 'To the Policeman.' I suppose, William, that means you; it's only some rubbish, I suppose."

She passed the envelope to her husband, who peered at the address as she had done.

"Let's have the lamp, Susan, you can't see to read in this here light. Not that I suppose it's anything worth reading, but mine ain't cat's eyes anyhow."

The lamp was lit and placed upon the table. Mr Granger studied what was written on the sheet of paper which he took from the envelope.

"Robert Champion was the name of the man who was murdered in the wood. The mistress of Exham Park, who calls herself Miss Arnott, was his wife. He came out of Wandsworth Prison to see her. And he saw her.

"Ask her why she said nothing about it.

"Then the whole truth will come out."

Mr Granger read this once, twice, thrice, while his wife and Mr Nunn were watching him. Then he scratched his head.

"This is rummy--uncommon. Here, you take and look at it, it's beyond me altogether."

He handed the sheet of paper to Mr Nunn, who mastered its contents at a glance. Then he addressed a question to Mrs Granger, shortly, sharply.

"Who gave you this?"

"What is it?"

"Never mind what it is, woman! Answer my question--who gave it you?"

"It's no use your speaking to me like that, Mr Nunn, and so I'd have you know. I'm no servant of yours! Some child slipped it into my hand, but what with the bad light and the flurry I was in because of what you'd been saying, I didn't notice what child no more than nothing at all."

Mr Nunn seemed disturbed.

"It'll be a serious thing for you, Mrs Granger, if you're not able to recognise who gave you this. You say it was a child? There can't be so many children in the place. I'll find out which of them it was if I have to interview every one in the parish. It can't have got so far away; perhaps it's still waiting outside."

As he moved towards the entrance, with a view of finding out if the bearer of that singular communication was still loitering in the immediate neighbourhood, he became conscious that someone was approaching from without--more than one. While he already had the handle in his grasp it was turned with a certain degree of violence by someone on the other side; the door was thrown open, and he found himself confronted by what, in the gathering darkness, seemed quite a crowd of persons.

"Is William Granger in?" demanded a feminine voice in not the most placable of tones. Mr Nunn replied,--

"Mr Granger is in. Who are you, and what do you want with him?"

"I'm his sister, Elizabeth Wilson, that's who I am, and I should like to know who you are to ask me such a thing. And as for what I want, I want justice; me and my daughter, Sarah Ann, we both want justice--and I'm going to see I get it too. My own cousin, Jim Baker, he's in prison this moment for what he never did, and I'm going to see that he's let out of prison double quick and the party as ought to be in prison put there. So you stand out of the way and let me get inside this house to see my brother."

Mr Nunn did as he was requested, and Mrs Wilson entered, accompanied by her daughter, Sarah Ann. He looked at the assemblage without.

"Who are all these people?"

"They're my friends, that's who they are. They know all about it, and they've come to see that I have fair play, and they'll see that I have it too, and so I'd have everyone to understand."

By way of commentary Mr Nunn shut the door upon the "friends" and stood with his back to it.

"Now then, Granger, who's this woman? And what's she talking about?"

Mrs Wilson answered for her brother.

"Don't you call me a woman, as if I was the dirt under your feet. And as for who I am--William, who's this man? He's taking some fine airs on himself. As what I have to say to you I don't want to have to say before strangers, perhaps you'll just ask him to take himself outside."

"Now, Liz," observed her brother, fraternally, "don't you be no more silly than you can help. This gentleman's Mr Nunn, what's in charge of the case--you know what case. He saw Jim Baker in Winchester Gaol only this afternoon."

"In Winchester Gaol, did he! Then more shame to them as put him in Winchester Gaol, and him as innocent as the babe unborn! And with them as did ought to be there flaunting about in all them fine feathers, and with all their airs and graces, as if they were so many peacocks!"

"What might you happen to be talking about?"

"I'm talking about what I know, that's what I happen to be talking about, William Granger, and so you'll soon learn. I know who ought to be there instead of him, and if you've a drop of cousinly blood in your veins you'll see that he's out of that vile place, where none of my kith or kin ever was before, and that you know, the first thing to-morrow morning."

"Oh, you know who did ought to be there, do you? This is news, this is. Perhaps you'll mention that party's name. Only let me warn you, Elizabeth Wilson, to be careful what you say, or you may find yourself in worse trouble than you quite like."

"I'll be careful what I say, I don't need you to tell me, William Granger! And I'll tell you who ought to be in Winchester Gaol instead of Jim Baker--why, that there proud, stuck-up young peacock over at Exham Park, that there Miss Arnott!"

"Liz! I've told you already not to be more silly than you can help. What do you know about Miss Arnott?"

"What do I know about Miss Arnott? I'll soon tell you what I know about your fine Miss Arnott. Sarah Ann, tell your uncle what you know about that there Miss Arnott."

Then the tale was unfolded--by Wilson the housemaid--by degrees, with many repetitions, in somewhat garbled form; still, the essential truth, so far as she knew it, was there.

She told how, that eventful Saturday, the young mistress had been out in the woods, as she put it, "till goodness only knows what hours of the night." How, the next morning, the key of the wardrobe drawer was lost; how, after many days, she, Wilson, had found it in the hem of her own skirt, how she had tried the lock, "just to see if it really was the key," of what the drawer contained--the stained clothing, the bloody knife. She narrated, with dramatic force, how first Evans and then Miss Arnott had come upon the scene, how the knife and the camisole had been wrested from her, how she herself had been ejected from the house.

When she had finished Mr Nunn looked up from the pocket-book in which he had been making copious notes of the words as they came from her lips.

"What you've said, Sarah Ann Wilson, you've said of your own free will?"

"Of course I have. Haven't I come here on purpose?"

"And you're prepared to repeat your statement in a court of law, and swear to its truth?"

"I am. I'll swear to it anywhere."

"You don't know what has become of that knife you've mentioned?"

"Haven't I told you that she took it from me?--she and Mrs Evans between them."

"Yes; just so. Well, Mr Granger, all that I want now is a warrant for the arrest of this young lady. And, at the same time, we'll search the house. We'll find the knife of which this young woman speaks, if it's to be found; only we mustn't let her have any longer time than we can help to enable her to get rid of it, which, from all appearances, is the first thing she'll try to do. So perhaps you'll be so good as to tell me where I shall be likely to find the nearest magistrate--now, at once."

"I am a magistrate. What is there I can do for you, Mr Nunn?"

Looking round to see from whom the unexpected answer came, they saw that Mr Hugh Morice was standing in the open doorway. Closing the door behind him he came into the room.

CHAPTER XXXIII
ON HIS OWN CONFESSION

Hugh Morice had been resorting to that medicine--in whose qualifications to minister to a mind diseased he more than half believed--a ride upon his motor car. Of late he had found nothing to clear the cobwebs from his brain so effectually as a whiz through the air. That afternoon, after he had left Exham Park, he had felt that his brain stood very much in need of a clearance. So he had gone for a long run on his car.

He was returning through the shadows, partially cured, when he found what, in that part of the world, might be described as a crowd, obstructing his passage through the village street. Stopping to inquire what was the cause of the unusual concourse, he realised that the crowd was loitering in front of Granger's cottage--the local stronghold of the County Police. As he did so he was conscious that a shiver passed all over him, which he was able neither to account for nor to control. The answers, however, which the villagers gave to his hurried questions, threw a lurid light upon the matter, and inspired him, on the instant, with a great resolve. Dismounting, he entered the cottage, just as Mr Nunn was addressing his remarks to Mr Granger. As he heard he understood that, if what he proposed to do was to be of the slightest effect, he had arrived in the very nick of time.

They, on their part, stared at him half bewildered, half amazed. He had on a long motor coat which shrouded him from head to foot; a cap which covered not only his ears but also part of his face; while his disguise was completed by a pair of huge goggles. It was only when he removed these latter that--in spite of the dust which enveloped him as flour over a miller--they recognised who he was. He repeated his own words in a slightly different form.

"You were saying, Mr Nunn, that you were requiring the services of a magistrate. How can I serve you in that capacity?"

The detective stared at the gigantic figure, towering over his own by no means insignificant inches, still in doubt as to who he was.

"I ought to know you; but, somehow, I don't feel as if I can place you exactly, sir."

Mr Morice smiled.

"Tell him, Granger, who I am."

Mr Granger explained.

"This is Mr Hugh Morice, of Oak Dene, Justice of the Peace for this division of the county. You can't have forgotten him, Mr Nunn; he used to be present at the coroner's inquest."

"Of course; now that Granger reminds me I remember you very well, Mr Morice. You have arrived at a fortunate moment for me, sir. I was just about to start off in search of a magistrate, and that, in the country, at this time of night, sometimes means a long job. I wish to lay an information before you, sir, and ask for a warrant."

Mr Morice glanced at the three women.

"In presence of these persons?"

"I don't know that Mrs Granger need stop, or Mrs Wilson either. Mrs Granger, you'd better take Mrs Wilson with you. It is partly in consequence of a statement which this young woman has just been making that I ask you for a warrant. Now, Mrs Wilson, off you go."

But Mrs Wilson showed reluctance.

"I don't know why I'm to be sent away--especially as it's my own daughter--"

Hugh Morice cut her short brusquely,--

"Leave the room!"

Mrs Wilson showed him something of that deference which she had hitherto declined to show to anyone else. Mrs Granger touched her on the shoulder.

"I'm coming! I'm sure, Susan Granger, there's no need for you to show me. No one can ever say I stop where I am not wanted."

When the two elder women had disappeared, Hugh Morice turned his attention to Wilson the housemaid.

"Who is this young person?"

Mr Nunn informed him. Her story was gone through again. When she had finished Mr Morice dismissed her to join her mother and her aunt.

"Now, Mr Nunn, what do you want from me?"

"A warrant for the arrest of Violet Arnott, of Exham Park."

"On what charge?"

"Wilful murder--the murder of Robert Champion."

"Of whom?"

"I said Robert Champion; but as it's not yet proved that was his name we'd better have it in the warrant--name unknown. I may say, Mr Morice, that that girl's statement is not all I'm going on. Within the hour I've received this anonymous communication."

He handed the communication in question to Mr Morice, who turned it over and over between his fingers.

"Where did you get this from?"

"I can't tell you just at the moment; but I daresay I shall be able to tell you before very long. Of course it's anonymous; but, at the same time, it's suggestive. Also a statement was made to me, of the most positive and specific kind, by James Baker, at present a prisoner in

Winchester Gaol. Altogether I'm afraid, Mr Morice, that the case against this young woman is looking very black."

"Are you in the habit, Mr Nunn, of making ex officio statements of that kind on occasions such as the present? If so, let me invite you to break yourself of it. A man of your experience ought to know better--very much better, Mr Nunn. I regret that I am unable to do what you require."

Mr Nunn stared; possibly slightly abashed by the rebuke which had been administered to him in the presence of Mr Granger.

"But, sir, begging your pardon, you've no option in the matter."

"Haven't I? You'll find I have--a very wide option. I shall decline to allow a warrant to be issued for the arrest of the lady you have named."

"But, Mr Morice, sir, on what grounds?"

"Very simple ones. Because I happen to know she's innocent."

"But that's no reason!"

"You'll find it is, since I also happen to know who's guilty."

"You know who's guilty? Mr Morice!"

"Precisely--Mr Morice. It is I who am guilty. Mr Nunn, I surrender myself into your custody as having been guilty of killing a certain man on a certain Saturday night in Cooper's Spinney. Is that in proper form?"

"Are you serious, sir?"

"I mean what I say, if that's what you are asking, Mr Nunn."

"Then what about the tale that girl was telling, and that knife she saw?"

"That knife is mine."

"Yours!"

"Exactly, and I'm afraid that knife is going to hang me."

"How came it in Miss Arnott's possession?"

"That's the simplest part of the whole affair. After I had used it she found it, and has kept it ever since."

"Do you mean that she's been screening you?"

"Something like it. That is, I don't know that she was sure of anything; but, I fancy, she has had her doubts. I daresay she'll tell you all about it if you ask her. You see, Mr Nunn, I've been in rather an awkward position. So long as it was only a question of Jim Baker it didn't so much matter; it's quite on the cards that in the course of his sinful career he's done plenty of things for which he deserves to be hung. When it comes to Miss Arnott, knowing that she knows what she does know, and especially that she has that accursed knife of mine, that's a horse of a different colour. Since she has only to open her mouth to make an end of me, I may as well make as graceful an exit as possible, and own the game is up. I don't quite know what is the usual course in a matter of this sort, Mr Nunn. My motor is outside. If it is possible I should like to run over to my house. You may come with me, if you please, and Mr Granger also. There are one or two trifles which require my personal attention, and then you may do with me as you please. In fact, if you could manage to let me have an hour or two I should be happy to place at your disposal quite a little fortune, Mr Nunn and Mr Granger."

"You ought to know better than to talk to me like that, Mr Morice. After what you've just now said it's my duty to tell you that you're my prisoner."

CHAPTER XXXIV
MR DAY WALKS HOME

It chanced that night that Mr Day, the highly respected butler at Exham Park, paid a visit to a friend. It was rather late when he returned. The friend offered to put him into a trap and drive him home, but Mr Day declined.

"It's a fine night," he observed, "and a walk will do me good. I don't get enough exercise out of doors. I like to take advantage of any that comes my way. I'm not so young as I was--we none of us are; but a five-mile walk won't do me any harm. On a night like this I'll enjoy it. Thank you, Hardy, all the same."

So he walked.

It was just after eleven when he reached the village. Considering the hour he was surprised to find how many people there were about. Mr Jenkins had just turned his customers out of the "Rose and Crown." A roaring trade he seemed to have been doing. A couple of dozen people were gathered together in clusters in front of the inn, exchanging final greetings before departing homewards. For the most part they were talking together at the top of their voices, as yokels on such occasions have a trick of doing. Mr Day stopped to speak to a man, with whom he had some acquaintance, in the drily sarcastic fashion for which he was locally famed.

"What's the excitement? Parish pump got burned?"

"Why, Mr Day, haven't you heard the news?"

"That Saturday comes before Sunday? Haven't heard anything newer."

"Why, Mr Day, don't you know that Sarah Ann Wilson, from up at your place, has been over to Granger's, trying to get him to give her a warrant for your young lady?"

"There's several kinds of fools about, but Sarah Ann Wilson's all kinds of them together."

"So it seems that Granger thinks. Anyhow he ain't given it her. He's locked up Mr Morice instead."

"What's that?"

Another man chimed in.

"Why, Mr Day, where are you been not to have heard that they've locked up Mr Morice for murdering o' that there chap in Cooper's Spinney."

"What nonsense are you men talking about?"

"It ain't nonsense, Mr Day; no, that it ain't. You go over to Granger's and you'll soon hear."

"Who locked him up?"

"Granger and Mr Nunn, that's the detective over from London. They locked him up between them. It seems he gave himself up."

"Gave himself up?"

"So Mrs Wilson and her daughter says. They was in the kitchen, at the other side of the door, and they heard him giving of himself up. Seems as how they're going to take him over to Doverham in the morning and bring him before the magistrates. My word! won't all the countryside be there to see! To think of its having been Mr Morice after all. Me, I never shouldn't have believed it, if he hadn't let it out himself."

Mr Day waited to hear no more. Making his way through the little crowd he strode on alone. That moon-lit walk was spoilt for him. As he went some curious reflections were taking shape in his mind.

"That finishes it. Now something will have to be done. I wish I'd done as I said I would, and taken myself off long ago. And yet I don't know that I should have been any more comfortable if I had. Wherever I might have gone I should have been on tenterhooks. If I'd been on the other side of the world and heard of this about Mr Morice, I should have had to come back and make a clean breast of it. Yet it's hard on me at my time of life!" He sighed, striking at the ground with the ferule of his stick. "All my days I've made it my special care to have nothing to do with the police-courts. I've seen too much trouble come of it to everyone concerned, and never any good, and now to be dragged into a thing like this. And all through her! If, after all, I've got to speak, I don't know that I wouldn't rather have spoken at first. It would have been better perhaps; it would have saved a lot of bother, not to speak of all the worry I've had. I feel sure it's aged me. I could see by the way Mrs Hardy looked at me to-night that she thought I was looking older. Goodness knows that I'm getting old fast enough in the ordinary course of nature." Again sighing, he struck at the ground with his stick. "It would have served her right if I had spoken--anything would have served her right. She's a nice sort, she is. And yet I don't know, poor devil! She's not happy, that's sure and certain. I never saw anyone so changed. What beats me is that no one seems to have noticed, except me. I don't like to look her way: it's written so plain all over her. It just shows how people can have eyes in their heads, and yet not use them. From the remarks I've heard exchanged, I don't believe a creature has noticed anything, yet I daresay if you were to ask them they'd tell you they always notice everything. Blind worms!"

Perhaps for the purpose of relieving his feelings Mr Day stood still in the centre of the road, tucked his stick under his arm, took out his pipe, loaded it with tobacco and proceeded to smoke. Having got his pipe into going order he continued his way and his reflections.

"I knew it was her from the first; never doubted for a moment. Directly I saw her come into the house that night in the way she did, I knew that she'd been up to something queer, and it wasn't very long before I knew what it was. And I don't know that I was surprised when I heard how bad it really was. All I wanted was to get out of the way before I was dragged into the trouble that I saw was coming. If I hadn't known from the first I should have found out afterwards. She's given herself away a hundred times--ah, and more. If I'd been a detective put upon the job I should have had her over and over again, unless I'd been as stupid as some of those detectives do seem to be. Look at that Nunn now! There's a precious fool! Locking up Mr Morice! I wonder he doesn't lock himself up! Bah!"

This time Mr Day took his pipe out of his mouth with one hand, while he struck at the vacant air with the stick in the other. Perhaps in imagination he was striking at Mr Nunn.

"Poor devil! it must have been something pretty strong which made her do a thing like that. I wonder who that chap was, and what he'd done to her. Not that I want to know--the less I know the better. I know too much as it is. I know that she's haunted, that never since has she had a moment's peace of mind, either by day or night. I've the best of reasons for knowing that she starts pretty nearly out of her skin at every shadow. I shouldn't be surprised to hear at any moment that she's committed suicide. I lay a thousand pounds to a penny that if I was to touch her on the shoulder with the tip of my finger, and say, 'You killed that man in the Cooper's Spinney, and he's looking over your shoulder now,' she'd tumble straight off into a heap on the floor and scream for mercy--What's that?"

He had reached a very lonely part of the road. The Exham Park woods were on either side of him. A long line of giant beeches bordered the road both on the right and left. Beyond again, on both sides, were acres of pines. A charming spot on a summer's day; but, to some minds, just then a little too much in shadow to be altogether pleasant. The high beeches on his left obscured the moon. Here and there it found a passage between their leaves; but for the most part the road was all in darkness. Mr Day was well on in years, but his hearing was as keen as ever, and his nerves as well under control. The ordinary wayfarer would have heard nothing, or, not relishing his surroundings, would have preferred to hear nothing, till he had reached a point where the moon's illumination was again plainly visible. It is odd how many persons, born and bred in the heart of the country, object strenuously to be out among the scenes they know so well, alone in the darkness at night.

But the Exham Park butler was not a person of that kidney. When he heard twigs snapping and the swishing of brushwood, as of someone passing quickly through it, he was immediately desirous of learning what might be the cause of such unwonted midnight sounds. Slipping his pipe into his pocket he moved both rapidly and quietly towards the side of the road from which the sounds proceeded. Just there the long line of hedge was momentarily interrupted by a stile. Leaning over it he peered as best he could into the glancing lights and shadows among the pines. The sounds continued.

"Who is it? Hullo! Good lord! it's her!"

As he spoke to himself a figure suddenly appeared in a shaft of moonlight which had found its way along an alley of pines--the figure of a woman. She was clad in white--in some long, flowing garment which trailed behind her as she went, and which must have seriously impeded her progress, especially in view of the fact that she seemed to be pressing forward at the top of her speed. The keen-eyed observer watched her as she went.

"What's she got on? It's a tea-gown or a dressing-gown or something of that. It's strange to me. I've never seen her in it before. So, after all, there is something in the tales those gowks have been telling, and she does walk the woods of nights. But she can't be asleep; she couldn't go at that rate, through country of this sort, if she were, and with all that drapery trailing out behind her. But asleep or not I'll tackle her and have it out with her once and for all."

Mr Day climbed over the stile with an agility which did credit to his years. As he reached the other side the woman in the distance either became conscious of his presence and his malevolent designs or fortune favoured her; because, coming to a part of the forest from which the moon was barred, she suddenly vanished from his vision like a figure in a shadow pantomime. When he gained the spot at which she had last been visible, there was still nothing of her to be seen, but he fancied that he caught a sound which suggested that, not very far away, someone was pressing forward among the trees.

"She did that very neatly. Don't talk to me about her being asleep. She both heard and saw me coming, so she's given me the slip. But she's not done it so completely as she perhaps thinks. I'll have her yet. I'll show her that I'm pretty nearly as good at trapesing through the woods at night as she is. I don't want to be hard on a woman, and I wouldn't be if it could be helped, but when it comes to be a question of Mr Morice or her, it'll have to be her, and that's all about it. I don't mean to let her go scot-free at his expense--not much, I don't, as I'll soon show her!"

He plunged into the pitch blackness of the forest, towards where he fancied he had heard a sound in the distance.

CHAPTER XXXV
IN THE LADY'S CHAMBER

Miss Arnott was restless. She had to entertain her two self-invited guests--Mr Stacey and Mr Gilbert, and she was conscious that while she was entertaining them, each, in his own fashion, was examining her still. It was a curious dinner which they had together, their hostess feeling, rightly or wrongly, that the most dire significance was being read into the most commonplace remarks. If she smiled, she feared they might think her laughter forced; if she was grave, she was convinced that they were of opinion that it was because she had something frightful on her mind. Mr Stacey made occasional attempts to lighten the atmosphere, but, at the best of times, his touch was inclined to be a heavy one; then all his little outbursts of gaiety--or what he meant for gaiety--seemed to be weighted with lead. Mr Gilbert was frankly saturnine. He seemed determined to say as little as he possibly could, and to wing every word he did utter with a shaft of malice or of irony. Especially was he severe on Mr Stacey's spasmodic efforts at the promotion of geniality.

Miss Arnott arrived at two conclusions; one being that he didn't like her, and the other that she didn't like him. How correct she was in the first instance may be judged from some remarks which were exchanged when--after the old fashion--she had left them alone together to enjoy a cigarette over their cups of coffee, the truth being that she felt she must be relieved from the burden of their society for, at anyrate, some minutes.

Mr Stacey commenced by looking at his companion as if he were half-doubtful, half-amused.

"Gilbert, you don't seem disposed to be talkative."

The reply was curt and to the point.

"I'm not."

"Nor, if you will forgive my saying so, do you seem inclined to make yourself peculiarly agreeable to our hostess."

Mr Gilbert surveyed the ash which was on the tip of his cigar. His words were pregnant with meaning.

"Stacey, I can't stand women."

With Mr Stacey amusement was getting the upper hand.

"Does that apply to women in general or to this one in particular?"

"Yes to both your questions. I don't wish to be rude to your ward or to my hostess, but the girl's a fool."

"Gilbert!"

"So she is, like the other representatives of her sex. She's another illustration of the eternal truth that a woman can't walk alone; she can't. In consequence she's got herself into the infernal muddle she has done. The first male who, so to speak, got within reach of her, took her by the scruff of the neck, and made her keep step with him. He happened to be a scamp, so there's all this to do. It constantly is like that. Most women are like mirrors--mere surfaces on which to reflect their owners; and when their owners take it into their heads to smash the mirrors, why, they're smashed. When I think of what an ass this young woman has made of herself and others, merely because she's a woman, and therefore couldn't help it, something sticks in my throat. I can't be civil to her; it's no use trying. I want to get in touch with something vertebrate: I can't stand molluscs."

Under the circumstances it was not strange that matters in the drawing-room were no more lively than they had been at dinner. So Miss Arnott excused herself at what she considered to be the earliest possible moment and went to bed.

At least she went as far as her bedroom. She found Evans awaiting her. A bed was made up close to her own, all arrangements were arranged to keep watch and ward over her through the night.

"Evans," she announced, "I've come to bed."

"Have you, miss? It's early--that is, for you."

"If you'd spent the sort of evening I have you'd have come early to bed. Evans, I want to tell you something."

"Yes, miss; what might it be?"

"Don't you ever take it for granted that, because a man's clever at one thing, he's clever, or the least bit of good, at anything else."

"I'm afraid, miss, that I don't understand."

"Then I'll make you understand, before I've done with you; you're not stupid. I feel that before I even try to close my eyes I must talk to some rational being, so I'll talk to you."

"Thank you, miss."

"There's a Mr Gilbert downstairs."

"Yes, miss, I've heard of him."

"He's supposed to be a famous criminal lawyer; perhaps you've heard that too. I'm told that he's the cleverest living, and, I daresay, he's smart enough in his own line. But out of it--such clumsiness, such stupidity, such conceit, such manners--oh, Evans! I once heard a specialist compared to a dog which is kept chained to its kennel; within the limits of its chain that dog has an amazing knowledge of the world. I suppose Mr Gilbert is a specialist. He knows everything within the limits of his chain. But, though he mayn't be aware of it--and he isn't-- his chain is there! And now, Evans, having told you what I wished to tell you, I'm going to bed."

But Miss Arnott did not go to bed just then. She seemed unusually wide awake. It was obvious that, if any sound data were to be obtained on the subject of her alleged somnambulistic habits, it was necessary, first of all, that she should go to sleep; but it would not be much good her getting into bed if she felt indisposed for slumber.

"The only thing, Evans, of which I'm afraid is that, if we're not careful, you'll fall asleep first, and that then, so soon as you're asleep, I shall start off walking through the woods. It'll make both of us look so silly if I do."

"No fear of that, miss. I can keep awake as long as anyone, and when I am asleep the fall of a feather is enough to wake me."

"The fall of a feather? Evans! I don't believe you could hear a feather falling, even if you were wide awake."

"Well, miss, you know what I mean. I mean that I'm a light sleeper. I shall lock the doors when we're both of us in bed, and I shall put the keys underneath my pillow. No one will take those keys from under my pillow without my knowing it, I promise you that, no matter how light-fingered they may be."

"I see. I'm to be a prisoner. It doesn't sound quite nice; but I suppose I'll have to put up with it. If you were to catch me walking in my sleep how dreadful it would be."

"I sha'n't do it. I don't believe you ever have walked in your sleep, and I don't believe you ever will."

Later it was arranged that the young lady should undress, take a book with her to bed, and try to read herself to sleep. Then it became a question of the book.

"I know the very book that would be bound to send me to sleep in a couple of ticks, even in the middle of the day. I've tested its soporific powers already. Three times I've tried to get through the first chapter, and each time I've been asleep before I reached the end. It is a book! I bought it a week or two ago. I don't know why. I wasn't in want of a sleeping powder then. Where did I put it? Oh, I remember; I lent it to Mrs Plummer. She seemed to want something to doze over, so I suggested that would be just the thing. Evans, do you think Mrs Plummer is asleep yet?"

"I don't know, miss. I believe she's pretty late. I'll go and see."

"No, I'll go and see. Then I can explain to her what it is I want, and just what I want it for. You stay here; I sha'n't be a minute."

Miss Arnott went up to Mrs Plummer's bedroom. It was called the tower-room. On one side of the house--which was an architectural freak--was an eight-sided tower. Although built into the main building it rose high above it. Near the top was a clock with three faces. On the roof was a flagstaff which served to inform the neighbourhood if the family was or was not at home.

Miss Arnott was wont to declare that the tower-rooms were the pleasantest in the house. In proof of it the one which she had selected to be her own special apartment lay immediately under that in which Mrs Plummer slept. It had two separate approaches. The corridor in which was Miss Arnott's sleeping-chamber had, at one end--the one farthest from her--a short flight of stairs which ascended to a landing on to which opened one of Mrs Plummer's bedroom doors. On the opposite side of the room was another door which gave access to what was, to all intents and purposes, a service staircase. Miss Arnott, passing along the corridor and up the eight or nine steps, rapped at the panel once, twice, and then again. As still no one answered she tried the handle, thinking that if it was locked the probabilities were that Mrs Plummer was in bed and fast asleep. But, instead of being locked, it opened readily at her touch. The fact that the electric lights were all on seemed to suggest that, at anyrate, the lady was not asleep in bed.

"Mrs Plummer!" she exclaimed, standing in the partly opened doorway.

No reply. Opening the door wider she entered the room. It was empty. But there was that about the appearance of the chamber which conveyed the impression that quite recently, within the last two or three minutes, it had had an occupant. Clothes were thrown down anywhere, as if their wearer had doffed them in a hurry. Miss Arnott, who had had a notion that Mrs Plummer was the soul of neatness, was surprised and even tickled by the evidence of untidiness which met her on every hand. Not only were articles of wearing apparel scattered everywhere, but the whole apartment was in a state of odd disarray; at one part the carpet was turned quite back. As she looked about her, Miss Arnott smiled.

"What can Mrs Plummer have been doing? She appears to have been preparing for a flitting. And where can she be? She seems to have undressed. Those are her clothes, and there's the dress she wore at dinner. She can't be in such a state of déshabille as those things seem to suggest; and yet-- I don't think I'll wait till she comes back. I wonder if she's left that book lying about. If I can find it I'll sneak off at once, and tell her all about it in the morning."

On a table in the centre was piled up a heterogeneous and disorderly collection of odds and ends. Miss Arnott glanced at it to see if among the miscellanea was the volume she was seeking. She saw that a book which looked like it was lying underneath what seemed to be a number of old letters. She picked it up, removing the letters to enable her to do so. One or two of the papers fell on to the floor. She stooped to pick them up. The first was a photograph. Her eyes lighted on it, half unwittingly; but, having lighted on it, they stayed.

The room seemed all at once to be turning round her. She was conscious of a sense of vertigo, as if suddenly something had happened to her brain. For some seconds she was obsessed by a conviction that she was the victim of an optical delusion, that what she supposed herself to see was, in reality, a phantom of her imagination. How long this condition continued she never knew. But it was only after a perceptible interval of time that she began to comprehend that she deluded herself by supposing herself to be under a delusion, that what she had only imagined she saw, she actually did see. It was the sudden shock which had caused that feeling of curious confusion. The thing was plain enough.

She was holding in her hand the photograph of her husband--Robert Champion. The more she looked at it the stronger the conviction became. There was not a doubt of it. The portrait had probably been taken some years ago, when the man was younger; but that it was her husband she was certain. She was hardly likely to make a mistake on a point of that kind. But, in the name of all that was inexplicable, what was Robert Champion's photograph doing here?

She glanced at another of the articles she had dropped. It was another portrait of the same man, apparently taken a little later. There was a third--a smaller one. In it he wore a yachting cap. Although he was no yachting man--so far as she knew he had never been on the sea in his life; but it was within her knowledge that it was a fashion in headgear for which he had had, as she deemed, a most undesirable predilection. He had worn one when he had taken her for their honeymoon to Margate; anyone looking less like a seaman than he did in it, she thought she had never seen. In a fourth photograph Robert Champion was sitting in a chair with his arm round Mrs Plummer's waist; she standing at his side with her hand upon his shoulder. She was obviously many years older than the man in the chair; but she could not have looked more pleased, either with herself or with him.

What did it mean?--what could it mean?--those photographs in Mrs Plummer's room?

Returning to the first at which she had glanced, the girl saw that the name was scrawled across the right-hand bottom corner, which had hitherto been hidden by her thumb, in a hand which set her heart palpitating with a sense of startled recognition. "Douglas Plummer." The name was unmistakable in its big, bombastic letters; but what did he mean by scrawling "Douglas Plummer" at the bottom of his own photograph? She suddenly remembered having seen a visiting card of Mrs Plummer's on which her name had been inscribed "Mrs Douglas Plummer." What did it mean?

On the back of the photograph in which the man and the woman had been taken together she found that there was written--she knew the writing to be Mrs Plummer's--"Taken on our honeymoon."

When she saw that Miss Arnott rose to her feet--for the first time since she had stooped to pick up the odds and ends which she had dropped--and laughed. It was so very funny. Again she closely examined the pair in the picture and the sentence on the back. There could be no doubt as to their identity; none as to what the sentence said, nor as to the hand by which it had been penned. But on whose honeymoon had it been taken? What did it mean?

There came to her a feeling that this was a matter in which inquiries should be made at once. She had forgotten altogether the errand which had brought her there; she was overlooking everything in the strength of her desire to learn, in the shortest possible space of time, what was the inner meaning of these photographs which she was holding in her hand. She saw the letters which she had disturbed to get at the book beneath. In the light of the new discoveries she had made, even at that distance she recognised the caligraphy in which they were written. She snatched them up; they were in a bundle, tied round with a piece of pink baby ribbon. To use a sufficiently-expressive figure of speech, the opening line of the first "hit her in the face,"--"My darling Agatha."

Agatha? That was Mrs Plummer's Christian name.

She thrust at a letter in the centre. It began--"My precious wife."

His precious wife? Whose wife? Douglas Plummer's?--Robert Champion's?--Whose? What did it mean?

As she assailed herself with the question--for at least the dozenth time--to which she seemed unlikely to find an answer, a fresh impulse caused her to look again about the room--to be immediately struck by something which had previously escaped her observation. Surely the bed had been slept in. It was rumpled; the pillow had been lain on; the bedclothes were turned back, as if someone had slipped from between the sheets and left them so. What did that mean?

While the old inquiry was assuming this fresh shape, and all sorts of fantastic doubts seemed to have had sudden birth and to be pressing on her from every side, the door on the other side of the room was opened, and Mrs Plummer entered.

CHAPTER XXXVI
OUT OF SLEEP

Miss Arnott was so astounded at the appearance which Mrs Plummer presented that, in her bewilderment, she was tongue-tied. What, in the absence of tonsorial additions--which the girl had already noted were set out in somewhat gruesome fashion on the dressing-table--were shown to be her scanty locks, straggled loose about her neck. The garment in which her whole person was enveloped was one which Miss Arnott had never seen before, and, woman-like, she had a very shrewd knowledge of the contents of her companion's wardrobe. More than anything else it resembled an unusually voluminous bath-sheet, seeming to have been made of what had originally been white Turkish towelling. The whiteness, however, had long since disappeared. It was not only in an indescribable state of filth, but also of rags and tatters. How any of it continued to hang together was a mystery; there was certainly not a square foot of it without a rent. On her feet she wore what seemed to be the remnants of a pair of bedroom slippers. So far as Miss Arnott was able to discern the only other garment she had on was her nightdress. In this attire she appeared to have been in some singular places. She was all dusty and torn; attached to her here and there were scraps of greenery: here a frond of bracken, there the needle of a pine.

"Mrs Plummer," cried Miss Arnott, when she had in part realised the extraordinary spectacle which her companion offered, "wherever have you been?"

But Mrs Plummer did not answer, at first to the girl's increased amazement; then it all burst on her in a flash--Mrs Plummer was asleep! It seemed incredible; yet it was so. Her eyes were wide open; yet it only needed a second or two to make it clear to Miss Arnott that they did not see her. They appeared to have the faculty of only seeing those objects which were presented to their owner's inner vision. Miss Arnott was not present at the moment in Mrs Plummer's thoughts, therefore she remained invisible to her staring eyes. It was with a curious feeling of having come into unlooked-for contact with something uncanny that the girl perceived this was so. Motionless, fascinated, hardly breathing, she waited and watched for what the other was about to do.

Mrs Plummer closed the door behind her carefully--with an odd carefulness. Coming a few steps into the room she stopped. Looking about her with what the girl felt was almost an agony of eagerness, it seemed strange that she should not see her; her eyes travelled over her more than once. Then she drew a long breath like a sigh. Raising both hands to her forehead she brushed back the thin wisps of her faded hair. It was with a feeling which was half-shame, half-awe that the girl heard her break into speech. It was as though she were intruding herself into the other's very soul, and as if the woman was speaking with a voice out of the grave.

Indeed, there was an eerie quality about the actual utterance--a lifelessness, a monotony, an absence of light and shade. She spoke as she might fancy an automaton would speak--all on the same note. The words came fluently enough, the sentences seemed disconnected.

"I couldn't find it. I can't think where I put it. It's so strange. I just dropped it like that." Mrs Plummer made a sudden forward movement with her extended right hand, then went through the motion of dropping something from it on to the floor. With sensations which in their instant, increasing horror altogether transcended anything which had gone before, the girl began to understand. "I can't quite remember. I don't think I picked it up again. I feel sure I didn't bring it home. I should have found it if I had. I have looked everywhere--everywhere." The sightless eyes looked here and there, anxiously, restlessly, searchingly, so that the girl began to read the riddle of the disordered room. "I must find it. I shall never rest until I do--never! I must know where it is! The knife! the knife!"

As the unconscious woman repeated for the second time the last two words, a sudden inspiration flashed through the listener's brain; it possessed her with such violence that, for some seconds, it set her trembling from head to foot. When the first shock its advent had occasioned had passed away, the tremblement was followed by a calm which was perhaps its natural sequence.

Without waiting to hear or see more she passed out of the room with rapid, even steps along the corridor to her own chamber. There she was greeted by Evans.

"You've been a long time, miss. I suppose Mrs Plummer couldn't find the book you wanted." Then she was evidently struck by the peculiarity of the girl's manner. "What has happened? I hope there's nothing else that's wrong. Miss Arnott, what are you doing there?"

The girl was unlocking the wardrobe drawer in which she had that afternoon replaced Hugh Morice's knife. She took the weapon out.

"Evans, come with me! I'll show you who killed that man in Cooper's Spinney! Be quick!"

She took the lady's-maid by the wrist and half-led, half-dragged her from the room. Evans looked at her with frightened face, plainly in doubt as to whether her young mistress had not all at once gone mad. But she offered no resistance. On the landing outside the door they encountered Mr Stacey and Mr Gilbert, who were apparently just coming up to bed. Miss Arnott hailed them.

"Mr Stacey! Mr Gilbert! you wish to know who it was who murdered Robert Champion? Come with me quickly. You shall see!"

They stared at the knife which was in her hand, at the strange expression which was on her face. She did not wait for them to speak. She moved swiftly towards the staircase which led to the tower-room. She loosed her attendant's wrist. But Evans showed no desire to take advantage of her freedom, she pressed closely on her mistress's heels. Mr Gilbert, rapid in decision, went after the two women without even a moment's hesitation. Mr Stacey, of slower habit, paused a moment before he moved, then, obviously puzzled, he followed the others.

When the girl returned Mrs Plummer was bending over a drawer, tossing its contents in seemingly haphazard fashion on to the carpet.

"I must find it! I must find it!" she kept repeating to herself.

Miss Arnott called to her, not loudly but clearly,--

"Mrs Plummer!" But Mrs Plummer paid no heed. She continued to mutter and to turn out the contents of the drawer. The girl moved to her across the floor, speaking to her again by name. "Mrs Plummer, what is it you are looking for? Is it this knife?"

Plainly the somnambulist was vaguely conscious that a voice had spoken. Ceasing to rifle the drawer she remained motionless, holding her head a little on one side, as if she listened. Then she spoke again; but whether in answer to the question which had been put to her or to herself, was not clear.

"The knife! I want to find the knife."

"What knife is it you are looking for? Is it the knife with which you killed your husband in the wood?"

The woman shuddered. It seemed as if something had reached her consciousness. She said, as if echoing the other's words,--

"My husband in the wood."

The girl became aware that Day, the butler, had entered through the door on the other side, wearing his hat, as if he had just come out of the open air, and that he was accompanied by Granger in his uniform, and by a man whom she did not recognise, but who, as a matter of fact, was Nunn, the detective. She knew that, behind her, was Evans with Mr Stacey and Mr Gilbert. She understood that, for her purpose, the audience could scarcely have been better chosen.

She raised her voice a little, laying stress upon her words.

"Mrs Plummer, here is the knife for which you are looking."

With one hand she held out to her the handle of the knife, with the other she touched her on the shoulder. There could be no mistake this time as to whether or not the girl had penetrated to the sleep-walker's consciousness. They could all of them see that a shiver went all over her, almost as if she had been struck by palsy. She staggered a little backwards, putting out her arms in front of her as if to ward off some threatening danger. There came another fit of shivering, and then they knew she was awake--awake but speechless. She stared at the girl in front of her as if she were some dreadful ghost. Relentless, still set upon her purpose, Miss Arnott went nearer to her.

"Mrs Plummer, here is the knife for which you have been looking--the knife with which you killed your husband--Douglas Plummer--in the wood."

The woman stared at the knife, then at the girl, then about her. She saw the witnesses who stood in either doorway. Probably comprehension came to her bewildered intellect, which was not yet wide awake. She realised that her secret was no longer her own, since she had been her own betrayer, that the Philistines were upon her. She snatched at the knife which the girl still held out, and, before they guessed at her intention, had buried it almost to the hilt in her own breast.

CHAPTER XXXVII

WHAT WAS WRITTEN

She expired that same night without having uttered an intelligible word. In a sense her end could hardly have been called an unfortunate one. It is certain that, had she lived, she would have had a bad time, even if she had escaped the gallows. She had left behind her the whole story, set forth in black and white by her own hand. It was a sufficiently unhappy one. It is not impossible that, having heard it, a jury would have recommended her to mercy. In which case the capital sentence would probably have been commuted to one of penal servitude for life. It is a moot question whether it is not better to hang outright rather than endure a living death within the four walls of a gaol.

The story of her life as recounted by herself--and there is no reason to doubt the substantial accuracy of her narrative--was this.

Agatha Linfield, a spinster past her first prime, possessed of some means of her own, met at a Brighton boarding-house a young man who called himself Douglas Plummer. Possibly believing her to be better off than she was he paid her attentions from the first moment of their meeting. Within a month he had married her. In much less than another month she had discovered what kind of a man she had for a husband. He inflicted on her all sorts of indignities, subjecting her even to physical violence, plundering her of all the money he could. When he had brought her to the verge of beggary he fell into the hands of the police; as he was destined to do again at a later period in his career. Hardly had he been sentenced to a term of imprisonment than his wife became the recipient of another small legacy, on the strength of which she went abroad, and, by its means, managed to live. Her own desire was never to see or hear of her husband again. She even went so far as to inform her relatives that he had died and left her a sorrowing widow. He, probably having wearied of a woman so much older than himself and knowing nothing of the improvement in her fortunes, seems to have made no effort on his release to ascertain her whereabouts. In short, for some years each vanished out of the other's existence.

On the night of the Saturday on which they returned from abroad, when Miss Arnott went for her woodland stroll, Mrs Plummer, whose curiosity had been previously aroused as to the true inwardness of her proceedings, after an interval followed to see what possible inducement there could be to cause her, after a long and fatiguing journey, to immediately wander abroad at such an uncanonical hour.

She was severely punished for her inquisitiveness. Exactly what took place her diary did not make clear; details were omitted, the one prominent happening was alone narrated in what, under the circumstances, were not unnaturally vague and somewhat confused terms. She came upon the man who was known to Miss Arnott as Robert Champion, and to her as Douglas Plummer, all in a moment, without having had, the second before, the faintest suspicion that he was within a hundred miles. She had hoped--had tried to convince herself--that he was dead. The sight of him, as, without the least warning he rose at her--like some spectre of a nightmare--from under the beech tree, seems to have bereft her for a moment of her senses. He must have been still writhing from the agony inflicted by Jim Baker's "peppering" so that he himself was scarcely sane. He had in his hand Hugh Morice's knife, which he had picked up, almost by inadvertence, as he staggered to his feet at the sound of someone coming. It may be that he supposed the newcomer to have been the person who had already shot at him, that his intention was to defend himself with the accidentally-discovered weapon from further violence. She only saw the knife. She had set down in her diary that he was waiting there to kill her; which, on the face of it, had been written with an imperfect knowledge of the facts. As he lurched towards her-- probably as much taken by surprise as she was--she imagined he meant to strike her with the knife. Scarcely knowing what she did she snatched it from him and killed him on the spot.

It was at that moment she was seen by Hugh Morice and Jim Baker, both of whom took her for Miss Arnott. Instantly realising what it was that she had done she fled panic-stricken into the woods with-- presently--Hugh Morice dashing wildly after her. Miss Arnott saw Hugh Morice, and him only, and drew her own erroneous conclusions.

Mrs Plummer gained entrance to the house by climbing through a tall casement window, which chanced to have been left unfastened, and which opened into a passage near the foot of the service staircase. Afterwards, fast asleep, she frequently got in and out of the house through that same window. Unknown to her the discreet Mr Day saw her entry. She had still very far from regained full control of her sober senses. So soon as she was in, seized, apparently, by a sudden recollection, she exclaimed, turning again to the casement, "The knife! the knife! I've left the knife!"

Mr Day, who had no particular affection for the lady, heard the words, saw the condition she was in, and decided, there and then, that she had recently been involved in some extremely singular business. Until, shortly afterwards, he admitted her himself, he was inclined to fear that she had killed his young mistress.

The impression Mrs Plummer had made upon his mind never left him. Spying on her at moments when she little suspected espionage, his doubts gained force as time went on, until they amounted to conviction. When the body was found in the spinney, although he had little evidence to go upon, he had, personally, no doubt as to who was the guilty party. It was because he was divided between the knowledge that it was his duty to tell all he knew and his feelings that it would be derogatory to his dignity and repellent to his most cherished instincts to be mixed up with anything which had to do with the police, that he was desirous of quitting Miss Arnott's service ere he was dragged, willy-nilly, into an uncomfortably prominent position in a most unpleasant affair.

Nothing which afterwards transpired caused him at any time, to doubt, that, whenever he chose, he could lay his hand upon the criminal. He alone, of all the persons in the drama, had an inkling of the truth.

CHAPTER XXXVIII
MISS ARNOTT'S MARRIAGE

The charge against Jim Baker was withdrawn at the earliest possible moment. Hugh Morice was released that night from the confinement which he had himself invited. When Mr Nunn asked what had made him accuse himself of a crime of which he was altogether innocent he laughed.

"Since you yourself were about to charge one innocent person, you should be the last person in the world to object to my charging another."

The next day he went to Exham Park. There he saw its mistress. By degrees the whole tale was told. It took a long time in the telling. Part of it was told in the house, and then, as it still seemed unfinished, he went out with her upon her motor car. The rest of it was told upon the way.

"It seems," she pointed out, "that, as the wretch married that poor woman before he ever saw me, I never was his wife at all. I don't know if it's better that way or worse."

"Better."

"I'm not so sure."

"I am. Because, when you become my wife--"

She put the car on to the fourth speed. There was a long, straight, level road and not a soul in sight. They moved!

"You'll get into trouble if you don't look out."

"I'm not afraid."

"I was about to remark that when you become my wife--"

"I wish you wouldn't talk to me when we're going at this rate. You know it's dangerous."

"Get down on to the first speed at once." She did slow a trifle, which enabled him to speak without unduly imperilling their safety. "I was saying that when you become my wife I shall marry you as Miss Arnott--Violet Arnott, spinster. That will be your precise description. I prefer it that way, if you don't mind."

Whether she minded or not that was what he did. No one thereabouts had the dimmest notion what was her actual relation to the man who had met the fate which, after all, was not wholly undeserved. So that the great and glorious festival, which will not be forgotten in that countryside for many a day, is always spoken of by everyone who partook of the bride and bridegroom's splendid hospitality as "Miss Arnott's marriage."

It was indeed one of those marriages of which we may assuredly affirm, that those whom God hath joined no man shall put asunder.

THE END

Made in the USA
Lexington, KY
26 December 2013